Stars
Over
Clear Lake

✦

Young Adult Novels by Loretta Ellsworth

✦

In Search of Mockingbird

Unforgettable

In a Heartbeat

The Shrouding Woman

Stars

Over

Clear Lake

✦

Loretta Ellsworth

≋
THOMAS DUNNE BOOKS
St. Martin's Press
New York

THOMAS DUNNE BOOKS.
An imprint of St. Martin's Press.

STARS OVER CLEAR LAKE. Copyright © 2017 by Loretta Ellsworth. All rights reserved.
Printed in the United States of America. For information, address
St. Martin's Press, 175 Fifth Avenue, New York, N.Y. 10010.

www.thomasdunnebooks.com
www.stmartins.com

Title-page photo courtesy of freeimages.com

The Library of Congress Cataloging-in-Publication Data is available upon request.

ISBN 978-1-250-09703-3 (hardcover)
ISBN 978-1-250-09704-0 (e-book)

Our books may be purchased in bulk for promotional, educational, or business use. Please contact
your local bookseller or the Macmillan Corporate and Premium Sales Department
at 1-800-221-7945, extension 5442, or by e-mail at
MacmillanSpecialMarkets@macmillan.com.

First Edition: May 2017

10 9 8 7 6 5 4 3 2 1

To all those couples who met at the Surf Ballroom over the years—

this dance is for you.

Stars
Over
Clear Lake

✦

One

✦

2007

"I haven't been inside this place in fifty years," I say softly as I pause in front of the sand-colored brick building. The outside of the Surf Ballroom hasn't changed from when it opened in 1948, its rounded roof making it look like a roller derby from the outside. A bedrock of Americana tucked in a small town in north central Iowa, the ballroom is often overlooked, despite its contribution to musical history. But to me it's so much more. The memories are like seaweed, pulling me down and threatening to suffocate me. It's only because they're honoring my late husband that I'm here tonight.

The marquee above me reads *Fireman's Ball*. Underneath the marquee is the empty ticket booth where bobbed-haired Violet Greenwood used to work. She's been dead for twenty-five years, but the image of her dispensing tickets with a cheery smile and pop of her gum is as fresh in my mind as this morning's coffee.

I take a breath and reach for the handle when the door bursts open. My daughter stands on the other side, her blue eyes wide at the sight of me.

"Where have you been? I called your cell phone five times!"

Daisy's red sleeveless dress shows off her thin frame and healthy tan, and complements her highlighted blond hair. Botox treatments have eliminated the inherited crease between her eyebrows. No one would guess she's in her forties.

But Daisy is standing stiff-necked, her veins sticking out on her throat as though my presence here is stressful.

"I had it turned off. Didn't want to run the battery low," I say evasively.

"Mother, what's the use of having a phone if you never have it turned on?" She shakes her head. "You shouldn't even be driving."

"What do you mean? I've never had an accident."

"That's because Dad did all the driving when he was alive. A person's reflexes aren't as good at your age."

"Why does that make me unfit for driving? Isn't that age discrimination?"

She lets out an exasperated sigh. "Oh, never mind, Mother. Come in before you melt out here."

I suck in a breath, blinking out the sunlight as my eyes adjust to the darkness.

The expansive lobby holds a gift shop, offices, a small hallway filled with pictures to the right, and the main hallway leading to the dance floor. The old coat check sits off to the left; a long counter with a red laminate top glistens in front of the numbered rows that lead to the deep recesses of hangers. I gape at the lobby's blue walls, the ones with the painted yellow pineapples. I'd forgotten about them! And the multicolored carpeting beneath my feet, bright colors that practically shout to be seen.

I grab Daisy's arm. "It's just like I remember it. The fancy lobby and swanky coat check room . . ."

"Yes, it hasn't changed," Daisy replies. "We had a terrible time trying to decorate. We couldn't use colored paper and the lighting was a nightmare, but I think it turned out okay. The bathrooms could use a renovation, though, and my husband is already on his second drink."

We pass a table full of paper flyers. I pick up one that advertises the

Winter Dance Party next February, a show honoring the original in 1959 when Buddy Holly, Ritchie Valens, and J. P. "The Big Bopper" Richardson gave their last performances. They died a few hours later when their plane crashed just north of Clear Lake.

"Kind of early to be advertising, isn't it?" I ask. "It's only August."

"Not really. The tickets go on sale in October and they sell out every year. Harry and I went in costume last year. We had a blast."

I crinkle my nose. "Almost seems morbid to celebrate their final performance."

"I don't think so," Daisy says. "You know what the Bible says: time to mourn and a time to dance."

"Yes, it does," I say, keeping to myself the irony of my daughter quoting Scripture when she only attends mass on scheduled holidays, and as far as I know, hasn't cracked open a Bible since her youth.

"Besides," Daisy says, "we went with the mayor and his wife. They might hire me to redesign their bathroom. I think they're coming tonight, too."

"The mayor? Isn't he related to Lance Dugan?"

"Yes. Lance is Chad's uncle."

"I went to school with Lance." I let out a soft sigh. "That was ages ago."

I take a tentative step onto the wooden floor of the ballroom, and despite all the people mulling about, the conversations and music around me, I feel as if I'm the only person here. Off to the left is the stage, the heavy red velvet curtains drawn back. It's flanked by fake palm trees trimmed with tiny white lights. I remember waiting for those curtains to part; how the stage would come into view, glowing under bright lights that dissolved everything else, as though I'd been hypnotized.

A band is playing a soft tune from an earlier era, "String of Pearls." One of Glenn Miller's hits. My kind of music. "Did you know the Glenn Miller Orchestra played on that very stage? And Jimmy Dorsey?"

"Lots of people have played here. Come on." Daisy pulls on my arm as though I'm an errant child.

Tiered wooden booths occupy one side of the ballroom and are tucked under green-and-white-striped awnings, each booth numbered for reservations. I search for booth 110 and when my eyes settle on it I have to fight back tears. I take in a breath to calm myself.

The walls above the booths are painted with oceanfront murals that used to whisk me away from the cold Iowa nights. I get a vague whiff of salt air and see the waves washing against the shore. I blink and look away.

How easy it is for my mind to travel back in time. It must be this place. The clouds that float across the arched ceiling to look like the night sky. The ocean waves on the back wall. The wooden booths and the lighted palm trees. Nothing has changed.

Tables with white linens occupy the center of the floor. Filling them are framed pictures and posters showing the development of the fire department, including historical fires in the community. I'm drawn to a photo of the original Surf Ballroom, which burned down a year before this one was built in 1948. Next to it is a newspaper clipping showing a crowd gathered around the burned remains. My throat tightens and I can almost the feel the smoke choking me again, my helplessness as the ceiling collapsed. Memories have a way of doing that to you, resurfacing despite time and distance and attempts to forget.

"Arson or natural causes?"

I jump and take a step back. "What?"

Harry, my son-in-law, hands me a glass of champagne. "I noticed you looking at the pictures of the original building. We were talking about it down at the firehouse, debating whether we could still solve the puzzle of that fire sixty years later. You were what, about eighteen when it burned down? Do you remember it?"

I fan myself with the flyer, feeling suddenly hot. "Vaguely. I heard it was bad wiring." My voice sounds tinny, higher than it should.

"I'm not so sure about that. I think by using modern technology and interviewing people who still remember the event, well, we might figure out what actually caused it."

As the town's fire chief, my son-in-law has a fascination with talking about anything fire-related. He has a receding hairline and hair that's turned mostly gray, a nice, firm chin, and a manner that puts everyone at ease. But I'm shaking, nearly spilling the champagne. I take a sip of the bubbly, which tickles my nose.

"You sound like an episode of *CSI*. You have a large crowd," I say, derailing the conversation.

"Yeah, half the town is here. Not to worry, though. We're within the fire code occupancy limit. That's part of the reason we chose this place."

"Why don't you take Daisy on a nice cruise after this is over? Or at least a weekend in Minneapolis to visit your son." Harry has two children from a first marriage. I don't see them often enough, but have always considered them my own. Maybe a trip would put this nonsense of investigating the old fire out of Harry's head.

"We just saw John two weeks ago when we went to the Mall of America. A cruise might be nice, though. If I could talk her into it, I'd do it in a nanosecond. But you know how she is." He takes another swig of his drink.

"If she's worried about me, she shouldn't be. I'd be fine."

"Maybe later. We're both so busy right now."

He doesn't say it, but I know I'm the reason she won't go.

"Mother," Daisy taps my arm, and I'm grateful for the distraction. "I was just telling my friends that you and Dad met here."

Her friends are all tanned and wearing dresses similar to Daisy's, like a high school clique thirty years later. And Daisy, just as she was then, is still at the center.

"Um, yes, we did," I say, not meeting her eyes. I feel twenty again, like I was at the grand opening of the Surf, just rebuilt after the fire. I'd worn a forest-green dress that had a tight waist and flared at the bottom. The place had been packed. I'd sat in booth 110. Our booth.

I look down, breaking the spell. Maybe it's too much being in this place again. Or maybe it's this particular occasion, seeing photos of the burned-down Surf, reliving the memories of that day.

"Did you spend every anniversary here?" one of Daisy's friends asks.

Daisy turns to me. "I don't remember you two ever coming here. Why not?"

"We came here before you were born." I clear my throat. "The farm took all our time later on."

Harry picks up a portable microphone from the center table and speaks into it as a wide circle of people forms around him. "Thank you all for coming tonight. We wanted to have the Fireman's Ball at the Surf because it holds a special place in the community. It's a piece of our history and, let's face it, a place where a lot of people have hooked up over the years."

The crowd laughs.

"Some of you may know that there was another Surf Ballroom, one that burned down sixty years ago. As an engineer, I've always thought that studying past fires can help us learn about fire dynamics. I spent the last few years in the fire investigator training program in Des Moines. And with the help of my squad, we're going to examine the file from the original Surf fire to see if we can use modern technology to determine what caused it."

The sound of clapping fills the ballroom and I bury my face in my glass of champagne. The bubbles no longer bother me.

"This also happens to be where my in-laws met. We lost Sid last year. He was a volunteer with the department for many years, and even though I wish he could be here with us, I'm sure he is in spirit."

More clapping. I nod and finish my drink. A shadowy figure standing near the stage waves at me and I squint into the darkness. It's a young man, but I don't recognize him.

"Do you have anything to add, Lorraine?" Harry motions to me to step forward and hands me the microphone.

Maybe it's the bubbly, but I'm overcome with an urge to set the record straight. "I didn't really meet Sid at the Surf."

I glance at my open-mouthed, wide-eyed daughter. I pause, wondering if I should say more. The young man is no longer there, but the attendance in the room has multiplied as people from my past mingle with the present guests. I see my brother Pete, looking like he did sixty years ago, swaying to the music. And now I see Pete's buddy Mike Schmitt, drinking his beer off to the side, a shy smile on his face.

I shake my head. What kind of illusion is this? They can't be here, of course. But I can see them as surely as I see Glenn Miller standing on the stage. And is that Roy Orbison? And that boy playing a guitar, I'm sure he's Buddy Holly. They're here, all part of this place, just as much as the maple hardwood dance floor beneath my feet.

The voices and songs crowd my head and suck all the air away, making it difficult to breathe. Flashes of light go off as people snap pictures. The room is hot and spinning. I try to fan myself but both hands are full. If only I could just breathe. The glass of champagne somehow slips from my hand. Then the microphone falls. I'm faintly aware of the shattering of glass on the wooden floor, the banging of the microphone as it hits, sending an explosion of high-frequency sound through the crowd.

My weight gives way as I fall into the arms of my son-in-law, who catches me just before my head hits the floor.

Two

✦

July, 1944

You're too young," Mom pleaded. "Just a child. We need you here on the farm. You can still get a deferment." She sobbed and latched onto my brother, Pete.

"It's a little late for that, Mom. I already finished basic training. We're shipping out now."

He insisted we say our goodbyes at home instead of at the station, likely because he feared Mom would make a scene, which was exactly what she was doing.

Pete calmly patted Mom on the back and pried her arms off him. He handled her better than me and Daddy combined. "Mom's like a clock that's been wound too tight," he once told me. "You have to let her wind down slowly or the whole thing will explode."

Mike laid on the horn. He was waiting in his Buick with his window rolled down, his hands trying to keep out the flies that swarmed his vehicle. It was already warm, even though dew still licked at the tips of the grass and sunlight had barely reached the top of the barn.

"It was only a matter of time before I got drafted anyway," Pete told Mom in a soothing voice. "Besides, I can't be the one left behind when all my buddies are going to fight the Nazis." He nodded toward Mike, who was revving the engine now.

Pete turned to Daddy, who shook his hand like he was a man instead of a farm boy. Pete's uniform did make him look a bit older.

"Sorry to leave you shorthanded, Pop," Pete said.

Daddy shrugged it off. "Duty to your country comes first. Besides, they're sending five German prisoners from the POW camp in Algona next week. We'll make it through the season if this hot weather don't kill everything off."

Pete was leaving for war and Daddy was talking about the weather?

"Takes five Germans to make up for one of me," Pete said, standing tall, "but I'll be back before you know it, Pop."

Daddy looked shrunken next to Pete in his overalls and work shirt. Daddy had always seemed taller, and I hadn't noticed when Pete passed him by.

I followed Pete to the car. In the distance a meadowlark whistled a carefree tune.

"Wait," I said, and straightened his tie. "Why do you want to go to the other side of the world when you've never even been out of your own state?" I couldn't imagine Pete in Europe, so far away from Iowa and out of his element.

"I just gotta go, Skippy. You'll understand when you're older."

Pete threw his duffel bag in the car, then tugged on my red braid. "Don't grow up while I'm gone."

I wanted to object that I was almost fully grown, only three years younger than him. But before I could say anything, the car pulled away, churning up a swell of dust in its wake.

"And don't touch my record player," Pete yelled, leaning out and flashing a quick wave.

Then he was gone.

Mom watched the car until it was only a faint dust cloud in the distance, her arms folded so tight that her knuckles were white. "He's not a fighter," she said.

"He wants to do his duty, the same as every other boy in this town," Daddy said.

"You mean the same as all those boys whose families don't even get a body to claim because they're buried on foreign soil? Is that what you want for your son?"

Daddy hugged her as she cried on his shoulder.

"Everything will be okay," he said.

Mom suddenly pushed him away. "Okay? This is anything but okay. It's all your fault. And I'm not having a bunch of Nazis on my land!"

She rushed toward the slanted porch off our kitchen. The screen door that slammed behind her was immediately dotted with flies trying to get in.

Daddy and I followed her inside.

"We already talked about this." Daddy touched her shoulder but she jerked away.

"*You* talked about it," Mom said in a shrill voice, then put a hand to her head. "I never agreed."

"I can't do this by myself," Daddy said, his voice impatient. "There was no other way."

Mom sniffed and shook her head. "I'm not going to discuss this now. I'm going to go lie down."

Mom had taken to her bed for a week when Pete had enlisted. How long would she be there this time?

I snatched up the dishcloth and scrubbed at a splotch of dried-up jam on the counter. I hated to see my parents fight. "You shouldn't have gotten POWs, Daddy," I whispered when I heard the creak of her shoes on the stairs.

Daddy adjusted his cap over his flattened reddish-brown hair. His face was tan and leathery from years of working in the sun. "Didn't have a choice. Not a single response to the notices I posted around town. Even women are filling in at the factories. I don't know why they put up a POW camp in the middle of Iowa, but I'll take whatever help I can get. She'll just have to get used to it."

"Maybe Mom is right about Pete staying home. He's just a farm boy," I said, wondering if we should go after him before the train left.

Daddy nodded. "Maybe when he comes back he'll be a soldier."

I didn't want Pete to change. And the house felt empty without him.

"He will come back, won't he, Daddy?" I clenched the dishcloth and felt my lower lip tremble.

Daddy readjusted his cap and wiped the back of his hand across his damp forehead. "We pray to God he will, sweetheart."

He headed toward the door. "I'm going out to the fields. Watch after your mother."

It didn't take much to send Mom to her bed. Her moods were like the weather, unpredictable and unrelenting. And I was left to take over the housework during those stretches.

I'd rather have been in the fields with Daddy, and had offered to help when Pete left. There was no way he'd get the baling done on his own. The last month he'd kept a grueling schedule: up before dawn and out late at night, managing to just kick off his work boots before falling asleep in the easy chair, sometimes not even eating, he was so tired. But Daddy wouldn't hear of me missing school and I had plenty of chores as it was.

Mom's feet shuffled across the floor above me. I grabbed a bowl off the shelf and plopped it down on the small, square wooden table in our kitchen. I didn't have the knack for making biscuits like Mom, getting them perfectly round in the pan the way she did, but it would be up to me to keep Daddy fed until she was recovered enough.

After I got the biscuits rising, I made strawberry Jell-O, Daddy's favorite dessert. Then I took out chicken and breaded it and put it in the oven. I'd learned from Mom to do the cooking before the sun got too hot and made the kitchen unbearable. I sang as I worked, softly so as not to wake her. I imagined myself on the stage of the Surf Ballroom belting out "We'll Meet Again" while Benny Goodman's band played behind me.

Pete owned that record. He'd told me not to touch his record player, but I felt drawn to his room, as though his leaving was a dream and he'd be sprawled out on his bed reading a *Dime Detective* magazine instead of on a train bound for another continent.

I snuck up to his room and sat down on his unmade bed, the sheets tangled like he'd been in a hurry. I ran my fingers across the ribbing of his blue bedspread and brought his pillow to my face, breathing in his boyish, sweaty smell. I studied the pin-up of Rita Hayworth that shared wall space with a Sacred Heart of Jesus picture. A suede bag filled with marbles and an old model airplane were perched on a blue bookcase next to some worn mystery comics and paperbacks, proof to me that my brother was still just a boy. His phonograph sat atop the dresser, records stacked neatly beside it. I remembered how he'd paid twenty-five cents a week for eight months to buy that record player. How long before it would be played again, before I'd hear music seeping underneath his bedroom door?

I opened the tan luggage-style case. Pete had left a record on the grille, the needle still in position. I turned the switch and it sputtered, then came to life as Dick Robertson's tenor reached out to me.

> *Oh, how I hate to get up in the morning!*
> *Oh, how I'd love to remain in bed!*

I shuddered as I thought of Pete. I missed him so much already.

"What do you think you're doing?"

I jumped at the shrill sound behind me and flicked off the switch.

Mom stood in the doorway, red-faced, her eyes ablaze with indignation. "He's gone one hour and you're rifling through his belongings?"

"I was only . . ."

"You're violating your brother's room. Get out! Get out!"

I'd never heard her yell like that before. I ran past her down the stairs, through the stuffy kitchen with its fried-chicken smell, out the back door and into the yard, not stopping until her screams were out of earshot.

I bent over to catch my breath and vowed not to set foot in Pete's room again until he returned.

Three

✦

1944

A week later Mom found her way downstairs. There was no mention of her yelling at me, but Pete's door was closed and the curtains in his room were drawn.

Daddy was finishing his morning coffee when a truck emblazoned with a white star on the door turned into our long driveway. Daddy flashed a worried look at Mom before he hurried out the door. I followed him before Mom could object. In the rear of the truck were men dressed in green fatigues, their shirts rolled up to the elbows. There were five of them, some wearing caps, all of them looking ruffled and disoriented and a bit malnourished. Algona was a good forty miles from our farm.

Beside them sat a man in military uniform. He held a rifle.

Daddy shook his head. "They're a poor-looking lot, if I do say so. But they'll have to do." He directed the truck to park over by the barn.

"Lorraine!" Mom's voice drew me back inside.

"Stay indoors," she told me. "I don't want you outside while they're here."

"But the cows need to be milked twice a day," I complained. "And

I have to collect eggs and feed the chickens. How am I going to do my chores?"

Mom just stared down at the table, her head in her hands. "God forbid! Nazis on our property. What was he thinking?"

I sighed, hoping she wasn't headed toward another spell. "I'll wait until Daddy has them in the fields before I go out to do chores."

I went up to my room and peeked out from behind the curtains of my open window. I could hear Daddy's deep voice, the familiar twang in the back of his throat and the slow speech he used when explaining something.

Another man was interpreting Daddy's words, one of the prisoners who wore a beret. They were a ways off so I couldn't hear much of what they were saying. I saw Daddy step forward and shake each of their hands as they introduced themselves. Mom would throw an absolute fit if she saw that!

One of the men glanced my way. He had dark hair combed to the side, just like Hitler, but without the mustache. He raised his eyebrows at the sight of me and I ducked, pressing my body into the wall as the curtains fluttered above me. My heart raced at the thought of the enemy just yards away from our own house. What *was* Daddy thinking?

Daddy didn't act scared. But when he didn't come back for his noonday meal, I began to worry.

"Daddy must be awful hungry," I remarked to Mom as I stood watch at the kitchen window.

Mom didn't look up from her crocheting. "He'll come in when he's hungry enough."

When she went upstairs to lie down, I wrapped a clean towel over a plate of cold chicken, two biscuits, and an apple, and headed out to the pasture. I walked across the flat gravel toward the fields behind our barn. My nose twitched at the smell of the chicken coop, which desperately needed cleaning, but that would have to wait.

The cows had drifted toward the far fence that bordered Mr. Murphy's property. They'd broken through enough times that Daddy was considering replacing the wooden fence with barbed wire. I summoned them back, using Daddy's call that sent them running.

The sun beat down enough that my skin glistened and my ponytail stuck to the back of my neck. I cut through the thick grove of trees behind the barn, then stopped in my tracks, almost dropping the food. Right in front of me was a man. No, not a man. He was more of a boy, not much older than Pete.

His blond hair was messy and he wore a sleeveless T-shirt stained with grass and dirt. I could see the outline of muscle through the shirt. His green jacket lay crumpled next to him. He was sitting against a haystack, smoking a cigarette, staring out at the field with a faraway look in his eyes.

I took in a breath at the sight of the enemy right in front of me. I thought of turning back and running, but this was *our* farm. I couldn't hide forever.

"You'd best be careful or you'll burn down the farm," I said, remembering how Daddy warned us to be mindful where we burned trash.

He jumped and almost dropped his cigarette, seemingly as spooked by my presence as I'd been by his.

He composed himself and looked at me as though I was a curiosity.

"Your cigarette?" I said.

He shrugged and kept on smoking.

I imitated his smoking motion.

He offered me a cigarette.

I shook my head. "No."

He pointed to the cigarette. "*Verboten?*"

"Yes, whatever you said."

"*Nein.*"

"No smoking," I said again, a bit louder.

He pointed across the field where other workers were taking a break. Several of them were smoking, too.

"We'll see about that." I walked on to find Daddy.

"*Fräulein,*" he called after me. I turned back.

He pointed at an apple on the ground. "*Haben Sie einen Apfel für mich übrig?*"

I picked up the apple and pointed at his cigarette. "If you get rid of that."

He tossed his cigarette on the ground and rubbed the toe of his boot across it.

I tossed him the apple.

He caught it and smiled as though I'd given him an exotic fruit. "*Danke.*"

"You're welcome," I said, but I didn't smile back. It seemed disrespectful to smile at the enemy.

I walked between the ribbons of freshly cut hay waiting to be pitched. Daddy stood next to the hay rack wagon. It was hooked up to the horses and the hay was piled as high as the pitchforks could reach.

I stopped and petted Prince and Pauper, who despite Daddy's training had never become well-broke for farm work. Daddy said it was because they'd been mail carrier horses, and working in the field was different work than clomping down a road.

Daddy was trying to get the prickly hay out from inside his cuffs. He gratefully accepted the food. "I was hoping you'd come."

"You got a lot done, Daddy."

"Ten times as much as I could do alone." Daddy looked at his full plate. "They'll be working here awhile and you know what hard work this is," he said in a low voice. "Seems we could feed them. They don't get more than a rabbit's portion of rations, not enough to keep up their strength doing this kind of work."

"You want Mom to cook for them?"

"It wouldn't be asking too much, seeing as how much work they're doing. I'd never get this finished if I had to do it alone."

"Mom won't . . ."

"I'll talk to her about it when she's more accustomed to the sight of them. But maybe tomorrow you could rustle up a little extra grub?" He gave me a wink, one that meant that this would be our secret.

"I'll see what I can do," I said, not making any promises. Maybe I could round up some apples and bread and molasses, things Mom might not notice were missing.

"Should they be smoking out here?" I asked. I knew Daddy liked his Lucky Strikes, but he could be trusted to be safe with his smokes. These Germans couldn't. The POW with the Hitler haircut snarled his lips around his cigarette, giving credence to my fears.

"They're fine. You worry too much," he said, patting my back.

Maybe Daddy didn't worry enough. I walked back the way I'd come, tramping through the plowed field, bits of grass sticking to my socks. The boy with the apple nodded at me. I ignored him. Didn't want him getting too friendly just because I'd given him an apple. But I couldn't help but look back at him after I'd passed. He was still watching me, and waved. I ran the rest of the way to the house.

Four

✦

1944

I put my towel and swim cap in the basket of my bike and tucked ten cents in my pocket for a Coca Cola as I escaped the heat of the farm and set off for town. My red braid bounced behind me as I focused on avoiding the ruts in the gravel. My only thoughts were of the cool lake water and Scotty Bishop. He hadn't asked me out yet, but recently he'd been particularly attentive. Today might be the day.

I traveled along the road next to the ditches filled with long grasses and spindly chicory plants, their pale blue flowers reaching up to the sky. I didn't meet any cars until I reached Highway 18, which cut across the full length of North Iowa from the Big Sioux River in South Dakota to the Mississippi River on the Illinois side. The highway ran parallel to the train tracks.

My back was hot and sweaty by the time I passed the Burma Shave sign and turned down the leafy, shaded roads leading to downtown Clear Lake. I rode past the Surf Ballroom and the library, then biked around the town square, where the bandshell stood across from the beach. People sat on benches, licking ice cream cones and catching the light breeze off the lake.

Clear Lake was an oasis in the middle of the flat Iowa landscape. The Sioux and Winnebago had used the spring-fed lake as a summer home before Nathan Boone, Daniel Boone's son, mentioned it in a land survey in 1832. Although it was a tourist attraction, our population remained small except in summertime.

The war made things quieter than normal, but people still flocked here on hot days. Some rode over on the trolley from Mason City. Others stayed at beachside resorts. Along the sides of the town square were small stands serving cotton candy, popcorn, and root beer floats.

I parked my bike and searched the crowded beach. I had almost given up hope that Scotty was ever going to ask me out. He was going to be a senior, and this summer might be my last chance to find out if he really liked me.

I arrived not a moment too soon. I spotted Stella sitting next to Scotty on the beach. Stella was leaning into him, giggling at something Scotty said, until she saw me. Then she bounced up and ran over, grabbing my arm. I quickened my step.

"I didn't think you were going to make it," Stella said. "What with your chores and all."

"Couldn't miss our last hurrah of the summer," I said. "Don't tell anyone, but Daddy called the POW camp. They sent some men to help." Stella was my best friend, but she liked to gab. I didn't want the whole town knowing that Germans were working on our farm.

"Ooh," Stella said, faking a shiver. "I wouldn't want those monsters on my property."

"Well, don't mention it to anyone," I repeated. "Mom's not too happy about it."

"Who can blame her?" Stella said. "But my lips are sealed."

Stella tugged at the bottom of her red swimsuit, the same one she'd had for the last two years. It was too small, spilling excess cleavage out the sides. Her family never had two cents to rub together, and Stella babysat to buy her own clothes.

Stella was four inches shorter than me, but nine months older, and she knew how to get boys to notice her. Her wavy dark hair curved around plump cheeks and bright red lips.

I smoothed back frizzy hair that had escaped my braid and fixed my gaze on Scotty as he flipped his brown hair out of his eyes. He was tall, his long legs lean from running back and forth across the basketball court, and had an easy confidence about him that came from excelling at everything. He stood up, took my towel, and set it down next to his. "I'm glad you decided to come."

How glad? Was he ever going to ask me out? I smacked my lips that had never worn lipstick and looked out at the lake, its blue hues reflecting the hot sun. Shouts and screams floated toward shore as Lance Dugan splashed water on girls and dunked the younger boys. He never got in trouble, of course. His dad owned the bank, and had given Lance a Packard for his seventeenth birthday.

I pulled off my top and pants and kicked off my shoes. Scotty's wet arm brushed mine as I sat down. I felt exposed in my white one-piece suit and tugged at the halter top.

Stella scooted away toward the other girls, making it appear as though she wanted us to have some privacy, although she was still close enough to hear everything we said.

"The beach is packed," I said. "Good thing you saved me a spot."

"I was saving it for *you*," he said reassuringly. "Stella just came over to tell me that the Monaghans were moving."

Stella lived blocks away from Scotty and they knew all the same people. Even though I only lived a couple miles out of town, it was a different world from city life.

"Have you been in the water yet?" I asked Scotty. "Is it cold?"

"Feels great," he said. "Want to go for a dip?"

I nodded and stuck my thick braid into my bathing cap, then followed him down to the water. The hot sand bit at the bottoms of my feet and I hurried to get to the wet slush at the lake's edge. The water was cool but not cold, and I couldn't help but remember the last time I'd been here with Pete. Last year on the Fourth of July, we'd gone to Bayside Amusement Park and then met Mom and Daddy at this beach later.

I glanced over at the dock where we'd sat with Mike Schmitt for the fireworks. Mom and Daddy had stayed on the blanket at the park but we'd wanted to be closer, to feel the boom of the explosions, and had crowded onto the dock. Now both boys had gone off to war and they'd banned fireworks this year because of the wartime need for powder and explosives. Pete would be watching a different type of fireworks.

"Come on." Scotty pulled me out deeper, past the rocks and seaweed that curled around my toes, to clear water and a sandy bottom. The lake stretched out before us like a blue carpet, still except for a passing sailboat and the swimmers splashing near the edges. We walked out until we were even with the end of the dock, until the water finally reached our necks, right before the drop-off.

"I'm not a great swimmer," I warned him. "I never learned properly."

Scotty ducked his head under the water, disappearing for an instant. Then he reappeared, closing the distance between us. "Don't worry. I won't let you drown." He was inches away, the water lapping against his bare chest, his wet hair dripping down the sides of his face, looking at me with his reassuring chestnut eyes. I felt aware of his body in the water, of our limbs nearly touching. I had a sudden urge to kiss him right there in front of the whole beach crowd.

But would he kiss me back? Scotty hadn't even asked me out, although he had walked me to class last year. Maybe he was like Pete, who had been shy until he'd finally gotten bold enough to ask Mary Scholl to dance at the Surf one night. That had seemed to break the ice with

Pete, who had danced with many girls since then, and had gone on plenty of dates.

Perhaps a kiss would break that barrier between us, the one we'd been tiptoeing near for most of our lives. We weren't little kids anymore. But should I act so forward? Mom would say that only a hussy would kiss a boy in public. What if that boy was going to war? Scotty wasn't, but I'd seen lots of girls kissing their army boyfriends in public. The war had changed many things.

Scotty spit out water and smiled at me. Stella had an advantage in living so close to Scotty. But Scotty liked me, not her. I felt emboldened and reached out and put my arms around his neck. But suddenly my feet were pulled out from beneath me and I sank down, gulping water.

The water stung my open eyes. I could see Scotty's knobby knees and his long, white legs. I flailed about, splashing, trying to discover what had pulled me under. Someone behind me, but I couldn't see who. As I tried to stand, Scotty's arms reached down and pulled me back up. I gasped for air and wiped the wetness from my eyes.

Scotty was saying something, but I couldn't hear him through my waterlogged ears.

"Who did that?" I whirled around, looking for the culprit.

"Lance," Scotty said, laughing.

"It's not funny," I said, turning back and splashing him.

"Hey. I didn't dunk you." He splashed me back.

Suddenly we were having a splashing war and others joined in. Kids and adults alike splashed each other. Scotty was much better at it, and I put my hand up to block the waves of water that were threatening to overtake me.

Finally, I turned and retreated to shore and sank down into the hot sand. I was used to Lance Dugan pulling girls' braids and knocking boys down in grammar school. Lately he'd even started busting windows out of cars and running wild at night. Only his father's influence kept him out of serious trouble. Now he'd managed to destroy my afternoon with one swift jerk of my legs underwater. Instead of a first kiss, I'd gotten soaked.

"So, you didn't answer me," came Scotty's voice from behind me.

"What was the question?" I wiped my face off with the towel, still a bit angry at him for laughing. The towel spread grains of sand across my forehead.

"Will you go to the movies with me? Next week?"

I stopped wiping and looked at him. I nodded, barely aware of the "yes" that came out of my mouth. Then I realized what a sight I must look with my swimsuit pulling at my rear, the bathing cap scrunching my forehead, and water dripping off my nose. I recovered and pulled off the bathing cap, shook out my hair, and smiled at Scotty. The moment had been saved after all, and I hadn't had to act brazen, even though a part of me still wished I had.

Five

✦

1944

The next morning I woke to the sound of a truck's wheels on our gravel. I rushed to get dressed and quietly slipped down the stairs. I took in a breath when I saw Mom sitting at the kitchen table, snapping the ends off string beans and dropping them into a bowl of cold water.

"Don't feed the animals just yet," she told me. "Have your breakfast first. There's a pot of fresh-made oatmeal on the stove."

"I'm not hungry."

Mom glared at me. "I don't want you out there where they can see you. Understand?" She snapped a bean, the movement quick and sharp, and reached for another.

I nodded. At least she was out of bed.

A copy of the *Globe Gazette* sprawled open on the table. On page three, right next to an ad for the Navy's WAVES, was an article titled "War Prisoners Provide Labor." I sat down and snapped beans with Mom while straining to read the article. It was about the Algona POWs and how they were willing farm workers. I wondered if Daddy had shown Mom the article, if that's what he'd used to convince her. Had he convinced her?

"Daddy got a good section of the field done already," I said, hoping that would impress her.

"He did? Then maybe they won't be here long."

I didn't remind her that the hay needed to be stored in the barn and the corn would need picking. Mom turned the radio on. News of the war flitted across the wire, filling the room with the drama of our boys half a world away.

"The Allies have reached the French capital of Paris, and Patton and his army continue their march over the Seine River."

"Do you think Pete is in France?" I asked.

"That's where all the fighting is taking place," Mom said, clutching a bean so tightly that a seed burst out from the end of the pod.

Bill Slocum interrupted the news for an Admiral commercial advertising for workers for its Chicago factories, noting that *"no experience is necessary and new workers will be paid while they learn."*

I used to wake to the songs of Dick Haynes. Now the only channel Mom listened to was the CBS World News Program.

"Scotty Bishop asked me to the movies," I said. "Can I go?"

Mom looked at me, a sudden focus in her eyes. She hadn't been interested in anything about me since Pete came home from basic training. Of course, she hadn't *ever* been much interested in me.

"We know his family from church. He's supposed to be such a good basketball player, isn't he?"

I nodded. "He's been offered a scholarship to college." Scotty was the golden boy of our school, smart, athletic, and good-looking. His father worked as an accountant.

"Well, I don't see what it would hurt as long as he brings you home at a reasonable hour."

I remembered my promise to Daddy, that I'd find a way to bring some extra food to the POWs today. But Mom didn't even want me anywhere near them. I'd always had so much freedom around the farm, and now I felt imprisoned by not being allowed to go out into the fields.

When noon came around I found Mom in the front breezeway iron-ing shirts. Three gigantic elm trees stood guard over the front of our house and kept the porch cooler than the rest of the house. But the air in the breezeway felt sticky today. A drop of sweat was running down the side of her face.

Mom kept her dark hair in a tight bun, and her fair skin always made her look pale. Even though she could pluck a chicken in record time, Daddy said she had a "fragile countenance," which I didn't understand.

"Are you going to town?" I asked her, knowing we needed some sup-plies. "I have a letter for Pete."

She glanced at the kitchen clock. "I'll go as soon as I get this ironing finished. Unless you'll finish it for me?"

"Okay." I ran to my room and retrieved the letter. Mom took off her apron and handed it to me. Then she put on her hat and picked up her purse. I was pressing Daddy's white church shirt as Mom got into the car and drove onto the road. Even with all the work he'd been doing, Daddy never skipped Sunday morning mass at St. Patrick's, although he did doze off during the sermon and Mom had to nudge him a few times. I waited until the gravel had settled back onto the road and Mom's car was out of sight before I cut up thick chunks of bread and smothered molasses in the middle of the sandwiches. Then I gathered a bunch of fresh tomatoes from the garden and some apples from the tree behind the barn. I covered the food with napkins and hauled it out in a deep basket with a handle that I could carry more easily. I knew Mom might notice the missing bread.

When I arrived at the field I spotted the boy with blond hair I had encountered yesterday. He and another man were raking the long rows of hay into piles. The boy was tall like Pete. The back of his T-shirt was drenched in sweat. When he saw me approach, he smiled as if we were long-lost friends.

Daddy was tamping down the hay in the wagon while four other men pitched round mounds filled with the freshly cut stalks into the side. The guard, who'd introduced himself as Norman, sat off to the side, watching.

I called out to Daddy. "Food's here."

"Time for a break, men," Daddy said. "Help yourself to grub."

Norman raised his eyebrows. "They're prisoners. They've had their rations."

"They're underfed," Daddy said, "and they won't last the afternoon. It's my farm."

Norman scowled. He stood tall, his gun at attention, as though he were in charge of guarding Hitler himself. When I set the basket down, Daddy stretched out his arm to the men. They came forward cautiously and took the food.

Daddy gave me a hug. "Where's your—"

"In town. I didn't tell her."

"She'll see it my way," he said. But I knew better. If Mom and Daddy had to name a favorite, Pete would be Mom's and I would be Daddy's. It was Daddy who encouraged me to dream, who clapped the loudest at my singing recitals.

Pete knew before he could walk that he'd work the farm. He grew up happy and secure in that knowledge. But I wasn't sure where life would take me.

"Maybe someday we'll be listening to you on the radio," Daddy always said. Mom rolled her eyes at the notion of me being anything other than a wife. But Daddy had opened up the possibility that I could do whatever I wanted. So much freedom was both exciting and scary.

I knew I had to get back home before Mom returned. My hand moved toward the empty basket, but the boy got there first. "Tank you," he said in a thick accent as he picked it up and handed it to me.

Our hands touched for a moment. I looked at him and his ears flushed red. Was it sunburn or was he shy?

"You're welcome," I said, and hurried away.

I thought about him on the way back. Did his family worry about him the way we worried about Pete? What if Pete were held prisoner? Wouldn't we want him to be treated with kindness? Maybe the little food we shared with this boy would make his time in prison less painful.

That's what I told myself, anyway.

Six

✦

1944

You won't be going to the movies next week," Mom announced in the middle of dinner.

"What? Daddy!" I shot a look of protest at my father.

Daddy cleared his throat. "I think with all that's going on, it would be good for Lorraine to get out," he said.

"She needs to be punished."

"Now, Gladys," he said.

"Don't 'Now, Gladys' me. She stole bread as if she was a common sneak thief."

"She did it for me. Those men would have dropped from exhaustion before the day was over."

"They're the enemy," she said. "Not houseguests."

"They're just men who speak German, like the Mennen family down the road. No difference."

"The Mennens have two sons in the United States Army. That's a huge difference."

"We're all caught up in the war, but we're all people. Can't you see that?"

"No. I see that my son is headed to a foxhole in France while Nazis are in my fields eating my bread."

"Pete *wanted* to sign up. You think an overprotective mother was going to keep him here?" Daddy pounded the table and I jumped. Silence filled the room. I wanted to find a dark corner to hide in.

Mom finally spoke. "No. I expected *you* to keep him here. You needed him. He'd have understood that."

"I couldn't ask him to give up his honor."

"There's no honor in death."

"Our son was of age. He didn't need our permission."

Mom's eyes were steely. "No, but I'll bet you gave it to him, didn't you?"

Daddy put down his fork and avoided Mom's eyes. "Heavens, woman! How long you gonna fret like this?"

"Until my son comes home."

Daddy sighed his I-give-up, can't-reason-with-her sigh.

"And you," Mom said, turning her wrath on me. "You should be ashamed of yourself, going behind my back."

I looked down at my potatoes, pushing them around with my fork. I hadn't expected this punishment, to miss out on my first date with Scotty Bishop. I wanted to scream. It wasn't fair. But I thought of what Pete would say, how to handle Mom with diplomacy.

I took a breath and put my hands together. "I'm sorry," I said. "I shouldn't have taken food without asking you first."

Mom looked as though she didn't believe me.

"I was just being a good Christian. You always tell me to think of others first. Didn't Father O'Connor tell us just last Sunday that even though we are at war we shouldn't forget that all men are our brothers, and when peace is restored and justice prevails we must heal as a nation? I couldn't go to confession without saying I'd sinned by letting those men go hungry. I couldn't eat the bounty of our garden and watch them starving."

"I'm sure they're not starving."

"You didn't see the measly rations they got," Daddy said. "A piece of dark bread, beans, and some kind of cooked intestines that looked disgusting. I was truly ashamed to eat in front of them. It's uncharitable to make men work on that. And one thing I pride myself on is charity." He nodded for emphasis.

"Well," Mom finally relented, looking between the two of us like a fish caught on a hook. "I guess it doesn't hurt to give them something while they're working here. We don't want people thinking we're not charitable."

"Thank you," Daddy said.

"And even though it was wrong of you to take the bread, I'm not going to spoil your date," Mom said, as though she was taking the higher ground on this whole thing. "I rather like that Bishop boy."

"Oh, thank you, Mom!" I was ecstatic. Daddy winked at me.

"From now on I'll decide what food of ours they eat," Mom said firmly, settling the matter. "And Lorraine will take it to them and come right back. No speaking to those men."

✦

Now Mom was making the meals, and she was never one to be skimpy with food. She prepared fresh biscuits, watermelon pickles, and even her apple pie, a bit tart because she didn't have sugar and had to substitute corn syrup. Sometimes she cooked fried chicken or roast beef sandwiches.

Pete wrote to say he'd arrived on foreign soil, that he'd never been so happy to be on solid ground because he'd been seasick. Mom placed Pete's old globe on the dining room table. I once caught her tracing her finger across the Atlantic Ocean, her mind long gone from our white clapboard farmhouse. She barely left the house except to tend the garden, go to mass, and do her weekly shopping. She never wandered out of earshot of the radio, and she cut out every piece of information from the newspaper that might pertain to Pete that she could get her hands on.

"Now that Paris is liberated, maybe the Soviet army will do their part on the other side of Europe and our men can rest a bit. Seems only fair, don't you think?" she asked anxiously one day.

"I suppose so." I didn't know much about war, but I doubted they'd sit around and wait for the Russians to work their way to France.

I grabbed the basket of food on the counter. "You hurry back," Mom called from inside as the screen door slammed behind me.

I looked up at the overcast sky. It was one of the wettest summers on record, and if I didn't keep my hair braided it would frizz out to twice the size of my head.

"Hi, Norman," I said to the guard when I found the group over in the east pasture beyond a line of pines that stretched across our property. He was fanning himself with a newspaper.

"Hiya, Lorraine. What'd you bring me?" he teased.

"There's plenty here. You're welcome to eat."

He stood and patted his gun. "I tried to enlist, ya know. I woulda been over there with your brother if I could. I was classified 4-F because I'm deaf in one ear. I got my deferment papers right here."

He took out the papers to show me.

"I wanted to go," he insisted again. "They wouldn't let me."

"I know," I said reassuringly, amazed that he carried his papers with him.

I searched for the boy soldier, who waited for me each day with a new English phrase he'd practiced. Sometimes I saw him take out a small dictionary when I approached. He never asked the interpreter to translate, but seemed intent on figuring it out himself.

"Goot morning," he said.

"Good afternoon," I replied, as it was past noon.

He frowned and turned away to check his dictionary. I kept walking. He pointed at his chest. "My name Jens."

"I'm Lorraine," I said, ignoring Mom's instructions to not speak to the men. Daddy talked to them all the time.

"Lorraine," he repeated. "Pretty name. Pretty *Fräulein*."

"Thanks, but I already have a boyfriend." Günther, the German with the beret who spoke English, laughed and translated. I put down the basket of food: warm corn biscuits and ripe apples. Jens turned red, retreated to a spot far away, and pulled out a cigarette.

"I think you embarrassed him," Günther said, taking a biscuit.

"I didn't mean to," I said.

While Daddy examined the tractor's engine, I took out an apple from the basket and walked over to where Jens sat. I held out the apple.

He shifted uncomfortably in his spot. The smile was gone from his face.

"How do you say this in German? Apple?"

He tilted his head as though he didn't understand.

"*Deutsch*? Apple?"

"*Apfel*," he said.

I pointed at the cigarette. "What's that?"

"*Zigarette*."

"Cigaretta? Wow! Almost the same!"

I handed him the apple. "Apfel for cigaretta?"

He smiled in spite of himself. He had a dimple in the corner of his right cheek. He handed me the unlit cigarette, which I stuck in my pocket, and I gave him the apple.

He showed me his dictionary then. "I teach Een-glish."

"You *learn* English," I corrected him.

"Ya. I learn English." He nodded firmly and took a bite of the apple.

I started to walk away but only took a few steps before I spun around.

"See you later."

He frowned as though he didn't understand.

"Later. Soon, as in tomorrow. Um, never mind. Goodbye."

He nodded then. *"Auf Wiedersehen.* Goodbye."

I turned and almost bumped into the man who'd reminded me of Hitler. I'd heard Günther call him Helmut. He was glaring at Jens.

"Fräulein," Helmut said in a curt voice, as though he was dismissing me. He turned to Jens and said something I didn't understand. Jens's face reddened, and he looked down at the ground.

I rushed back to the house.

Seven

✦

1944

Imagine me, Lorraine Kindred, singing with a big band! At the Surf Ballroom!"

Mom was driving me to church for choir practice. She grimaced and shook her head. "Forget about it. You're needed at home. There's a war going on, in case you've forgotten."

"For crying out loud, Mom, the war isn't taking place here. The Navy Band is performing at the Governor's Ball, and Miss Berkland asked me to sing one number with them. It's the biggest celebration of the year!"

"I know what it is. I've lived here my whole life, and you'll watch your tongue, young lady. If they had any sense of decency, they'd cancel the celebration this year. How can you even think of singing when your brother is in harm's way?"

Anger settled in my chest, and I bit my lip and looked out the window before I said something that would completely ruin my chances.

"If you'd only talk to Miss Berkland," I said in what I thought was a reasonable voice.

"That old maid? She's past thirty. Can you believe it?"

"What does that have to do with singing?"

"If she was a mother, she'd understand that things are different now that we're at war. She shouldn't have asked you without my permission first."

"Honestly, Mom."

"Besides," Mom continued, "why do you want to sing for a bunch of strangers? It's not as though you're going to make a career out it."

"Miss Berkland said I sing as well as Vera Lynn," I said with a bit of pride in my voice.

Mom pursed her lips. "She shouldn't be encouraging such ideas."

"Why not?"

"Because you're young and impressionable. How many Iowa girls do you know who sing professionally?"

"None," I admitted.

"We're simple people, Lorraine. Poking your head up in the clouds will only end up hurting you. I'm telling you this to protect you."

I gave up and stared at the cornfields out the window. Neither of us said anything for a while. When Mom finally did speak, her voice was strained. "Did you hear that Steven Powers died last week? He was in France."

"I heard," I said. "His brother is in my class at school." Steven had worked at the Decker Plant and was engaged to a girl from Mason City. They had planned to get married as soon as he got back from the war.

Mom whispered, "Pete is probably in France."

"Pete's going to come back," I said.

Mom turned and squinted at me. "How do you know that?"

"I just know." In reality, I just couldn't imagine it any other way. Life wouldn't make sense if Pete wasn't in it. "I pray for him every night," I said, to convince her. Not that I prayed as much as Mom, whose mottled black rosary beads spent more time in her hands than in the white ceramic box with the cross on it.

"You think Steven Powers's family didn't pray for him?"

"I guess they did."

"They most certainly did. But that didn't keep him from getting killed."

"Bill Burgen's brother came back," I said, as proof that not everyone who went off to war died.

"He came home shell-shocked. And it was a miracle he lived."

"Daddy doesn't think Pete's going to be killed. Why do you have to be so sour all the time?" I said, then immediately regretted it when Mom pulled the car over to the shoulder and stopped.

I braced myself for a slap on the face for mouthing off. But Mom closed her eyes and shook her head. I almost wished she *would* slap me. Instead, Mom put her head down on her white knuckles that were gripping the steering wheel.

"You don't know what's happening," she said. "Your father has already accepted the course of this war as far as your brother is concerned. He's only interested in duty and honor. He'd rather have a dead hero than a live coward." She lifted her head and looked at me. "So don't say that I'm sour. I'm worried, is all."

Worry? It seemed to be more than that.

We were silent the rest of the way there. When Mom pulled up to let me off, I knew I should just let it go. But I was more like Dad; I had his reddish hair and light complexion and the conviction that I could make everyone see things my way, and that if I believed something hard enough I could make it true. Mom had Swedish roots in her past, and her family had always been kind of gloomy. She had an uncle who'd shot himself in the barn when one of his hogs died.

"Mom," I said before I got out, "I know you're worried about Pete. I've seen you getting worse with worry, like it's taking over everything else. But worry didn't ever save anyone's life."

"Maybe not," she said. "But I can't just stick my head in the sand like everyone else in this family. And tell that woman you're not singing at the Governor's Ball."

I got out and Mom drove away. I walked into church and knelt in the last pew. I could hear the organ above me, Miss Berkland playing a slow rendition of "Ave Maria." The afternoon sun cast a hazy sheen upon the altar.

"Dear God," I prayed, "please keep Pete out of harm's way. End this war and bring him home soon, before Mom loses her mind. And if You have time after that, please allow me to use this talent You gave me. If it is Your will."

✦

"*Salve, salve, salve Regina,*" I sang as Miss Berkland played the pipe organ in our church balcony. My voice echoed off the empty pews below.

She held the last note for an extra beat, then clapped her meaty arms together. "The Lord gave you beautiful vocal cords, Lorraine. You've got the voice of an angel. We're so lucky to have you in the church choir."

Church was supposed to be about God, not me or my singing. But I felt a certain satisfaction in showing off my voice, even if it was just during mass at St. Patrick's.

That's why I was spending one afternoon a month under Miss Berkland's tutelage. I told Mom it was for the church choir, but in reality, I wanted to learn how to sing professionally.

Miss Berkland had a plain, round face framed by short, tight curls, and carried her extra weight beneath a collection of long jumpers that she wore over frilly lace blouses. She directed the choir at school during the day and at St. Patrick's on the weekends. Her voice was like silk, and I wondered why she wasted her time on a bunch of high school kids.

Miss Berkland made a *tsk* sound. "It's a shame your mother won't let you sing at the Governor's Ball. It would be a feather in your cap to add to your résumé."

She said "résumé" as if I actually had such a thing. Other than a few recitals at school and a solo in the church choir, my biggest audience was the chickens in our coop.

"If it would help, I could talk to your mother. You know, I toured with a local band when I wasn't much older than you. I could tell her what a good experience it would be for you."

I shook my head. Mom would just wonder why Miss Berkland hadn't landed a husband while she was on tour.

"Mom isn't what you'd call musical," I explained. "She doesn't see how singing fits into farm life."

"It doesn't," Miss Berkland answered. "A talent such as yours shouldn't be wasted on the cows."

I swallowed hard, thinking, *That describes my future to a tee.* "Sometimes this all feels like a pipe dream, Miss Berkland."

She sighed. "Don't feel that way. And I don't mean to dishonor your mother, Lorraine. It's just that I remember when I sang 'Look for the Silver Lining' at the Governor's Ball when I was your age, and how my mother cried when my picture was in the newspaper. It was the proudest moment of her life."

She stopped and dabbed at the corner of her eye with a tissue. "I know your mother only has your best interests at heart. You're young. There will be other opportunities."

"Will there be?" I asked.

Miss Berkland smiled at me and nodded. "Of course. How about we sing something fun?" She looked around to make sure Father O'Connor wasn't within earshot before she started playing "Boogie Woogie Bugle Boy."

I took the high part and Miss Berkland sang the low harmony. I laughed at the pipe organ's version of the song as it floated down the steep pews of the old balcony, past the wooden railing, and rattled the stained-glass windows of St. Patrick's.

Eight

✦

1944

Missing out on singing with the Navy Band nearly broke my heart. Mom said it was for the best, that we shouldn't encourage such revelry during wartime.

"But it's patriotic," I insisted.

"We're patriotic enough," Mom said. "Look at all we've sacrificed already."

"My cousin's friend is the drummer for Ray Gray's Orchestra," Stella said at school the next day, trying to comfort me. "They're playing at the Surf next week. Maybe they'll let you sing a number with them."

"Mom would never allow it."

Stella put an arm on her hip. "And who says she has to know? Just tell her you're going to the dance with me, stag, like lots of girls do."

Pete had started bringing me along with him to the dances last year, and Mom had never objected. All the kids went stag, except for the serious couples. But I hadn't gone since Pete had left.

"No, it's too risky," I said, not wanting to jeopardize my date with Scotty.

Cooking for the POWs kept Mom busy, and even though the radio was still on and the globe took up table space, she had taken an interest in her chores again. The lack of letters from Pete was a source of worry, though. Mom made frequent walks to the mailbox and would wait for the mail carrier if he was late.

Each day when I brought the food I was thanked by soft-spoken Günther, whose beret sat lopsidedly on his head while thick, round-rimmed glasses framed a kind face.

"How do you speak English so well?" I asked.

"I studied philosophy at Cambridge University in England," he said.

"This must be hard for you, doing menial farm work," I said.

"It is better than being on the war front," he replied. "We are lucky. We are safe from the fighting here. And we feel useful."

I told Daddy what Günther said.

"They're saving our crop," Daddy said. "They're hard workers, and they like getting away from the prison camp."

"They're forced labor," I reminded him.

"Not exactly. We pay them. Not what they're worth." He nodded at the basket of food. "That's why I like you bringing out extra vittles for them."

"They earn money as prisoners?"

"They get coupons that are like money. They use them to buy cigarettes and stationery at the prison camp canteen."

It was hard not to like some of the men, even when Mom acted like having them on our farm was a treasonous crime.

Large-framed, quiet Ludwig had been a mechanic before the war, and helped Daddy tune up the tractor engine. He showed me a tattered photo of his daughter, a chubby toddler with curly blond hair looking wide-eyed at the camera. His eyes were misty as he kissed his first two fingers and touched them gently to her image.

Jakob was a jovial man who laughed a lot and loved to eat. He was preparing for a chess tournament at the camp. Daddy brought out his old chess set, and Jakob and the prison guard Norman spent lunch in fierce competition.

Günther loved to read. He asked Daddy lots of questions about farming and the United States. Daddy said he thought Günther was trying to reconcile all he'd been told about our country with what he was seeing.

Helmut was different from the rest. He had a permanent scowl and refused to eat with the others. I couldn't understand what he was saying, but when the other men were helpful or friendly, he barked at them in German, and he never thanked me for the food. When he took off his sweaty shirt, I saw a tattoo under his arm. The letter A.

I asked Günther about it.

"It is a mark of the SS," Günther said quietly. "A mark of authority."

"What do you mean?"

"It is his blood type. It assures him first treatment if he is wounded. That very likely saved his life when he was shot in the stomach."

It seemed unfair. I'd read about Hitler's elite. Helmut conducted himself like one of those Aryan types who thought he was above others.

Jens was still a mystery to me. He was so much younger than the other men, only a year older than Pete.

The first week I ignored his attempts to talk to me, even as he met me with a smile and a friendly "hello," and offered to carry my basket. I just nodded and walked away.

But he was persistent, his smile ever-hopeful. And his blue eyes were kind and vulnerable. I slowly began to talk to him, at first just a few words, then more as his vocabulary improved. He waited for me each day with his dictionary. He had also signed up for a language class at the Algona camp, taught by Günther. I didn't know all that much about him except that he wanted to learn English and was too stubborn to ask Günther to translate for him.

His expression was one of constant struggle as he searched for words to communicate with me.

"Buska? *Scheisse!*" he said, pointing at the basket, his mouth failing to form the word.

Günther looked up from his book and laughed. "*Nein, mein Kamerad.*"

"Basket," I said, and waited for him to repeat it.

"Basket," he said then looked at me. "You help?"

"Help?"

"He wants you to tutor him," Günther said.

"That's your job," I said.

"Not enough time," Günther said. "He is impatient to learn."

"I couldn't," I said, shaking my head at Jens.

"*Verboten?*"

"He wants to know if it's forbidden," Günther said.

"Forbidden? I don't know. Mom wouldn't—well, tell him I'll think about it."

I looked to Günther, who translated.

"Okay?" I said.

"Okay," Jens said. "Basket," he said firmly, and handed it to me, as though he wouldn't take no for an answer.

Nine

✦

2007

I focus on the white plastic pitcher with a pale blue cap as it sweats cold water down its side. I remember wiping the condensation off a similar pitcher as my husband lay dying last year, as if I could somehow wipe away the cancer that was slowly consuming him.

And now here I am, in a room with the same hospital-grade pitcher. I shiver and pull the blanket up over the flimsy hospital gown. I'm still spooked. I don't believe in ghosts. I know I couldn't possibly have seen those people at the Surf. But they looked so *real*.

Just then Daisy's voice echoes from the hallway. "I want that doctor to see my mother now!"

I'm embarrassed by her shouting. Sugar leaves a sweeter taste in your mouth.

"I'll page him right away," the nurse says.

Well, you can't argue with success.

Daisy enters the room. "He'll be here soon, Mother. Nurse!"

A woman who looks roughly the same age as Daisy hurries in. She's plump, with fine lines around her eyes.

She checks the monitor and wiggles a flashlight in front of my eyes. "Can you tell me what your name is and what the date is?"

"Lorraine Deters. It's Saturday, August eleventh, two thousand and seven, and I'm fine, really. I just think the champagne got to me. I don't usually drink."

Daisy crosses her arms. "You should have better sense than that, Mother."

"Now, don't get your pantyhose in a twist, Daisy. It was only a toast."

"Of course you had a toast. It was a special occasion," says the nurse, whose nametag reads Janet. "Just the same, I think we should let the doctor look at you."

I give the nurse a grateful nod. I want Daisy to go back to the ball, but of course she won't think of it. She's duty-bound and will go to her grave that way, even though it's killing her that all her country club friends are back at the Surf enjoying chicken Florentine without her.

"You don't need to stay. I'll call you after the doctor examines me," I promise. "Someone can come pick me up."

"I'm not leaving you alone," Daisy states firmly. "Not after what happened. Mother, you were talking nonsense right before you passed out."

"What nonsense?"

"You've always told me you met Dad at the Surf. And now today you said that wasn't how you met? Honestly, Mother, how could you have forgotten?"

"There's nothing wrong with my mind, if that's what you're implying."

"So the champagne caused a memory lapse, too?"

I sigh and wait for the nurse to leave. "There's something I haven't told you," I start to explain, but just then Dr. Baker rushes into the room. He's thin with a receding hairline, a man hitting his mid-sixties who is always in a hurry and doesn't have any notion of retiring soon. I'm amazed at how he keeps going.

"Is my favorite girl causing trouble?"

"It's nothing, really," I reassure him. "Just a bit light-headed."

"Well, after what you've been through this year, that's perfectly under-standable. Still, let's check you out and make sure you're in the same great shape as you were six months ago."

Daisy leaves. Dr. Baker puts the cold stethoscope on my chest. "Your heartbeat is kind of low, but you've always had a bit of a slow heartbeat, haven't you?"

"Isn't that supposed to be good?" I ask.

"Yes, but if it drops too low, which sometimes happens as we get older, that might explain why you felt light-headed and fainted. Were you short of breath before you passed out?"

"Yes, a little," I confess. I'd thought my breathlessness was just a response to being at the Surf again.

He continues his exam. I let my gaze wander to the window, where billowy clouds are passing by, reminding me of the clouds that move across the Surf's ceiling. The ones at the Surf aren't real clouds, of course; just an illusion, like the ghosts I saw. Except they didn't look like ghosts. They looked as real as the people standing next to them, laughing and talking. But they weren't real. They couldn't be.

I've always hated needles and shots. I tense up just at the thought of feeling that sting when the needle pricks my skin. But today I'm glad to feel the poke when the nurse comes to draw blood. At least that feels real, when everything else around me doesn't. Yes, the pain is definitely not an illusion.

+

Afterward, Daisy insists on pushing me out in a wheelchair.

"Honestly, Daisy! As if I can't walk because I had one little fainting spell."

My daughter ignores me.

Daisy maneuvers the wheelchair into the elevator. On the way down, the elevator stops at the floor below us and another wheelchair is pushed inside, creating a tight fit. I look at the man next to me, his head hung low against his chest. I take in a breath at the sight of him. He's a shell of his former self. His skin sags like loose clothing, and his face is sunken and pale. A plaid blanket covers his legs and lap. He shows little reaction to his surroundings.

But he happens to look my way. I freeze, wondering if he'll remember me.

His eyes flare with recognition.

"Hello, Lance," I say. "It's good to see you."

He leans forward and squints. It's been years since we last saw each other, longer than that since we've spoken. He looks so old. A faded scar traces the side of his face, down his neck.

"The Surf," he says, nodding at me. "That's where I know you from." His voice is weak and hoarse, as though it takes great effort to speak. A sharp contrast to the cold, intimidating sound I remember from my youth.

"Yes," I admit.

"I used to go there all the time," he says.

"I remember."

He turns toward the young man pushing him. "I may not look it now, but I used to be quite a dancer in my day."

"I'll bet you were, Mr. Dugan."

"And I'll bet you didn't know that the Surf used to be on the lake."

"No, I didn't know that. I guess that was before my time."

"Everything was before your time," Lance snarls. "You're just a snot-nosed kid."

The young man rolls his eyes. "You got that right, Mr. Dugan."

Lance gives me a sideways glance. "The old Surf burned down, you know."

My heart races at his words. Besides me, he's the only one who knows what happened that night.

Lance reaches up and runs a finger along his scar, a puzzled look in his eyes.

The elevator stops and the door opens.

"Take care, Lance," I say, as the young man unlocks the wheelchair's wheels to move him away.

Lance nods at me. "Good to see you again."

Daisy waits until the door closes. "That frail-looking man is Chad's uncle? Chad said he moved back to be close to the Mayo Clinic for his cancer treatment, but I didn't realize how sick he was."

"It looks as though Lance is losing his battle."

Daisy is unusually quiet on the drive back. I stare out the window. What an odd coincidence to see Lance again, especially when I've just come from the Surf.

Finally, I feel the need to fill the silence. "You should have let Harry bring me over here," I say.

"What kind of daughter would I be if I let my husband drive my mother to the hospital after she was unconscious while I stayed and partied? Really, Mother."

I pick at a piece of lint on the car seat. "Then you should have let me take a cab back."

"Now you're just being ridiculous," Daisy says, glancing my way. "So, what did you want to tell me at the hospital?"

I wave my hand. "Oh, nothing."

"Where did you actually meet Dad?"

"Um." My mind races. "The parking lot. Outside the Surf."

"Well, that's nitpicking. It's still the Surf."

"I guess so."

"That's a relief. I thought you were going to tell me some dark family secret."

"And would that be so bad?"

"Chad said that his uncle left town suddenly after some accident that happened years ago. It makes him nervous whenever he's up for office that there might be some old family scandal he doesn't know about."

"I heard Lance moved because he married a woman from out east. There's nothing scandalous about that," I say, trying to keep my voice even. "And I didn't think you were interested in politics."

"Well, just the same, I'm glad we don't have any skeletons in our closet." She looks over at me. "We don't, do we?"

I force a small laugh. "I'm sure if you dig deep enough, every family has skeletons."

"In that case, Mother," Daisy says, her voice deadpan, "I'm hiding all the shovels."

Ten

✦

2007

I squint into the fading sun and turn my car into the Surf's parking lot for the second time in two days.

I lied to Daisy. I told her I was exhausted from yesterday, that I was going to bed early and would call her in the morning. Now, as the blue letters of the Surf Ballroom stare out at me, I realize how anxious I am to be here again.

When Sid and I moved to the farm, we started a new life and put the past behind us. Sid insisted, and I went along with it. The ballroom held powerful memories, ones that I reasoned were better kept at bay. But coming here last night, I felt such a strong connection to the Surf; a place that has survived changes in music over the years, tough times, leaky roofs, closings and reopenings, changing owners and extensive renovations. Like me.

This morning's paper was the real culprit. In big block letters on the second page of the *Clear Lake Mirror Reporter,* right under the obituaries, was an announcement.

THE BIG BAND BEAT IS BACK!

A GREAT TRADITION CONTINUES!

Sunday nights from June-Sept. Big Band Concert Series.

Dance the night away to memorable orchestrations of the swing era.

Doors open at 5:30 P.M. with dancing from 6–10 P.M. nightly.

I haven't been dancing in years. I doubt my old body could manage many dance moves. And yet, when I saw that advertisement, I had a sudden desire to go to the Surf, if just to prove to myself that what I saw yesterday was a fluke.

Dark clouds roll across the lake, blinking out the setting sun, and I tuck my umbrella under my arm. The marquee out front advertises a Rock and Roll Revue for the coming week. Just yesterday I saw Buddy Holly. Or thought I saw him. Am I just a grieving widow whose memories of the past are so strong that I'm hallucinating? My aunt Nelly saw nonexistent butterflies on the wall of her hospital room the last few days before she died, but we all thought that was due to the strong drugs.

I stop at the table inside the lobby and pay for a ticket, spending extra money to reserve a booth, one on the side not far from the stage. I place my umbrella on the seat next to me and settle in my spot. The band is onstage warming up. They're a younger group of men in their fifties and sixties. I've never heard of them. But I haven't kept up with music for years.

There's a small crowd present, not the mobs I remember from my youth. It's refreshing to see people dressed to the nines in suits and dresses, instead of golf shirts and Capri pants. I'm so glad I wore a dress.

"Can I get you something to drink?" A waitress who's much too young to be familiar with the big-band era stands next to my booth.

"How about a root beer? I haven't had one of those in ages."

"Sure enough. Are you expecting anyone else?"

"No. It's just me."

"A pretty woman like you? You won't be sitting here alone for long, I guarantee it."

Such a nice young girl, I think as she leaves. But she probably just said that to get a bigger tip. I've long since given up any pretense that I'm attractive, not at seventy-eight years of age. Even though I've always been thin, my shoulders have become rounded and I move more slowly. I stopped dyeing my hair its natural red color and let it grow out to a grayish-white tint. And I don't wear makeup. The wrinkles and spots that have taken over my skin are like the unwanted mosquitoes that swarm the lakeside. Both are expected, yet impossible to get rid of. But at least they're well-earned wrinkles.

I check out the crowd. Almost all of the people here are senior citizens, a few even older than I. Some I recognize: the former pastor of the Lutheran church and his wife, a couple from my own church, the man who used to run the cruise ship off the city seawall years ago. Most I don't know, though. I imagine the dance draws people from all across North Iowa.

I look up to see Eddie Johnson standing in front of me. He's not a ghost, but he's as close to being one as you can get without actually dying. Eddie is younger than me by five years but he hasn't aged well.

"Lorraine! First time I've seen you here. How the hell you doin'?"

"I'm fine, Eddie. How about yourself?"

"You know how it is. Gettin' by." He's a short, heavy man, bent over and mostly bald except for a rim of white that runs from ear to ear. His breathing is loud, as though it takes great effort. He adjusts the hearing aid in his right ear, then taps it once.

"I'm sorry to hear about Sid's passing. A good man and a fine farmer." His voice is loud.

I nod. "Thank you."

The waitress returns with the root beer. "See?" she says, her eyebrows raised.

I give a slight shake of my head. The last person I want sitting with me is Eddie Johnson. Although I feel sorry for him and all his health issues and financial woes, which I'm sure I'll soon hear about, Eddie is one of those people who you have a hard time sympathizing with. Years ago Sid hired him for the harvest, but Eddie quickly tired of the hard work and stopped showing up less than a week into it. Eddie now makes a habit of living with widows who can support him financially until they get sick of him and throw him out. I wonder if he reads the obit page regularly to keep up on who's available.

"I'll have a beer," Eddie says, handing the waitress a ten-dollar bill. "Keep the change."

"Yes, sir. Thank you."

I was never good at getting rid of unwanted guests, but I'm not interested in subsidizing Eddie's lifestyle.

"Actually, I'm expecting someone," I say as Eddie tries to fit his enormous belly into the space across from me in the booth. "But thanks for stopping by. It was good to see you again."

He looks wounded, and I almost have a change of heart. He nods and stands up. "I'm meeting someone, too. She's a well-off widow who wants to marry me. I don't know, though. Been there a few too many times, if you know what I mean. But you never know; I might be tying that knot again."

I can't imagine any woman who'd be that desperate. But I wish him luck as he shuffles off. I take a sip of my root beer, thinking of those rich widows who go through their entire inheritance on sleazeballs like Eddie after their husbands pass away, all because they're lonely. Or maybe they realize how fleeting life is and are trying to squeeze every bit out of their remaining years. I'll never understand it. But I was lucky. I had Sid.

The band is playing now, a tune I recall but can't name. I close my eyes and let the music take me away, back to another time and place. I think of all the people I wish were here tonight, but mostly I think of Sid.

What I'd give for a few moments with him again. That would be worth all the money in the world.

When I open my eyes, everything is the same, except couples fill the dance area now, shuffling across the maple hardwood floor.

Why am I here? I'm not interested in dancing or meeting a man. I'm going nuts, thinking I'd see my husband again. It was silly of me to come here tonight. Tomorrow I'll say a novena and ask the intercession of Saint Dymphna, patron saint of crazy people.

The band starts another tune, "Embraceable You." Sid loved that song.

How much I've missed this music, the deep sounds that come from the saxophone, the way the notes fill the air and make everything more exciting.

"May I have this dance, miss?"

A man stands next to my booth, his arm outstretched, a slight twinkle in his eye. He looks to be in his forties, wearing a suit he must have borrowed from his grandfather because it's definitely from another time: white, single-breasted, with wide trousers. A neatly folded black kerchief sticks out the front pocket, and his black bow tie matches the small corsage on his lapel. His dark hair is combed back in a way that reminds me of Daddy's hair when he was younger.

"Oh, I couldn't," I say, shaking my head.

"Oh, you can," he replies, and the twinkle becomes more pronounced.

"I'm afraid I wouldn't be able to keep up," I say in protest. "I haven't danced in years."

"I promise I won't fling you across the dance floor. I'm too much of a gentleman to do that. And we'll stop if you get tired out."

I hesitate. I'd feel foolish dancing with a man half my age. But he doesn't withdraw his hand, and there's something about him that seems familiar.

"I won't take no for an answer," he says, smiling.

I sigh and take his hand. He sweeps me onto the dance floor. His movements are smooth and flowing. He's obviously had lessons to dance so well. He has a way about him that's charismatic, like a movie star of a long-ago era.

"This isn't so bad now, is it?" he says.

"This is one of my favorite songs," I confess as we glide almost magically across the floor. He makes it seem so easy, almost like second nature. I'd forgotten how fun it was to dance. And he's so good at it.

"A wonderful song, but my band played it better and I'll bet you could sing it better," he says. "At least you could, back in the day."

Back in the day? I doubt he'd been born yet, back in the day.

"How did you know that I sang? What was the name of your band?" I ask.

He takes my hand as we foxtrot and presses it against his chest. "I'm offended. Truly, I am. You don't even recognize me?"

"I'm sorry. I haven't been to a dance at the Surf for many years. I doubt you're old enough to have played in one of the bands I sang with."

He spins me around once, slowly, and brings me in close. He has a natural flair and people are beginning to watch us. He smells like cigarette smoke, although smoking is banned at the Surf.

"Well, I remember you," he says. "You were just a wisp of a girl back then. You had long red hair and those sultry turquoise eyes. I called you the Tangerine Girl, and we played that song for you."

My skin tingles. I remember that, but it was so long ago, when I was just eighteen.

He smiles. "The night I heard you sing."

He must be joking. "You couldn't be talking about the original Surf Ballroom? That place burned down years ago."

He nods. "Sixty years ago. My band played there the night it burned. We should have been the first to open this new place, too. But instead Ray Pearl and His Orchestra played here. Go figure!"

Suddenly, I remember him. But he can't be who I think he is! How can I possibly be dancing with the famous Jimmy Dorsey? A man who made so much memorable music and who died fifty years ago?

"You're. . . ." I try to choke out the name, but it won't come.

"Shh, we don't want any unwanted attention. Let's just enjoy this dance, this song, this music."

He pulls me close and I feel weak. I lean my head on his shoulder. I try to quell the trembling of my hands. The saxophone player on stage is performing a solo in the middle of the song.

"You know, I used to play the saxophone," Jimmy says. "I was damn good at it, too, pardon the expression."

"I remember," I say, still in shock.

"We saxophone players appreciate good singers. You were one of them."

"Thank you." Jimmy Dorsey only heard me sing that one time. I can't help but feel honored by the compliment.

"Yes, you did a good job. You could have become famous like me. Bad timing, is all. Never expected the place to burn down."

"No. Of course not." I feel warm and a bit breathless. I should sit down before I faint again. But something keeps me here. I need to hear what he has to say. After all, it isn't every day you get to dance with Jimmy Dorsey, even if he is a figment of my imagination.

"They never did figure out what started the fire," he says. "'Course, it doesn't really matter now, does it? Water under the bridge, you might say. It wouldn't change anything if people did know."

"I suppose." I frown and stop dancing. "Is that why you're here? To keep me from telling?"

He shrugs. "You have nothing to be afraid of. The past is past. You can tell whoever you want. But maybe some things are best left secret."

"I don't understand."

"You remember my brother, right? He was hot-headed and stubborn. But he played a decent trombone."

I nod. Tommy Dorsey was more than decent. He was a legend. Jimmy and Tommy had started out together in a band, then had parted and formed their own bands. After World War II they'd joined up again. People joked that they were like opposite ends of a magnet.

Jimmy winks at a woman dancing past. The woman giggles. Jimmy was always the laid-back one, the charmer. He looks at me with those big brown eyes. "Well, Mac and I, I called him Mac, we didn't always get along. Everybody knows that. But we were still brothers, even though he was a short-tempered son of a gun. So we settled our differences after the war and got back together again. That's what you have to keep in mind. The past is like sibling rivalry, and believe me, I know a thing or two about that. Sometimes it drives you apart before it brings you back together again."

The music ends and people are clapping. Jimmy bows then walks me back to my booth. I sit down and he glides his fingers across the side of my face. "Thank you for the dance. Take care, my Tangerine."

And then he's gone. I blink and look around as though I'm coming out of a trance. Or was it a dream? I'm left with the sensation of being touched on my face, the words "Take care, my Tangerine" echoing in my head.

Eleven

✦

2007

I've always been a light sleeper, but I feel as though I've pulled an all-night shift at a Walmart. My poor old bones are sore and I have a splitting headache. I left the Surf shortly after dancing with Jimmy Dorsey, but what little sleep I was able to get was interrupted by vivid and disconcerting nightmares. I dream of the night the Surf burned down, and half expect to smell smoke when I wake. I'm relieved to be in my own bed, looking out at the lake, not in a burning building. My dress is a clump at the end of the bed. I didn't even bother to hang it up.

I get up and make myself some tea and toast, humming the music from last night. I should be more concerned. But whether Jimmy was a ghost or a hallucination or a dream, either way, it was a wonderful evening. For a short time I felt like a young girl again.

After eating my breakfast, common sense sinks in. I wonder if I even left my booth the night before. The music was so therapeutic that perhaps I dreamed the whole dance. I decide to take a walk to clear my head. I stroll along the sidewalk winding around the lake. Our move to the condo had been a good decision, and necessary once we got Sid's diagnosis. The condo was a great place to enjoy life again. Sid and I often took long walks and stuck our feet in the water. In the winter we watched from our window as ice houses appeared on the frozen lake.

I pass through the walkway between the two beige brick buildings that angle away from each other, apparently so that more units have a view of the lake. I live on the second story of the second building near the center, close to the elevator and a neighbor I barely know, a young single man named Garrett who once helped me get Sid from the hall into the living room when his strength had given out. He said to call on him anytime, but he's never home and is always in a hurry when I do see him.

I stop at the bench we christened Little Way after I encouraged Sid to walk just a little way each day to keep up his strength. I sit down and stare at the water lapping against the rocky shore, its steady rhythm comforting. The water stretches out beyond my vision, meeting the sky somewhere out in the distance. Clear Lake isn't that big, but it has bends and twists that make it appear larger.

This is my favorite spot. It's "our" spot, where we spent hours together. Sometimes I would read to Sid. He'd close his eyes and I wouldn't be sure if he had fallen asleep, but then he'd make a remark or ask a question— "What happened next?" or, "Is that the end?"—when it was obviously not the end, but he wanted to kid me. And sometimes he did fall asleep and I'd hear him snore and pretty soon he'd lean into me.

Just last year I sat here with Sid beside me. I miss not only his voice and presence, but the physicality of having someone close. I miss his touch, and almost a year later I still take his sweaters out of the drawer to inhale his scent. I still break down, not as much as before, but when something hits me just right, like when I read a piece of news that I know he'd be interested in, or when I hear his words in my head.

But I'm also angry at Sid. I'm angry that he died and left me alone. And I never agreed with his philosophy that the past was past, something to be forgotten. If he hadn't made me promise, none of this would have happened. If he hadn't left me . . .

"Thought I'd find you here."

Harry stands in front of me. He's wearing a striped golf shirt, khaki pants, and his country club hat. I'm struck by the fact that he knows where to find me. I wonder if Daisy would have had that same inclination.

He holds two cups in his hands. "You still like a latte with extra milk?" he asks, handing me one of the cups.

"I do, although I don't have it very often. It's not good for the figure," I say, accepting the cup. "As if I should be concerned with that at my age," I add with a laugh.

"Hey, you're as young as you feel, Lorraine. What was Sid's motto? Live each day to the fullest? No reason to stop now."

"I won't," I promise, although with Sid's death, life hasn't felt as full or worth living.

He sits down next to me on the bench and stretches out. Even though he's starting to look older, his thinning hair more gray than brown now, he still has boyish good looks.

"I was headed out to the golf course anyway, so I thought I'd stop by. When you didn't answer the door, I decided to look here. Kind of warm out today."

I hadn't noticed the heat yet. I've been too deep in my own thoughts to take in much of my surroundings. There are a few boats on the lake that I now observe: two sailboats, a fishing boat, and a pontoon boat in the distance. Funny how they suddenly appear in my line of vision as though they are ghostly apparitions, too.

"Do you miss the farmhouse?" he asks.

"Sometimes, but life is easier here. The condo is newer and smaller, and all on one level. I can walk around the lake and watch the fishermen, or hang my feet off the dock, or wade in the water. It's like being on vacation. We didn't travel much, you know." I don't add that even the smaller condo feels huge and empty without Sid in it, that it's no fun being on vacation by myself.

"You can still travel."

"It's harder now," I say, sounding like those women I detest, who think that life stops when you reach a certain age. But I also don't want to be one of those people on the cruise ship who needs a walker just to get to the pool and back.

I reach across and lightly touch his arm. "Why are you really here? Other than to discuss my travel habits."

He sighs. "You know me too well. I was going through some of the pictures we have on file at the firehouse. Pictures of the Surf Ballroom fire. There's one that I want you to take a look at."

He pulls a folded sheet from his pocket. "This is a copy of an old newspaper article. The picture's not the best quality, but I think there's a remarkable likeness."

He hands me the black-and-white photo, one taken from the top of Curly's Café, which used to be next door to the ballroom. It shows the ballroom being consumed by black smoke and flames. The picture was taken at night, but some of the spectators' faces are visible, highlighted by the fire.

"Here," he says, pointing to a woman in the far right corner of the photo. She's huddled beneath a blanket and the picture captures her profile, the upturned nose I've always hated and the high cheekbones that have dropped over the years. But the resemblance is still undeniable.

"Is that you?" he asks.

"I've never seen this before." I'm paralyzed for a few seconds. The evidence in front of me unnerves me so. What else does Harry know?

"So you were there at the fire?"

"I guess I was. I must have forgotten." Even to my own ears, my excuse sounds hackneyed.

"I'm surprised you forgot. This was a pretty big deal back then, wasn't it?"

I hand the picture to him. "There were a lot of 'big deal' moments back then. The war, and all that. And when you're as old as I am, they tend to run together."

He frowns and cocks his head to one side. "I suppose so. I was hoping this photo might jog your memory a bit."

I can barely look at it, the memories are so strong. I didn't know anyone had taken my picture, but I remember the cold biting into my ankles, feeling distraught and helpless. "I'm sorry. It was so long ago."

"That's too bad. I believe we can learn a lot from reexamining the past."

"I'm not so sure," I say. "I mean, what can you learn from a sixty-year-old fire?"

"Many things. It's becoming somewhat common to question conclusions now that we know more. For instance, have you ever heard of 'spalling'?"

"Can't say that I have."

"It's the breakdown of concrete during a fire thought to be caused by flammable liquids. Many people went to jail over concrete spalling because it looked like arson. But science and testing have discovered that crumbling is a normal phenomenon from moisture in the concrete over-heating during a fire, and is unrelated to a flammable liquid. That's just one example of how things have changed."

"That sounds terribly complicated. And to my knowledge, no one went to jail when the Surf burned down."

"I know," Harry says, standing up. "But that's the point. Maybe someone should have."

Twelve

✦

August, 1944

The truck with the white star on the door arrived at six in the morning. We loaded jugs of cold well water onto the back and wrapped them in burlap. By noon the August heat gleamed off the pitchforks and Daddy's cap was damp around the edges.

"You're to wear pants when delivering food to those men," Mom chastised me as I grabbed the basket of food. I reluctantly ran up to my room to change into my overalls. Her words followed me up the stairs. "I'm not allowing my daughter out there in a dress. I don't want to encourage those men to think of you in inappropriate ways."

Mom didn't understand. All the men, with the exception of Helmut, were kind and gracious. Helmut acted disgruntled much of the time, and he learned only enough English to say things like "Water" and "More" and "Eat." One day when I brought the food basket, Norman refused to let him eat.

"He didn't want to work this morning. No work, no eat," he said, nodding at the prisoner. Helmut clicked his heels and gave Norman the Nazi salute, then handed him an apple with a swastika carved into it. He said something in German to Günther and nodded at him to translate.

"He says to tell you he went long periods on the Russian front living on leaves and roots. This does not bother him."

Norman took a bite of one of Mom's biscuits and smacked his lips. "Fine and dandy with me. Tell him if he doesn't start working I'll tell the camp commander to put him on another detail. He'll be putting asphalt on roofs instead of working in this field. And there won't be any biscuits or chicken or pie."

Günther translated. Helmut said something that sounded like a swear word, then sneered and lit a cigarette. Norman smiled and winked at me. Later, when I came back out, Helmut was working alongside the other men.

Daddy gave me a look that said *Don't mention this to Mom.* I nodded. Of course I wouldn't tell her. Because Mom was right in this case. We did have a Nazi on our farm.

+

A few days later, Daddy came to find me after I had just finished hanging a load of laundry on the line. I wondered if the clothes would dry in the humid heat.

"I need your help," Daddy said, pointing at the distant horizon, which until moments ago had looked sunny. There it was: a looming thundercloud that threatened rain. No storms had been in the forecast.

"We have to finish getting the pitched hay into the barn," he said. "I need you to go out with the other wagon and collect the rest of the cut hay. Take two of the men with you."

I started tearing down the clothes from the lines, the ones I'd hung with painstaking care, tossing them into a pile. I threw the basket down on the porch and followed Daddy to the barn.

Daddy had a wagon attached to the back of the tractor. "Get as much as you can and we'll park the load in the barn. Günther, you and Jens go with her. Norman, do you want to go along?"

Norman shook his head. "I'll stay here. You might need my help." He nodded at the large grappling hook that Daddy used to lift the clumps of hay from the wagon up to the second-story haymow in the barn. It took three men to work the rope and lift, to distribute the hay above, and to handle the horse that pulled the rope.

Daddy had taught me to drive the tractor when I was thirteen, although Pete learned at eleven. Still, I had to practically stand on the clutch to push it in. Jens and Günther got on the wagon and I drove them out to the east fields. They jumped off and started pitching the piles into the wagon. I tamped down the hay, keeping one eye on the gathering clouds. Then I put the tractor in low gear. Sweat poured off Jens and Günther as they kept up with the moving wagon, running from pile to pile.

I caught my breath as a clap of thunder shook the ground. Jens looked at me, his eyes wide. We still had a quarter of the row left to pitch. We wouldn't make it that far.

After five more minutes, I yelled at them to stop. The rolling thundercloud loomed just beyond the field, followed by a darkened sky. Flashes of lightning threatened more than rain. We'd seen twisters drop from those types of clouds.

I revved the tractor as Jens and Günther stood on the giant pile of hay in the wagon and tried to keep their balance. The cloud chased us to the barn, where Daddy was pulling up the last of the hay.

I stopped the tractor near the door and we unhooked the stacked wagon. The men pushed it into the barn. That's when I noticed the empty stalls.

"The cows are in the far pasture!"

Daddy was working with the grappling hook and didn't hear me. I knew he would say to leave the cows. But we usually left them close to shelter, where they'd trot to the barn when the weather turned, letting out a low moo as though to warn us. The sky held an eerie, dark glow.

"I help," Jens said as he followed me to the cow pasture behind the barn. The clouds burst open. I could barely see through the downpour and almost ran smack into the gate. Daddy usually kept it open so they could wander back and forth, but they'd been too lazy to seek out the new grass on the far end of the pasture, so he'd been forcing them down there for the past week.

The cows were just on the other side of the gate, huddled together under a tree. They made low mooing sounds as if to berate me for locking them in. I tugged at the latch and Jens added his strength, then together we pulled the wide gate open. The cows didn't move, so I cupped my hands and tried to imitate the sound Daddy used to call them home. "Here Bossy, Bossy," I yelled.

Petunia was the first to come, and the rest followed her. After the last one had passed, Jens closed the gate. The cows hurried toward the safety of the barn. The rain fell in torrents around us, and the wind was picking up. I could barely take a step without being pushed back. Jens took my hand and pulled me toward the barn.

A large crack blasted the air, and a branch from a nearby tree fell not twenty feet from us. Mom would usually herd me down to the cellar in bad weather, then sit and worry about Daddy and Pete until they showed up dripping and cold from the fields.

We finally made it to the side door of the barn. I could hear the men's voices on the other side. It took both of us to open the door against the strong winds. I knew it wasn't safe here; I'd heard of barns blowing down, trapping the animals inside. But we were too far from the cellar. The cows had moved into their stalls. Daddy was probably standing at the open barn door, watching the skies for a funnel cloud that might ruin his crops.

I looked at Jens, whose shirt was completely soaked and streaked with strands of golden hay. The shirt clung to his body, showing off his muscular physique. Water dripped down his tanned arms. It was then that I realized he was still holding my hand. His wet palm was a natural fit in mine, as if meant to be there.

"Thank you for your help." I was suddenly aware of my drenched dress that stuck to my skin, of what it might reveal.

He blinked away the water that was falling from his hair onto his face. "*Bitte schön.* Welcome?"

"Yes." I nodded. "That's the right word."

The storm raged outside and another clap of thunder shook the door. His hand tightened around mine.

"*Unheimlich. Der Regen!*" He widened his eyes and pointed at the door.

"I don't know what you're saying," I said, shaking my head.

"Lorraine!" Daddy's voice called out. Jens quickly let go of my hand.

"Over here!"

Jens sighed and looked toward the other side of the barn, as though he was reluctant to go back to work. I thought of how hard he'd been trying to learn our language.

"I could help you learn English."

"You help?"

"Yes. Help. Teach you."

"Ya," he said. He looked unsure, but then his dimple deepened as he grinned at me.

"Okay?" I said.

"Okay!" Jens repeated. "Help." Then he laughed and shook his head like a dog, splattering me with wetness.

Thirteen

✦

1944

W here are you from?" I asked him. "What part of Deutschland? Munich?"

He shook his head. "Emden, Ostfriesland." He opened his dictionary and turned the pages. "North," he said, although it came out sounding more like "nort."

I made a mental note to look it up on Pete's globe later.

I'd been tutoring Jens every day for the last week. He was quick to learn, better than I was at picking up German. I reasoned that he'd helped us so much during the storm that it was the charitable thing to do. A good Christian act: helping out a boy who wanted to learn. Maybe he'd also discover that Americans were kind and generous. Daddy said that was part of the intention of putting a POW camp in the middle of Iowa: to show them what good people we were, and to discount all the propaganda they'd been fed by the Nazi party. But part of me also worried that Mom was right and that Jens was a Nazi, and no amount of good treatment or home-cooked food would change that.

It surely hadn't worked on Helmut, who glowered at Jens during our tutoring sessions.

"Brothers or sisters?" I asked.

Jens put up two fingers. "Edward *und* Herman."

"Where are they?"

"*Wehrmacht.* Ah, *Deutsche* ar-mee. Edward and Herman fight."

"Oh."

"You?" he asked.

I put up one finger. "One brother. Pete."

Jens looked around. "Where Pete?"

"France. Fighting," I replied.

"Oh." He sighed.

We looked at each other for a long moment. The irony of the situation filled the space between us: my brother and his brothers could be shooting at each other right now, and here we were, sitting in the middle of a freshly mown field sharing food and talking.

"We should study," I said, breaking the spell. I nodded at the words on the notebook paper I'd brought. I pointed at the first word on the paper and then at myself. "I."

"*Ich,*" Jens said, then "I."

The second word was you. I pointed at Jens. "You."

He nodded and pointed at me. "You."

A strand of hair fell out of my braid as I bent down to touch the third word. "We," I said, pointing at both myself and Jens.

He looked at me and pointed at himself, then carefully picked the strand of hair away from my face and touched my nose. "We."

It felt like a brotherly gesture, the kind that Pete would have made, but I flushed when his finger brushed my cheek.

"You already know this. Don't you?"

"Ya," he replied.

"You should have told me."

"Good practice," he said, and shrugged. He picked up a thick blade of grass and pulled it tight between his thumbs, then blew on it, making a whistling sound.

He looked at me. "You?"

I shook my head. I'd tried lots of times but could never make that sound.

"Easy," he said. He picked out a long blade and showed me how to hold it between my thumbs. He blew through his lips and nodded at me.

I made a pathetic attempt that sounded like I was spitting wind.

He laughed.

"Not easy," I said.

He took out his dictionary. "Easy than learn."

"Easier," I corrected him.

"Easier," he said.

"Why do you want to learn English?"

He opened his dictionary and scanned the pages, frowning as though he'd given this a great deal of thought and wanted to make sure I understood. Finally he looked up at me.

"When I see you," he said, pointing at me. "First day."

I didn't understand. "The first day you saw me?"

"Ya," he said. "I want talk you."

"You're learning English so you can talk to me?"

He nodded. "So I can talk you."

✦

"A group of hooligans visited the POW camp last night," Daddy told me the next morning as he poured a cup of coffee, pointing at an article in the newspaper. "They painted threats on the poles surrounding the camp. A poor way to show your patriotism. What poor excuses for human beings."

I wondered if Lance Dugan was involved. He seemed more like a schoolyard bully than the kind who would do this, though. "Has anything happened to the men who are working out of the camp?"

"Not yet." Daddy took a deep breath and shook his head. "I'll keep a lookout, and if I see anyone poking their noses around here, they'll get a load of buckshot in their rear ends."

"You can't go around shooting people just because they're on our property, Daddy."

"I got a right to protect myself and my boys." Daddy put that page of the newspaper under his arm. "Tell your mother I spilled coffee on this section and threw it out."

His boys? Had Daddy adopted a crew of German prisoners?

✦

"What movie are you seeing?" Mom asked later as she sat at the table nursing a cup of tea. It was too hot for tea, but a habit of hers this time of day. The kitchen smelled of liver and onions, and there was a swelling heat that held the promise of rain.

It figured that Mom's new excitement for my social life coincided with my date with Scotty Bishop. I tucked my yellow blouse into my gray skirt and picked up a white sweater, even though I didn't think I'd need it.

"*Meet Me in St. Louis.* It's a musical. Supposed to be really good."

Mom swatted away a fly that lingered on her cup of tea. Old newspapers were riddled with black smudges as we tried to keep them under control throughout the summer.

"And what time do you plan on coming home?" she asked.

"When do you want me home?"

"At a respectable time. You can spend half an hour in town after the movie is over, but I expect you home soon thereafter."

I couldn't decide whether to wear my hair up in a ponytail or down.

In the end the humidity decided for me and I put it up. But even with the heat I shivered at the memory of how close I'd come to kissing Scotty at the beach. Maybe tonight we'd share one.

"Your first date," Mom said wistfully. "I wish Pete could be here for this."

I let out a breath that sounded like a balloon deflating. Why couldn't it just be about me tonight?

"I remember his first date with Dixie Waverly," Mom was saying. "He was so nervous he forgot his money and had to borrow some from Mike Schmitt."

"Maybe he'll bring home a French wife," I said.

Mom was aghast. "Lorraine Kindred. Don't say such a thing!"

"I was just joking."

"He would never . . ."

"Besides, what would be so wrong with that?"

"Your brother is *not* bringing home a French wife. He doesn't even *speak* French."

"It's the language of love," I said.

"He's going to marry an Iowa girl the same as his father. Besides, Pete's always been sweet on Dixie."

I thought of mentioning that Dixie was dating someone else, but Mom's face was pinched together like a shriveled raisin, as though my suggestion had opened up a terrifying possibility she'd never considered before.

A black Buick turned into the long gravel driveway. Scotty must have borrowed his father's car. I grabbed my sweater and headed toward the door.

"You'll wait until he knocks on the door proper and introduces himself," Mom warned.

I rolled my eyes and went back up to my room so it wouldn't look as though I'd been waiting for him.

A few moments later I heard a knock at the door. Mom's voice carried up the stairs.

"I think she's almost ready, Scott."

I bounded down the steps before Mom got started on war talk, reciting who all was in the service from the area and who had died and how the Allies had just liberated Florence, because before he knew it she'd be showing him Pete's globe and we'd never get out of there.

"Hi, Scotty. I'm ready to go," I announced as soon as I reached the bottom of the stairs.

Mom flashed her *you know you're not supposed to run down the stairs* look.

"We should go so we're not late. I hear there's going to be a long line," I said as I hurried him out the door.

Scotty shrugged. "Nice seeing you again, Mrs. Kindred."

"Tell your parents hello," Mom said, following us to the door. Then she watched us out the window with moon eyes. She and Daddy never went to the movies. Mom said Daddy couldn't stay awake for a whole movie and his snoring would disturb the entire theater. Maybe farm life took too much energy. Or maybe they were just too old.

We'd almost made it to the car when Daddy drove up in the tractor. He waved at us but thankfully didn't stop. He was followed by the truck carrying the POWs.

I let Scotty open the door for me and didn't make eye contact with anyone as the truck wound around us. Hooting sounds drifted from the back of the truck, most likely Jakob. I was sure Daddy would hear about this from Mom.

Scotty stared at them. "Who are those guys?" he asked when he'd started the car.

"They're the men Daddy hired to help while Pete's gone."

"Where are they from?"

I paused, wondering what to tell him. It would be hard to explain the PW insignia on their shirts. "The POW camp in Algona."

His eyes widened. "*German* prisoners?"

"They're German POWs," I admitted, although they no longer seemed like prisoners but more like hired help.

"Holy buckets, Lorraine! You've got Germans on your farmland? Is your father nuts?"

"No, he's not nuts," I said, sticking out my chin. "He's got a farm to run and no one to help him. I don't see what harm there is in using those men to do chores for us while my brother is off fighting for our country."

"Sorry, I didn't mean to sound like a preacher's son," he said. "I'm just worried about you."

"Well, you don't have to be. The camp sends an armed guard."

"Wow. An armed guard. It sounds like the stuff of movies."

It actually felt very normal. Even Norman seemed okay with it now. He had become part of the background and the men had become part of Daddy's crew.

The truck had stopped to unload the water jugs.

"That one German looks really young," Scotty mentioned, and when I looked up I saw Jens sitting at the very back of the truck with his jacket slung across his sunburned neck. Our eyes met for an instant and I shifted my gaze, embarrassed.

Scotty drove to town in silence and I worried I'd been too harsh with him, or that I'd betrayed something in the look I exchanged with Jens. But Scotty took my hand when we got out of the car and held it all the way to the theater line, which wound out front and down the sidewalk past the corner drugstore.

His long fingers were interlaced with mine, making them look like a little child's next to his. His hand felt strong, but softer than Daddy's.

"What a mob!" Scotty shouted as we hurried to the back of the line.

I'd been to a few movies in my life, but hadn't ever seen a line this long. Scotty saluted two men in uniform who stood not far in front of us. They were home on leave from boot camp and they were laughing, their spirits high on this warm August night.

I remembered Pete bringing me to see *Bambi* two years ago. Even though I'd been almost fourteen, I'd cried when Bambi's mom was killed and Pete had put his arm around me. Where was he right now? What was he doing while I was standing in line at the Lake Theater?

"Hey, give us cuts." Lance Dugan pushed his hefty frame into line behind us. His shiny new Packard sat curbside in a no-parking area, but Lance didn't seem worried. No doubt his father would take care of any tickets he incurred. I held back a gasp when I saw Stella with him. My eyes widened and Stella replied with a small shrug. Why hadn't she mentioned she was dating Lance?

The line finally moved and we crowded into the cool theater, where Scotty found seats near the middle. The theater was one of the few places that had air conditioning, and that alone was worth the price of admission. Stella sat between Scotty and Lance. I caught my breath as the room darkened amid hushes and excited voices. The movie newsreel played first. It showed American soldiers sweeping the streets of Rennes for mines hidden by retreating Nazis after the liberation. The next clip showed cheering crowds along the streets as U.S. soldiers marched by. Could Pete be one of those soldiers? He'd only been gone six weeks, but as I searched among the faces the camera panned by quickly and I wished I could see the clip again. The reel ended with an angry mob trying to attack two collaborationists as soldiers took them away.

"Kill those Nazi sympathizers!" Lance yelled, and people cheered.

Scotty cheered as well. "See?" he whispered. "Who knows what those Germans are burying in your father's field?"

I flinched. What if Scotty was right? I could imagine Helmut doing something to undermine our crops. And I didn't really know the other men well. Neither did Daddy. I thought of Jens and his eagerness to please me, of Ludwig's helpfulness with the machinery, of Günther's curiosity about American life. Could it all be a ploy to gain our trust? Why would they want to help provide food for the enemy?

Mom said that Daddy and I had our heads in the sand. Maybe Daddy's devotion to the farm had given him rose-colored glasses, and maybe a smile from a blue-eyed boy with a dimple and disheveled blond hair had done the same for me.

Scotty squeezed my hand, wrapping his long fingers around my smaller ones. His hand felt sweaty now and I held my arm out awkwardly, trying not to think of how differently Jens's hand had felt in mine.

Fourteen

✦

1944

How you say this?" Jens pointed at a word in his book.

"Saxophone," I replied, stretching out the sound of the *o*.

"Saxophone," he repeated, emphasizing the vowel like I had.

We were sitting under an apple tree next to the barn, hidden from view of the house. The sweet smell of ripe fruit hung above our heads. Daddy had the men in the loft moving hay today. It was dusty, dirty, hot work, and Jens smelled of sweat and the barn. His tanned arms held a layer of dirt and he had a piece of straw stuck in his hair that I had to resist plucking out.

Daddy was downright smitten with Ludwig. The two spent their break time together fiddling with the tractor or the truck or whatever else needed fixing around the farm. Pete had been the one to help Daddy with such things, and Ludwig now filled a lonely gap that Daddy must have been feeling without Pete around.

Maybe that's why Daddy didn't mind me tutoring Jens, although we had an unspoken agreement not to mention it to Mom. Daddy and I were learning about their culture while teaching them our Iowa ways, but Mom would never understand.

The rest of the men were on the other side of the barn. Norman didn't seem bothered by the fact that Jens was sitting beneath the tree with me and Ludwig was with Daddy, completely out of his vision. Norman had become more at ease with the men, even Helmut, whose disgruntled complaining had become commonplace, but I noticed Helmut's body had filled out now that he was eating Mom's cooking, and his pale face had color now. When cigarettes became hard to get, Norman traded Jakob his wristwatch for four packs, as Jakob was able to buy cigarettes with his ration stamps from the camp canteen. Jakob said he hid the watch under his mattress so it wouldn't be confiscated.

Now Norman often left his gun locked in the truck so he didn't have to carry it around. The men teased him about his nightly shenanigans at the White Elephant Tavern in Algona, which he related with a certain pleasure. He relished their attention. I had to admit, my time with Jens was a nice break away from Mom, whose slippers I heard padding up and down the stairs all hours of the night and whose moodiness I had to face during the day.

As I sat with Jens, I remembered Scotty's warning. But sitting in the hazy afternoon sun surrounded by the chirping grasshoppers and clucking chickens, I refused to believe that Jens was my enemy.

His eyes brightened whenever he saw me, and I couldn't help but be awed that I was capable of lighting up his face that way. He'd been practicing hard and was able to carry on a basic conversation, although there were words he still struggled with. Günther said he was the hardest-working student in the class he taught.

"You have fun on date?" Jens asked, his tone sounding a bit accusatory. He picked at the grass and looked up at me from beneath furrowed brows.

The question startled me. I didn't feel comfortable talking about Scotty in front of him. I'd started wearing my hair down sometimes instead of in a braid. I wanted Jens to see me as older, so I bragged, "Yes. We went to the movies."

"Good," Jens said, making a wiping motion atop the grass with his hands. "Nice American boyfriend."

"Well, he's more than nice. He's on the basketball team and he's the smartest boy in our school. He's going to college next year."

Jens flashed a confused look. "College?"

"University," I said. "He's going to the University of Iowa."

"Oh. You go too?"

"I don't know," I said. "I'm a junior now. I have two more years of high school."

"You are smart. You go."

"I'm thinking of going to California." Of course, those thoughts had nothing to do with studying, and more to do with singing.

"Not be with boyfriend?"

I looked away. I hadn't really thought about it. Definitely not something I wanted to talk to Jens about.

"How about you?" I asked. "Do you want to go to college?"

He shook his head. "I no go, three reason." He held up one finger. "One, not smart. Two," he said, holding up another finger, "I must work, support family. And three," he said, holding up a third finger, "I am in prison camp."

"Number three will change," I reassured him. "The war will be over and you'll go back home."

He squinted into the sun. "I want go home. I hate war."

"Then why did you join the German army?"

"No choice. They come to my town, say I must fight. Make brothers fight, too. If resist we are traitors. Will be shot."

Jens hadn't wanted to fight. He wasn't like Pete who was performing his patriotic duty, who felt it was an honor to serve his country. I had heard Germany had a draft system. He ran his hand across the grass. "I am not Nazi. I am just soldier who no good fighting. That why I end up in prison camp after first skirmish."

"Is it terrible there? In the camp?"

"No terrible." He sighed. "Beds bumpy, no good to sleep, some guards hate us, treat us bad, not like Mr. Kindred. Other men from camp work canning factory. I am outdoors, learn about American agriculture. I prefer here. I am better farmer than soldier." He ran a finger along the grass. "Helmut say I disgrace Deutsch army."

"Why does he say that?"

"My *freundschaft*"—he stopped and pressed his lips together—"friendship with daughter of farmer. He say I face discipline when Germany win war."

"I didn't realize," I said, angry that Helmut was threatening Jens.

Jens shook his head. "I do not care."

"I care. And Germany isn't going to win the war. We are. So you won't be disciplined when you return."

"I will miss this farm. I will miss you." He looked up at me with eyes that were bluer than Clear Lake. I leaned over and took the piece of hay from his hair. My fingers lingered on a strand of hair and I had an urge to run them down his cheek and across his lips. I wondered what his lips would feel like against mine.

Then I remembered the newsreel. The collaborationists. Is that what I'd be if I let him kiss me? Would I be arrested and marched through the streets with people shouting and hitting me? What would Pete think? Mom would disown me.

I pulled my hand back. "What work will you do in Germany?"

"I play in band."

"What instrument? Oh, let me guess. The saxophone?"

He nodded. "I play in camp band."

"The POW camp?"

He nodded. "We play for prisoners and American officers."

"I want to sing with a band," I said. "That's what I really want to do." I didn't confess that to many people, but talking to Jens was different. Our moments together were too brief, like sand flitting through fingers.

"Like Judy Garland? We watch camp movie." He made a spinning motion with his fingers.

"Tornado? *The Wizard of Oz.*"

"Ya. Like on farm."

I remembered him pulling me against the strong winds, our damp skin touching, and fought an urge to look away. "That wasn't exactly a tornado. But yes, I want to sing professionally."

"You sing for Jens?"

"Here? Now?"

He nodded.

I looked around. Could they hear me? "Maybe a few lines." I started singing a Judy Garland song from the movie *Broadway Melody,* one I often sang around the house.

> *You made me love you*
> *I didn't want to do it*
> *I didn't want to do it*
> *You made me want you*
> *And all the time you knew it.*
> *I guess you always knew it.*

I stopped, realizing how the lyrics might sound to Jens. He was staring at me. I put my hands on my hot cheeks. Had I meant to sing that song to Jens?

"You sing good. No, not good," Jens said, struggling.

I scrunched up my nose. "Not good?"

"Great. You sing great."

"Thank you. Maybe someday I can hear you play the saxophone," I said, my voice shaky.

"Maybe you come hear band?" Then he shook his head. "No civilians in prison camp."

"Then you'll have to bring your saxophone here."

"Camp property."

"Oh."

He touched the end of my hair. "What this called?"

"Hair."

"No. Color."

"Red."

"Is my favorite color." He looked at me. "*Now* is my favorite color," he whispered.

I felt the heat rise in my cheeks again, imagining them slowly turning the color of my hair.

I stood up, reluctant to leave. "I'll be going back to school tomorrow. I won't be able to tutor you over lunch anymore." I hoped Daddy would keep the men working through the supper hour like he sometimes did. But most days they were gone by five o'clock.

Jens had a stricken look on his face. "I see you again?"

"I'll still bring out an afternoon snack," I said. We stood there looking at each other for a long moment. I wanted to say something, but what was there to say? My stomach fluttered at the thought of his smile. I wasn't supposed to feel this way.

"Someday I will hear you play." I said. "See you soon." I started to leave.

He looked confused. "When?"

"It's a different way of saying goodbye," I told him.

"Oh," he said, "Why not say goodbye?"

"Because goodbye sounds like forever."

He smiled. "See you soon. Maybe I find way to play for you."

I left, thoughtful, my mind full of maybes.

Fifteen

✦

2007

Daisy parks in front of the community center and turns off the car. "How long is your meeting?"

"It's scheduled for an hour and a half."

She huffs out a breath. "I suppose I can find some errands to do while you're there."

"If it's such a bother, I could have driven myself."

"You know how bad your night vision is. I'm not complaining."

It sounds like complaining to me.

"By the way, Harry showed me that picture. I didn't know you were at that fire."

My daughter has a way of unnerving me. Her comments often sound like accusations. It takes an effort not to become defensive. "It was so long ago I barely remember it."

She waves her hand dismissively. "I told him people aren't going to remember a sixty-year-old fire. I don't know why he's so interested in that project anyway."

Daisy's never held much interest in my past, as though it's too far re-moved from her to matter. She's concerned about the usual things:

whether anyone in our family has ever done anything fame-worthy, which they haven't, or whether anyone has ever been incarcerated, which they haven't. But she's never asked about my childhood, accepting what I offer up on occasion without much comment. She was closer to her father. And Daisy's father never mentioned the past, which seemed fine with Daisy.

She squints at me. "So what is this new activity you'll be doing?"

"We're making memory sculptures of Clear Lake's past. It's sort of like the memory-tile activities that they do in retirement homes, only we're making them for the fall festival as part of the history center."

"I didn't know you were artistic," Daisy says.

A sigh escapes me now that we're here. Daisy is right. I've never been great at doing anything artsy, and dredging up old memories isn't a good idea. "I'm not. The director of our condominium association asked if I'd participate. She thought I'd enjoy it since it involves history. I think she worries about me since your father died last year. And you know I have a hard time saying no."

Daisy focuses on her image in the mirror. "Didn't Dad always say that the past is past, that you should look to the future?"

"Yes, but a person's past defines him."

"I never heard Dad say that," Daisy says.

"That's because he didn't say it. I did."

"I like Dad's saying better."

I try not to resent her statement, even though the two of them always seemed like a club from which I was excluded. Sid had tried to bridge the gap between Daisy and me. Now that he's gone, all that's left is an empty chasm that neither one of us is able to cross.

Daisy gets out and rushes over to take my arm. I glance at her.

"The sidewalk is wet. I don't want you to fall, Mother," she says.

Sid is gone and my daughter's arm now holds mine. Is this sudden act of affection just for show? Is it the start of something? A connection between us? I don't want to get my hopes up too high.

Daisy continues. "I think what's important are the examples we set, like how Dad worked hard as a farmer and was a volunteer fireman."

"I wasn't exactly twiddling my thumbs that whole time," I say.

"I didn't mean it that way. Of course you worked hard, too. Dad used to say you handled the tractor better than he did. And you directed the Clear Lake Choir for years. I doubt I'd own a business and serve on three boards if it weren't for your examples."

I stop outside the community center and glance at the lake, which is a bit choppy tonight. Even though we volunteered in the community, we'd always kept a polite distance. Sid and I had no close friends. We had each other, and now that he's gone I feel so alone. "Like you said, our farm and volunteer work was an important part of this community's history. And that history is also our past. So you see, the past *is* important. It's what shapes us into who we are today."

"I just don't see why Harry wants to dredge up an old fire. The present Surf Ballroom has been here for over sixty years. That place is the one we know, not the one that burned down. No one even knows the other building existed. Who really cares what happened?"

I care. I don't want Harry to know who started the fire. Sixty years doesn't seem like enough emotional distance. For me or for the community.

"I suppose you're right," I say.

A pretty brunette meets us at the door. "So glad you could make it, Lorraine."

"This is my daughter, Daisy. Daisy, Jane is the activities director at our condominium."

Daisy shakes her hand. "Nice to meet you."

"Are you interested in making a memory sculpture, too?"

"Heavens, no. I'm just dropping off my mother. Excuse me," she says as she makes eye contact with a friend of hers.

"Lisa!" Daisy waves, and her voice becomes more animated.

"Your daughter is gorgeous," Jane says as she watches her walk away.

"She works hard at looking good," I reply, then flush as I realize what I just said about my daughter. How ungrateful I sound, and after Daisy drove me here. "She has her father's looks, too. She's very fortunate."

"Let me introduce you to our artists-in-residence." Jane leads me around the room and introduces me to the two artists and some of the other people in the group. There are about fifteen of us who will be making tiles, mostly senior men and women, but with a few younger women in their forties. I guess that I'm the oldest person here. It doesn't bother me as much anymore. I'm becoming used to the reality that most of the people in the world are younger than me.

The two artists are both women in their fifties who wear long, flowing skirts. One has on a peasant top and her hair is piled messily on her head. The other wears a tank top under an open blouse, has long dark hair with streaks of gray, and a chain around her neck that holds glasses with a bright orange design on the rims.

Daisy leaves with a small goodbye wave and holds up her cell phone, meaning that I should call her when it's over. Thank goodness I remembered to bring my phone. It spends more time charging on the counter than in use, a complete waste of money in my mind. But Daisy insists I have one.

I'd hoped she might stay and do this activity with me. She was such a loving, attentive child, but became more distant in her teen years. We butted heads all the time; it seemed we couldn't get through a day without a fight. After all I'd been through with my own mother, I desperately wanted to be close to my daughter. But a wedge had been created between us, and it remained, like a splinter that works its way under the skin and leaves a permanent mark.

I glance around the community center at the long tables they've set up, the kind with uncomfortable seats. I find a spot at the end. We watch a slideshow of previous memory sculpture classes. The results are so impressive that I think of calling Daisy now before I embarrass myself. There's no way I can make something as good as that.

"We'll work with each one of you individually," Tess, one of the artists, says. "And you'll be surprised at how wonderful your own creations will be." She passes out sheets of paper. "Some of you already know what you're going to sculpt. But you might want to sketch out your design first. And think about how your memory of our town relates to the sculpture, as you'll be writing down the memories to go along with the sculptures."

The other participants are already hard at work. I'm equally bad at drawing. This is a mistake. I shouldn't have come. I study the sun's setting reflection on the lake across the street, then watch as the Lady of the Lake, an authentic paddle boat, prepares to depart for an evening cruise. I wish I was on that cruise instead of in here.

Tess walks by. I hold up my blank sheet of paper. "I'm afraid I can't think of anything."

"That's okay. Sometimes I let my fingers think for me," she says, tossing her long hair back. "Just let go and don't worry about it. Your instincts will take over and your art will flow freely. Start drawing and see what happens."

Right. Let my fingers do the work. I spend a few more minutes watching everyone else work, their friendly chatter making me even more distraught. My thoughts drift. I've been part of this community my entire life. It shouldn't be this hard. Finally, I put my pencil to the paper and start drawing, hoping something will come of it. I draw a rectangular building. Then I draw turrets on the sides. I keep drawing, vaguely aware of what I'm doing, the noise of the room fading away. At least my hands are moving.

"How fascinating! What is that?" Jane stands over my shoulder a few moments later.

I look down at my drawing, startled by what has taken shape on the page.

"Are those flames coming out of the top of a building?" Jane asks.

"Yes," I reply, trying to keep my voice steady. "That's the original Surf Ballroom, the one that burned down."

"You saw this? This is your own memory?"

"Yes. I was there that night."

"Amazing! You were an actual witness. I've always wondered, how did the fire start?"

"They never found out what caused it."

Jane points at a scribble next to the Surf. "And what is that?"

"It's supposed to be firemen carrying out a couch. The Fox family lived in an apartment above the Surf. They tried to save as much of their furniture as they could. There was nothing left of the building by the time the fire was put out. Fortunately, no one was hurt."

"And who is that figure in the corner?"

My voice softens. "That's a boy I knew."

Jane bends down and peers at the drawing. "What's he doing?"

I stare at my primitive sketch. He's the one figure I've actually drawn somewhat well. Of course, I didn't mean to draw him or his wispy, blond hair or the instrument clutched to his side. It just came out, as though my hand was moving of its own volition.

I suck in a breath. My voice sounds distant. "He's leaving."

Sixteen

✦

2007

Y ou've turned into quite the social butterfly," Daisy says, turning around in the front seat. We're on our way to a dance hosted by the condominium association. "I'm going to have to get another calendar just to keep track of your activities."

As usual, it sounds like she's complaining.

"Keeps you young, right, Lorraine?" Harry says, his voice light. The front seat holds a tense atmosphere, as though an invisible fence separates the two of them. I wonder if it has anything to do with all the time he's devoting to the investigation. Daisy said he's become obsessed with it.

"I could have gotten another ride, but thank you for bringing me. I know how busy you both are. And this will give you an opportunity to meet more of the residents of the condominium association, Daisy."

She doesn't look back, but I can tell she's rolling her eyes. "If I didn't meet them before, why would I want to now?"

"Potential clients," Harry says. "Did you bring any business cards with you?"

"I always carry my cards with me," she snaps. Her voice softens, as though she realizes how she sounds. "I suppose you're right. From what

I've seen, most of the units are in desperate need of updating, and they're only five years old."

"They should have hired you as a designer when they built the place," Harry says.

"I agree," I chime in from the back seat. We sound like her adoring followers.

Harry guides his SUV into the blacktop parking lot next to the Surf and takes my arm as we walk to the door. The air is warm but holds a sprig of chill, a welcome respite from the August heat.

He looks up at the star-filled sky. "You forget to look up sometimes," he says. "You forget to see the stars."

"Harry, that sounds downright poetic."

"You'd think after all the calls I've been on in my life I wouldn't get shook up anymore, but we had a bad one late last night. A teenager from Minnesota who just got his license last month."

"I heard something about it on the news. Will he be all right?"

He shakes his head.

"Oh, I'm so sorry." I couldn't handle seeing such tragedy, especially a child. I don't imagine anyone can ever get used to that. "I understand if you don't want to be here tonight."

"No. A day like this makes you want to be around others so you don't think about it too much. Besides, I need a drink."

We pass the Buddy Holly memorial on the way in. Harry sighs. "Today we added another ghost to our town."

Funny that he would mention ghosts. It's been two weeks since I saw, or thought I saw, Jimmy Dorsey. Hopefully tonight I won't have any unwelcome visitors. I'll sit in a booth and refuse to dance with anyone.

"We better keep an eye on his drinking," Daisy whispers as Harry opens the door for us.

She waits until he's ahead of us before she adds, "I don't want him wallowing in liquor."

"I wasn't aware Harry had a drinking problem," I whisper back.

"Not so much a problem as a solution on days like today."

Who could blame him after what he'd witnessed?

Music floats out the open doorway. The band is already playing an upbeat number, not big band music, but still enjoyable. I'm glad for Harry's sake that it isn't too melancholy.

A sign in the expansive lobby welcomes the Clear Lake Condominium Association members. In my nervousness, I had eaten a light supper and now I clutch my growling stomach.

There are already a good number of people present. I know some of them from my own condo, people I've met over the last two years, although none of them have become close friends. I've been so preoccupied with Sid for the last year and a half that I haven't really made an effort to get to know them.

Jane is talking to a couple near the bar. She has on a yellow sundress that highlights her thin frame and brown hair. I wait until the music stops, then introduce Jane to Harry and Daisy.

"This is Jane, our activities director. And Mr. and Mrs. Cullen, who live on the first floor."

Harry nods at them, then reaches out to shake each hand. "Nice to meet you, Jane," he says, then greets both of the Cullens.

Daisy regards Jane. "We met before, at the community center."

"Yes, so nice to see you again. Lorraine, will you be there next week?" Jane asks me.

"I plan to be there," I say, glancing at Daisy. I'm not sure if I should use the design I created, but I made a commitment. I want to at least see the project through.

"What are you doing at the community center?" Harry asks.

"Residents are creating memory sculptures for our history center," Jane explains. "Ones that relate to the community. Last week they sketched designs for the tiles. Next time they'll be working with the clay and writing down the memories that go with the tiles."

"What's your design, Lorraine?"

"Well, I'm not sure what I'm going to make yet. . . ."

"She drew a sketch of the Surf Ballroom," Jane says. "And she did a wonderful job."

Harry's eyebrows go up. "You don't say."

"But not this Surf. It's the original one that used to be across the street," Jane adds.

"The one that burned down?"

"When you showed me that picture I thought I'd try to tap into this ancient memory," I say, nervously tapping my skull. "That's why I drew it for my sculpture. But I'm still not sure if that's the one I'll use."

"Oh, I hope you do," Jane says. "People need to know about it. It's part of this Surf in a way, too. They wouldn't have rebuilt it unless it meant a lot to them."

I shake my head. "I don't know. My memories of that place are very hazy."

Harry holds up his beer bottle. "I've been hearing some interesting stories about that place. Here's to remembering."

I want to know what he's heard, but Mr. Cullen mentions that his favorite band is the Whitesidewalls and the conversation drifts.

A long table with trays of finger food flanks the opposite wall. I excuse myself and make my way over, filling a plate with miniature pinwheel tortillas stuffed with spinach and cream cheese. Then I find a spot near the end of the table. If I stay here for a reasonable amount of time maybe Harry will dance with Daisy and he'll forget about my sculpture.

I'm on my second pinwheel when a voice startles me. "You really think that will work?"

I turn, dropping the pinwheel on the floor. A man leans against the wall, his arms folded as he watches Harry and Daisy. It's as though he's materialized from the dark wood behind him. Has he been here the whole time?

"Sorry. Didn't mean to scare you." He's a thin, older man with rugged skin, white hair, and glasses, dressed in jeans and a black T-shirt.

"I'm fine," I say, shaking off the jumpy feeling as I bend down to pick up the sagging pinwheel, leaving a messy smear on the wood floor. "What do you mean?"

He shakes his head. "Retreating to the appetizer table so they can dance? Their body language tells me that it's never gonna happen," he says, nodding his head in Daisy and Harry's direction.

"Maybe not," I say, wondering if he saw me staring at them. Either way, he has a lot of nerve to say something like that. He hasn't even introduced himself.

"I wouldn't place any bets on it," he says.

"Well, I'm glad I'm not a betting person," I say, hoping he'll take the hint and leave. I'm still holding the limp pinwheel in my hand, waiting to find a wastebasket.

"Are you kidding me? Isn't that why you're over here?"

"I was hungry."

"Nah. You're betting they're going to dance. Well, if they're going to make up, this is the place it'll happen. I've seen hundreds of couples meet and fall in love right on this dance floor."

How does he know they've been arguing? Is it that obvious? "You must spend a lot of time here," I say.

"More than you know." He raises his eyebrows. "I used to work here," he says, as though my silence is encouragement to continue talking. "I did all sorts of things, but mainly helped the acts set up backstage. I saw them all. The legends. The great performers. The big bands . . . Those were the days."

I study him more closely and resist the urge to poke him, to see if he's real. Jimmy Dorsey felt real, too.

The man motions toward the dance floor. "This place has an energy all its own. That's why people fall in love here. You step onto the dance floor, search out the flickering lights of the palm trees and the clouds floating across the ceiling, and you're no longer in Iowa. You're outside under a dark sky on some South Sea island. You gather under the striped awning and order a drink, and settle into your special booth.

"Your favorite band is onstage, and you feel the swell of the crowd. Not just the people in attendance, but the ones who came before you, whose essence sweeps overhead in the clouds and whose initials are engraved underneath the wooden table of your booth. They're drawn here just as you are, nostalgic for that glow of music and dancing that is a piece of their history and maybe one of their best memories."

I feel a shiver move up my back. I stand absolutely still, mesmerized by his voice and his words.

"The magic of this place originated long before the bricks and mortar were even bought. Even before the original Surf that used to be across the street. It's part of all of us. It's in our blood."

He looks at me when he mentions the other Surf. My face flushes and I turn away, feeling overcome once again. I've been seeing people who have been dead for years. I bumped into Lance, and drew a sketch of the old Surf. Now this man is spinning tales of magic. What is it about this place?

"Most people don't even know about the other Surf," I say.

The man winks at me as though we share some private joke, as though he knows me. "Maybe it's time they did."

"Y-yes," I stammer, feeling as though I'm under a spell. And perhaps I am, because his words feel as true as anything I've ever heard.

He nods at Harry and Daisy, who are now dancing to a slow country ballad. "I didn't think he'd get her to dance. Guess even I underestimated the magic of this place."

I watch them dance for a moment, feeling a bit self-satisfied. But when I turn to say something to the man, he's no longer there.

✦

I open the door of my condo and place my purse on a small table. Daisy walks up behind me and I flinch.

"You've acted jumpy all night, Mom."

"Just tired."

"I hope you didn't overdo it," she says. "Don't forget you have a doctor's appointment tomorrow morning. They're running tests."

I haven't forgotten.

"I doubt I overdid it," I say defensively. "I spent the entire time at the appetizer table."

Harry gives me a kiss on the cheek. "Get some rest, Sleeping Beauty. Don't think we didn't see you flirting with that man over by the table half the night. The way you were looking at him, well, I wondered if I'd be your ride home tonight."

Seventeen

✦

September, 1944

Scotty and I were the talk of the new school year. Girls I barely knew congratulated me as though I'd won a prize, although some did so with fake smiles and insincere tones. Who could blame them? Scotty was the most sought-after boy in school. And I was a farm girl.

I honestly didn't know what Scotty saw in me. Daddy said I was adorable, but fathers are supposed to say those things. I had a few freckles on my nose and a thicker, lighter version of my father's hair. I was tall and skinny and didn't fill out my sweaters like Stella did.

Maybe Scotty liked me because we'd both been fast runners in grammar school and I was the only girl who came close to beating him in a race. But Stella assured me it was a good thing I'd lost. Winning would only make boys *dislike* me.

When I was with Scotty, I felt lucky. He was the golden boy, and just being near him made me shine, too. He made me feel special just by association.

But after the first day of school, there was someone else I wanted to see. I rushed up the long, dusty driveway toward our white house, hunkered down and surrounded by tall trees on three sides except for the back, where the gravel curved around the rear of the house all the way to the cement walkway that led to the back porch.

I grabbed the food Mom had prepared, barely saying hello, then hurried to the barn. I didn't even take time to change out of my skirt and blouse. Daddy had the men painting the barn today. He had brought out the radio and Bing Crosby was crooning a love song. Daddy never mentioned war news to the men. The war was far away across the ocean and Daddy wanted to keep it that way.

Jens was painting the trim, carefully dabbing his brush at the edge of the window frame as though he was working on a masterpiece.

Jens's face lit up as I approached. "You come after school?"

"Yes. Are you ready for your lesson?" I asked, breathless from my run. Then I noticed his bruised left cheek.

"What happened?"

Jens glanced at Helmut before replying. "Fall down."

"At the camp?"

He nodded. "Ready learn," he said a bit defiantly, grabbing a biscuit with his free hand.

"I gotta go into town to get some more paint," Daddy said. "You men get an extra-long break today."

He tossed one of Pete's footballs to Jakob as he left. Jakob turned the ball in his hands curiously, as though he'd never seen the object before. Ludwig tried to take it away, but he ducked and tucked the ball tight in his arms. Ludwig ran after him, saying he wanted to try this "amerikanisches Spiel."

They called Günther to join them, but he'd already retreated into a book he'd gotten from the camp library, *Huckleberry Finn*.

"Play with us," they teased Jens. "*Lass' das schöne Mädchen sein.*"

"What did they say?"

"Not important." Jens shook his head at them.

"Please tell me."

Jens set the brush down and wiped his hand on his pants. "They say let pretty girl alone."

The men tossed the ball back and forth, not really knowing what they were doing. Norman finally explained the game to them and had Günther translate the rules. Then Norman showed them how to release the football. Soon they had a game going with Norman against Ludwig and Jakob. Soft-spoken Ludwig was quick and had good hands for catching the football. Jakob enjoyed tackling Norman, once he figured out that he wouldn't get in trouble. Helmut stood to the side, laughing every time Norman was tackled.

"You want to try to take me on?" Norman teased Helmut, who finally rolled up his sleeves and joined the game.

"I think I'm going to enjoy this," Norman said as he watched Helmut take a spot on the makeshift field.

"I'm not taking it easy on you," Norman warned him.

Jens had brought a book, a beginning reader that he'd gotten from the camp library. I helped him with the words, but it was hard to pay attention while the men were making all that racket in the background. Jens kept looking up at them. He smiled when Norman threw Helmut to the ground.

"Come on," I finally said. "We need quiet." I led him to a spot behind the barn, under the shade of the apple tree, where the ground was littered with yellow leaves and a few rotten apples. Norman wouldn't miss him for a while.

Jens was struggling more with the words today. He kept looking up, cocking his head, losing his place in the book.

The music still floated back, along with the yelling of the men as they were tackled or scored a touchdown. Bing Crosby was singing "I'll Be Seeing You." I sang along softly, my voice floating out across a breeze toward the corn fields.

"You like song?" he finally asked me.

"Yeah. This is one of my favorites."

"You dance?"

"Sure. We have a big ballroom in town. Everyone dances."

He looked back down at his book, but he was frowning. "I dance, too. I dance great."

Jens glanced toward the sound of the men on the other side of the barn. He cleared his throat. "You want to dance?"

"Oh, um. I don't know."

He stared down at the book. His ears were pink.

"Okay," I finally said. I could tell it had taken a lot for him to ask.

I stood and put out my hand. He clasped it in his paint-stained one, and the warmth of his hand filled mine. His fingers were long, and his palms were callused from working the fields.

Then he put his other arm around my waist and took a small step. I followed awkwardly, trying to keep distance between us. But he moved confidently, his hands guiding me across the crunchy leaves. I imagined myself in a flowing gown and him in a black suit and tie, weaving around the Surf Ballroom dance floor as others watched us with adoring eyes. He moved gracefully and made me feel like we were walking on air. Or maybe that's just because I was in his arms. I barely noticed that the distance between us had disappeared, that I was pressed against his hay-strewn shirt.

"You were right. You *are* great," I told him. "How did you learn to dance so well?"

"In Germany, everyone know how to dance. My mother teach me, too."

A breeze fluttered, whirling up the edges of my skirt and making my hair fly into my face. Jens released my hand and pushed the strands of hair back, and I stared into his eyes.

I touched his bruised cheek and he flinched. "Did you really fall?"

He didn't answer but took my hand back and once more swept me away to the music.

Bing Crosby was singing his melancholy tune and I wondered if Jens thought about me when he was in the prison camp. What was it like for him there?

I knew this was wrong, the two of us dancing together. We were supposed to be enemies. What would Norman say if he saw us? Or Daddy? And what would Pete think? Was I betraying my own brother? I was definitely feeling like a collaborationist now, because more than anything I wanted Jens to kiss me. I wanted him to never let go.

The song ended and we stopped dancing, but Jens still held me, as though he didn't want this moment to end. Finally, he opened his hand and pulled it away. "Thank you for dance with me."

My hands felt heavy, and I didn't know what to do with them. "Someday when you're back home in Germany you'll ask a girl to dance and you'll remember how you danced on a little farm in Iowa," I said, trying to dismiss the closeness I'd felt.

"No," Jens said, his eyes serious. "I will remember the girl I danced with. I will never forget *mein Schatz*."

"What does that mean?"

"My treasure."

"I won't forget either," I said, meeting his eyes.

We stood there for a long moment, neither one of us willing to look away. The distance between us was intoxicatingly small. I was a girl and he was a boy sharing a small respite from the war. A simple dance. A simple promise not to forget.

Eighteen

✦

1944

S o, did Scotty kiss you yet?"

I stopped on the cement steps leading up to our school and jabbed Stella with my elbow. "Stella!"

She tucked her books under her arm and fluffed her bangs. "What? You've gone on two dates. That's a reasonable amount of time. More than *I'd* need with Scotty Bishop."

"What about you and Lance Dugan?"

Stella shook her head. "You think we're a couple? No, silly. I wanted to go to the movie, and I didn't have any money."

That sounded calculating and mean, even if it *was* Lance. Stella could get in trouble, leading on a guy like him.

I followed her into the two-story brick building that ran the length of a long town block. Pete's class had been the third to graduate from this newly built school. "So you're not dating him?"

"No. But that doesn't mean I'm not going to the Surf with him in two weeks. He's got four tickets and Del Courtney and his Orchestra is playing. Three-dollar tickets! We can double date."

"Del Courtney? I love the song 'Journey to a Star'!" And three dollars was more than I could ever afford.

"It's not a teen dance, but Lance says he can get us in. You and Scotty have to come with us. I don't want to be alone with Lance."

Stella and I had never had dates at the Surf. Last year we'd gone stag to the teen dances like most of the girls, lining up along the wall until a boy asked us to dance. And the boys did. Everyone danced. We knew all the bands, had even made up rhymes for them. *Groan and grunt with Earl Hunt. Swing and sway with Sammy Kaye!*

"Should you be leading Lance on like that?"

Stella tucked her shirt into her tight skirt. "He's mostly harmless. I just have to keep him at arm's length. So, will you go? It's free!"

"I'll ask Scotty." I hoped to see him during lunch.

The bell rang. "See you later," Stella called over her shoulder. "And you still didn't answer my question."

Scotty hadn't kissed me yet. After our last date I'd lingered on the back doorstep for several long seconds, waiting. He'd started to lean in and I'd prepared myself by moving closer, but then Mom had made some noise in the kitchen and he'd backed down and left. I felt relieved as I saw his car pull out of the driveway.

Last year he'd been all I could think of, but now when I thought of kissing him, a different face pushed his out of my mind. The memory of dancing with Jens still brought a flush to my cheeks, as though we'd done more than dance.

I hurried to class, passing Lance, who was shoving a young, skinny kid into the boys' bathroom to torture him as only Lance knew how.

"Hey, Lorraine," he said, one arm around the boy's neck. I recognized the red face of Tommy Moser. His twin sister was in my class, but Tommy had been held back a year. He'd supposedly stopped breathing when he was born and had been a bit slow ever since. But Tommy always had a smile on his face and, unlike Lance, didn't have a mean bone in his body.

"Stop being such a bully, Lance. You're late for class," I said, thinking that he was one boy I wouldn't mind seeing go off to war.

"Just taking care of some business first," Lance replied, and disappeared behind the heavy door.

Daddy said that some people have hearts of stone and minds to match. That seemed to fit Lance to a tee. Stella was crazy to date him.

I hurried to history class, where Mr. Burns spent the next hour denouncing President Roosevelt for replacing former Iowan Henry Wallace as his running mate for the upcoming election and disgracing our state by picking a Missouri man instead, Harry Truman. Daddy agreed with Mr. Burns, but he still planned to vote for Roosevelt.

In English class I sat next to Betty Lou, who was the richest girl in town. Unlike Lance, she didn't flaunt her money. But she always had nicely manicured nails and matching outfits. Her older brother was a combat pilot who had enlisted the day after Pearl Harbor was attacked. As I slid into my desk, I noticed her once-beautiful nails had been bitten to the quick.

Our new English teacher was a young woman recently graduated from college and completely inept at handling boys like Lance Dugan. I counted three times that Miss Sterling cried in class, and my copy of *The Grapes of Wrath* had drawings in the margins made by a previous student of Hitler being smashed by Superman.

When the bus drove up to my house after school, I saw Mom waiting at the end of the driveway. She still wore her white apron over her housedress, her hair in a messy bun. She never met the bus. There could be only one reason.

Pete.

The voices of the other students on the half-empty bus faded into a chilling buzz. The wheels squeaked to a stop, and I suddenly didn't want to get off. If I stayed here in this seat, everything would remain the same.

The driver looked at me in the mirror and I forced myself to stand. My throat immediately went dry and my heart pounded as I walked up the aisle of the bus, my books propped against my chest. When I stepped off, Mom took one look at me and shook her head.

"Pete's fine," she reassured me.

"Oh," I choked out. "I thought. . . ." I couldn't say it out loud. It was too horrid a thought.

"I didn't mean to scare you," Mom said. "I just wanted to give you this." She put her hand in her apron and pulled out a letter addressed to me. "It's from Pete."

Finally. A letter from Pete. Addressed to me! Mom had received two other letters from Pete, but this was my first. I looked at Mom's anxious face. "You could have opened it."

"I certainly thought about it. But it's addressed to you, and just seeing his handwriting let me know he's okay. For now." Her voice gave out at those last words.

I stared at the familiar handwriting, thinking about the long trip this letter had made all the way from Europe.

"Open it!" Mom said.

I normally would have taken it to my room to read in private, but I tore it open right there in the lingering fumes of diesel exhaust and read it out loud.

Dear Skippy,

Never thought I'd miss home so much I'd be dreaming of fresh-tilled Iowa dirt and Mom's meatloaf and my squeaky bed with the broken spring. I even miss you, Skippy. There. I said it. Happy now?

Letters are slow in getting to us. I just got two of yours today. A letter from home does more for our troop's morale than ten Betty Grable pin-ups. We take turns reading our letters out loud, except of course for some of the more personal stuff. They all think you're too smart for your britches, which I knew all along. I mean, you started school when you were four. Mom says it was because you couldn't stand me being so far ahead of you, but you were smart even then. And I told everyone how you sing better than Vera Lynn, although none of them believe me when I say that. I guess that's why Dad talks about you doing something besides farm work.

I didn't look up at Mom but felt her frown cross the distance between us. She still hadn't considered that I would be anything but a farm wife, even when Pete bragged about my singing.

I'm looking out my foxhole right now. Can't tell you where in case the Germans get hold of our mail. But it's hilly here like along the Mississippi River and kind of scenic. If I wasn't stuck in this hole I'd be enjoying the sight of it, real peaceful and quiet, but then the artillery starts and ruins the mood. The Germans got a truckload of another battalion's mail and Axis Sally tried to stir up anger and discontent over the radio waves by using their letters against them, telling them that their girlfriends were being taken away by the guys at home. They just laughed, though, so the joke's on them. There are a couple of other Iowa boys in my troop and we reminisce about buttered corn and even fried Spam sand-wiches, which, by the way, I had some Spam last week. The other soldiers call it "4-F ham" but to me it's a little taste of home.

I'm writing Mom and Dad next but may not make the post before the mail gets shipped out. Tell Mom I'm fine, that is, if she isn't reading this right now.

I stopped and looked at Mom and saw the corners of her mouth turn up slightly, then continued reading.

You have a lot of time on your hands when you're sitting in a foxhole, and I keep thinking that the last words I said to you were to keep your mitts off my record player. But if anything ever did happen to me, you're the only one I'd want to have it, even though you're clumsy and likely to break it. Just to let you know.

Keep the Blue Star in the window and I'll be home before you know it. Word is, Hitler is on the run and we're going to follow him all the way to Germany. Even though I'm seeing the world, when I get back I'll be more than happy to spend the rest of my days in North Iowa. Well, I gotta go. Keep singing and don't grow up too fast while I'm gone.

Love, your big brother, Pete.

I glanced at the blue star fastened in our front window, barely visible from the road. Mom was wiping her eyes with the back of her hand but quickly stopped when she noticed my gaze on her. We Iowans kept our crying private, limited to our tear-soaked pillows, never out on the gravel road in plain view.

"Pete's fine," she repeated. "He's alive, and he's okay."

"I know, Mom." It felt good to hear her say it. Maybe she wouldn't be so gloomy now.

We walked down the long driveway littered with leaves from the ash trees in the front. Pete had been gone two months. It made me think of how lonely the holidays would be without him this year. He'd never spent Thanksgiving or Christmas away from home. I'd have to send an extra-special care package to him and hope he received it. Maybe I'd send a can of Spam. But I didn't want the Germans getting Pete's Christmas present.

"Why don't you take a food basket to your father and show him that letter?" she asked.

My mood lightened at the thought of seeing Jens. I carried out the basket of food to the cornfield where Daddy and the men were picking corn. When I saw the men crouching over the cornstalks, joking with one another, it struck me how I no longer viewed them as the enemy. They were just people. I knew how Günther wanted to learn more about the US and return to his country and teach philosophy, but that he was afraid to stand against Hitler because of men like Helmut and the Nazi sympathizers at camp. He'd mentioned that three men had reported themselves as anti-Nazi and were transferred to a different camp for their safety. They would have been beaten or forced to commit suicide if they'd stayed.

I knew that even though Ludwig missed his wife and young daughter, he liked it at the POW camp because no one was shooting at him and he was learning about mechanics from Daddy. Jakob thought the camp conditions were better than the cold-water flats he'd come from in Germany and he was glad the Russians hadn't captured him. Günther had told me that the camp offered sports, theater, chess games, and even a camp newspaper.

Helmut wanted freedom and said that American farmers weren't smart as they wasted too much land with long driveways, but even he seemed less threatening now. He'd learned that his family home had been bombed, that his wife and sons had barely made it out alive, and that his parents had died. Günther said that seeing the cost of war on his homeland had made Helmut question the value of it. Helmut now said "thank you" to me and even smiled on occasion, though he still remained confident in the German army.

And I knew that Jens was a quiet, thoughtful boy who preferred to play his saxophone rather than fight; who, if we met under different circumstances, would have been the kind of boy Mom might approve of.

The men had transcended their POW status as Daddy and I got to know them. Daddy had been learning about life in Germany, and often had some story to share at dinner about one of the men, although Mom would get up from the table and excuse herself when he started in.

The letter in my hand, I rushed to Daddy. "This is great," he said after reading it. He wiped a hand across his eyes, pretending he had a piece of hay in them even though I knew it wasn't the hay that was making them mist up. "The war will be over soon and he'll be coming home," Daddy said. He patted the letter before handing it back.

The men gathered at the basket, none of them shy now about the midday snack. But someone was missing today.

"Where's Jens?" I asked Günther, finding him apart from the others with his food and a book, per his custom.

"He's practicing with the band. They're performing a concert this weekend, very important because some government officials will be attending."

"Oh." I swallowed back the disappointment, trying not to let it show.

"I'll tell him you asked about him," Günther said. "I know it will make him happy." He gave me a knowing smile.

"Will he be back next week, then?" I asked.

Günther shrugged. "We have no way of knowing."

"Oh," I said again. I'd taken it for granted that Jens would be here. And now I was as unprepared as I'd been when Pete had signed up, thinking that things would be the same when clearly so much change had come into our lives.

Günther took a step closer and spoke in a low voice. "I would like to thank your mother personally for this good food she makes us. Is it possible I can do that when we leave today?"

Mom didn't want to even see the POWs. But Günther spoke the best English of them all. Maybe Mom would see that he was a polite man, not the monster she'd created in her head. "Yes, of course. Just knock on the back door when you're done."

My voice held a hopefulness I didn't really possess.

Nineteen

✦

October, 1944

You're going to get us all killed!" Stella kept her head down so the cloud of dust wafting up from the gravel road wouldn't get in her eyes. She propped a hand on top of her headscarf to protect her perfectly coiffed bun, which teetered to the side.

Riding in the back of Lance's red convertible with Scotty made me feel free. The wind whipped my hair and I knew it would take forever to comb it back in place, but I was just glad to be going out, even if Lance was showing off by driving at ridiculous speeds.

The last two weeks had been depressing, but I'd convinced myself that it was for the best. When I told Mom that Günther wanted to thank her personally, she had gotten a stricken look on her face.

"He's not coming inside. He just wants to thank you for the food, Mom," I had said, convincing her to open the door. Mom finally agreed, but when Günther had expressed his gratitude in his best English, she'd just nodded, then shut the door on him. Mom would never see Günther or any of the men as anything other than the enemy.

Her reaction made me realize that I had no future with Jens. He was a prisoner, a boy on the wrong side of the war, and nothing could change that. After the war was over he would go back to Germany and he'd find some pretty German girl and forget all about me. I should concentrate on the boyfriend by my side.

Lance picked us up early so we could eat at Decker's Hamburger Stand, which was connected to the Surf. Stella wore a tight-fitting blue dress with pink flowers on it. I had on a white blouse and green jumper and my dressy loafers, and had my hair pulled up to the side with a comb.

"It always reminds me of a castle," I said, as the turrets of the Surf came into view.

Lance laughed and adjusted his tie in the mirror. He had on a blue tweed suit with a matching waistcoat. "The Fox family actually lives there. You know what they say, a man's house is his castle."

"Who needs a castle for a home? I'd settle for a nice house on the lake," Scotty said, shaking his head. He wore a medium-gray wool suit that rode a bit short in the sleeves, as though he'd outgrown it.

"I don't," I replied, and he squeezed my hand.

"Drive past once so everyone can see me in this swank car," Stella exclaimed. "I'm so excited!"

"Hell, it's just hamburgers," Lance said.

"I'm talking about this car. It's the cat's meow!" she said. "Who cares what we eat?"

I felt like Stella in that regard. I didn't care if we ate at all. Scotty was holding my hand, my fingers barely peeking out of his large palm. This was the night he was finally going to kiss me; I was sure of it.

We parked down the block and entered the small restaurant. It was crowded since it was a Saturday night and Del Courtney would be performing. There wasn't an empty table.

"I know the owner," Lance said. "Give me a minute."

Scotty, Stella, and I waited while Lance pushed his way to the kitchen, his wide frame barely squeezing through the space between the tables.

A few minutes later he came back with the owner, who led us up the stairs to the rooftop where a handful of tables overlooked the lake. "If you don't mind dining alfresco, there's a great view of the lake up here and no wind tonight," he said. "We seat special patrons up here."

Lance nodded his approval. There were only six others seated on the roof.

Stella shrieked. "It's fabulous!"

It *was* fabulous. We could see the boat taxis from up here, the ones that took people across the lake and ferried them up to local restaurants or the beach. We could see the stone sea wall overlooking City Beach and the fishermen off the distant peninsula to the right.

"Look at those people walking along the beach," Stella pointed. "They look like little ants from up here. It's positively making me dizzy!"

"Let's order," I suggested, before Stella fainted from excitement. We ordered hamburgers and fries and Cokes.

"Have you heard the band play before?" I asked Scotty, who was taking in the view.

"No. This is my first time here. Always too busy with sports. Gotta say it's gol-darn nice. I'm glad we came." He flashed his million-dollar smile at me, the one that melted the hearts of all the girls at school, and I felt so lucky to be there with him.

The food arrived and Scotty flexed his arm as he reached for the ketchup, the arm that would play basketball at Iowa next year, the arm we'd all be talking about for years to come because Scotty was the best player to come out of our school. He and Lance talked basketball even though Lance would have died of a heart attack if he'd dribbled a ball down the court. But Lance knew all about college ball just the same.

"You should reconsider teams, my man," he said. "Iowa State made the final four at the NCAA conference this year. Why waste your time on a team that won't take you there?"

"Aren't they rivals?" I asked, although I rarely followed basketball. I knew that Iowa State was in Ames and the University of Iowa was in

Iowa City. I didn't plan on attending either school. I was determined to go far away, although that came with the worry that Scotty would forget about me.

"Yes," he said. "But I'd probably sit on the bench at Iowa State, at least the first year. Besides, I like the Iowa coach. This is assuming I don't get drafted."

"The war will be over by then," Lance said with certainty, and I hoped he was right. "Our boys have Hitler cornered like a rat."

"Where are you going next year?" Stella asked Lance. Even though Lance spent more time flushing kids' heads in the toilet than in class, his father had money to keep him out of the draft and send him to college. And since most college-aged boys were off fighting, there were plenty of open spots.

"Haven't decided. Out east somewhere. My mom wants an Ivy League school."

"How exciting! I'm dating an Ivy League man!"

Everything was exciting to Stella tonight. Honestly! She'd made it sound as though she didn't care for him, as though she was using him. But here she was, fawning over Lance like *he* was the cat's meow. I knew Stella's family wasn't all that well off, that she had four younger brothers and her dad had been sick and did part-time carpentry work when he was feeling up to it. Stella had confided that her uncle helped them out with money sometimes, that her mother was embarrassed about it. Would she really go out with Lance just because he had money? The thought of dancing with him sent shivers up my back.

"Well, Dad went to Columbia so he's leaning that way. But college isn't for everyone," Lance said, glancing at me. "It's a waste of money for girls, if you ask me."

I consistently earned top honors at school in my subjects. Did he know my teachers had encouraged me to attend college?

"Why is it a waste of money?" I asked, glaring back at him.

"Because girls are only there to find a husband. You can do that at home."

"Not every girl wants to find a husband."

"All the ones I know do," Lance said dismissively.

Scotty squeezed my hand under the table, and I held my tongue.

We could hear the band warming up below while we ate. I barely touched my food. Although I'd lost my appetite, I was glad to be away from the farm, away from Mom and her endlessly depressing mood. At least Daddy had the farm to keep him occupied. I had to be around Mom more than he did. But I couldn't complain without looking like an uncaring, selfish brat. Which maybe I was.

"Is your father caught up with his field work?" Scotty asked.

"Yes. He's ahead of schedule, actually. Picking corn now."

"Are *they* doing it?"

"Yes," I said quietly.

"Who are they?" Lance asked, suddenly interested.

"Germans from the POW camp," Stella offered. "Her father's using them while Pete's gone." Then she clamped her hand over her mouth and widened her eyes, as if she'd just remembered her promise not to tell.

"You've got Nazis working for you? I'd like to see that!" Lance said with a smirk. I pictured him heckling them, making remarks that would embarrass Daddy and the men.

I scowled at Lance. "You're not allowed. They're under strict supervision."

"They have an armed guard," Scotty said.

"You don't say?" Lance took out a pack of Camels and tapped the end against the table, producing a long cigarette. He played with it between his fingers. "So, what do you think of having Nazis on your farm?"

"I don't think about it, to be honest," I said, not meeting his eyes. "They're just filling in until the war ends and Pete comes home."

"But you must see them now and then," he persisted. "Any of them try to escape?"

The thought almost made me laugh. "No. Where are they going to go in the middle of Iowa?"

He stuck the cigarette in his mouth and flicked a match to light it. Then he sucked a deep puff and let it out slowly. "If I were one of them, stuck in a prison camp away from women, I'd go visit the farmer's daughter."

I felt my cheeks heat up but didn't look away. I didn't want to give Lance the satisfaction.

"It's giving me chills just talking about those monsters," Stella said, rubbing her arms. "I'm freezing now."

Stella's words stung. I had chills, too, but they were from Lance's leering gaze. They weren't monsters, I wanted to insist. The only monster was sitting across from me.

Lance and Scotty split the bill. "Let's go downstairs and I'll introduce you to Carl Fox, the owner of the Surf," Lance told Scotty, as though he was trying to impress him. Scotty was the class president, a star athlete, and strikingly handsome. Everyone wanted to be his friend. Why he'd want to be friends with Lance Dugan, though, was beyond my understanding.

But Lance turned on the charm when he introduced us to Carl Fox, a dark-haired man who'd built the Surf and three other ballrooms around the Midwest. Mr. Fox lived in an apartment in one of the turrets above the Surf with his family.

"It's the cat's pajamas! You're living in a castle!" Stella said.

"Well, it does offer a good view of the lake," he said.

Mr. Fox found us a prime table next to the dance floor, one that was reserved for prominent guests.

"We're right up where the rich folks sit," Stella said, nudging me. "Did you ever think we'd be sitting here?"

"It's not *that* swell," I replied, even though I did like sitting closer to the stage. As much as I hated being with Lance, I was always enthralled by the ballroom. The stage was surrounded by palm trees, and murals along the walls depicted ocean waves and sailboats, even a lighthouse!

The furniture was rattan and a large window to the side of the stage opened up to the lake. Pinpoints of light in the middle of the lake were boats making their way to the Surf.

Del Courtney and his Orchestra filled the stage, the men dressed in matching black suits and red ties. Their insignia was printed on a big drum. A woman wearing a long black jacket-dress stood in front of them, singing into the microphone. She had a sultry Peggy Lee quality to her voice and I felt jealous watching her. What would it be like to stand up there in a flowing gown and sing with the band? I'd come close to being on that very stage for the Governor's Ball. But Mom wouldn't allow it.

People were already on the dance floor. There was a mix of dancers, but mostly older people. Not many teens could afford the steep ticket prices for Del Courtney, and the few that were present were accompanied by their parents.

Scotty had a worried look on his face. "I'm not a big dancer," he told me. "I can manage a waltz but nothing more."

"I'll show you," I promised. "You'll be doing the Lindy Hop like Fred Astaire."

"Or I'll be falling on my face like Charlie Chaplin," Scotty said, not convinced.

"Don't worry," Lance said. "Either way you'll make an impression."

Lance drew a hand through his thin hair and took Stella's hand. "Let's show him how it's done, babe." Stella was a good dancer and loved to show off. She jumped up and followed Lance out onto the floor.

We sat for the first few songs, then Scotty's face lit up when the music turned slow. "I can handle this," he said, pulling me up. Scotty managed a reasonable waltz, although with his lanky build he towered above me.

I looked over at Stella, who had her head on Lance's shoulder. If I hadn't gone swimming that day, would Stella be dancing with her head on Scotty's shoulder right now instead? She was too short, I decided. Her head would be pressed against his chest.

"I wish we didn't have to ride back with Lance," I told Scotty as we danced.

"Aw, don't mind him."

"Why are you friends with him? He's such a bully."

Scotty shrugged. "I guess he doesn't bother me much. And his father is a friend of my dad. Mr. Dugan promised to help me find work after college, especially if I do well in basketball. Why is your best friend dating him?"

I couldn't imagine what Stella saw in Lance other than his father's money. But I never imagined that Stella would be a money-grubber. I'd thought she had more class than that.

At the break Stella grabbed my arm and pulled me to the women's restroom.

"That Lance is a wolf on a scooter," Stella said as she fixed her hair in front of the large mirror. "His hands were everywhere except where they were supposed to be."

"Stella, you should have slapped him! You shouldn't have to put up with that kind of behavior."

She smeared a thick layer of red lipstick on her lips and stared at me in the mirror. "Don't be a prude, Lorraine. It's all part of the game. I let him think he's got a chance, then shoot him down later."

The way she'd been leaning into him made me wonder if she really would shoot him down. "I'd be careful around Lance Dugan. I don't trust him."

Stella laughed. "We town girls can take care of ourselves. You country bumpkins are the ones who need help."

On our way out of the bathroom Stella almost bumped into a young man carrying a tray of dirty dishes. He dropped a glass, which clattered and broke on the floor.

"Watch out, clumsy!" she yelled as she made her way around him.

I shook my head, wondering at how Stella was changing before my eyes into some kind of spoiled hussy. I stopped and bent down to pick up a piece of glass that had slid over by my foot. I stood to hand it to the worker, meeting his eyes.

A small gasp escaped my lips. It was Jens.

Twenty

✦

1944

J ens! What are you doing here?"

"Washing dishes," he said, shifting the tray so he didn't lose another glass. His white apron was stained with coffee and red sauce.

"Günther said you were practicing for a concert."

"Ya, we did play. A good concert. A man from City Chamber asked me to help out here. Later they need saxophone player, and they use me."

"You're going to be playing here tonight?"

"Yes. Other musician is sick."

"Will you be coming back to the farm?"

He shrugged. "I go where they tell me." He looked at my dress and nodded. "Pretty dress. You here with boyfriend?"

"Yes," I admitted.

"I must go work," he said, busying himself with picking up pieces of broken glass, avoiding my eyes. "Goodbye."

"Wait!"

Jens looked up at me. "What?"

"I, um, just want to tell you that . . ."

"You miss Jens?" he said, a smile teasing the corner of his mouth.

"Yes, I mean, I miss seeing you every day, and bringing you food, and, uh, tutoring you. By the way, your English is sounding good."

"I work hard at it. Soon I will be more skilled in speaking."

"You're already proficient," I said. "At least, you are in my opinion. And this is a good opportunity for you. I've never heard of any, uh, guys like you, getting to play at the Surf Ballroom."

"Yes. Very good opportunity."

"I'll finally get to hear you play."

He nodded. "Yes. But I prefer to be at your farm. I miss you," he said, suddenly more serious.

A lock of hair fell into his eyes. My hand reached down, but I stopped myself from touching him. He stood, and for a long moment our eyes locked.

"What are you doing?" Stella's voice burst out. "I thought you were behind me."

I jumped.

She cast a suspicious glance toward Jens, then saw the mess on the floor and the piece of broken glass in my hand. "Oh, you shouldn't be doing that, Lorraine. You'll ruin your dress. Let him pick it up."

"Yes. Let me do it," Jens said quickly. "You go with your friend."

I handed him the piece and followed Stella back to the table.

"Who was he?" she demanded.

"Just a worker here."

"He had an accent."

"I think he's from France," I lied.

Stella stopped and tugged on my arm. "That was no French accent. I saw the way you were looking at him. Who is he really?"

Stella could always tell when I was lying. "He's one of the POWs who worked on our farm. Please don't tell anyone," I said when I saw the distressed look on her face.

"Why would they have them here?" She peered around the room as though she suspected every worker in the place to be a Nazi.

"They needed a saxophone player. It's just for tonight, I think."

Stella shook her head. "You shouldn't be associating with him. People will talk if they find out."

"Find out what? That I know him because he worked on our farm? He's just a boy. Honestly, Stella. You're making a mountain out of a molehill."

"Well, I'm not going to say anything, but I don't approve of them having German prisoners right under our noses. He could be a spy. He could be planning to blow up the Surf. You ever think of that, Lorraine?"

I nodded toward the boys waiting at our table. "He's not. I swear he's not going to do anything of the sort. Just don't tell anyone. Especially Lance. Promise?"

She bit her lower lip for a moment before she finally nodded.

I pulled her arm. "I can count on you this time?"

"Of course," she said, tugging out of my grasp. "He was cute, though, wasn't he?"

"Jens?" I shrugged. "I didn't notice."

The band was playing an upbeat swing tune. Lance pulled Stella onto the floor and they attempted the Lindy Hop. Lance could barely bend over and his suit looked like it was going to burst wide open on his full frame. After less than two minutes he collapsed on his chair, red-faced and breathing heavily.

Scotty laughed and patted him on the back. "Nice try. Maybe next time you'll make it through a song."

"Maybe next time you'll drop dead," Lance said between breaths.

The set included slow tunes and ballads and Scotty and I danced the entire time. Then the bandleader held up his hand. "Who wants to hear a rockin' number?"

Everyone shouted and clapped.

The band started with "Straighten Up and Fly Right," a King Cole Trio song, and that's when I saw him. Or rather, I first saw Norman, dressed in his uniform, standing off to the side of the stage. He didn't have his rifle visible. He could have been a fan for all anyone knew.

I followed the sound of the saxophone to the stage. There he was, dressed in a black suit and red tie like the other band members onstage. I'd never seen him dressed in anything other than work clothes. His hair was slicked back. Jens stood up and performed a solo, improvising the arrangement with a rhythm I'd never heard before. People cheered and hopped up onto the dance floor.

"The guy's got a good beat," Scotty said.

I could only stare.

Scotty wanted to try the fast dance. He was too tall and lanky to do the jitterbug without bumping into people around him, but I gave him an encouraging nod. Mostly I kept my eyes on the stage, on Jens, who had a chance to catch his breath while the other musicians performed. He searched the crowd and his eyes settled on me. I smiled at him and nodded. Then he started playing again.

Scotty followed my eyes to the stage. "He looks familiar," he said. "Do you know him?"

"No," I said quickly. "I'm exhausted. Let's sit down." But Scotty continued to stare at Jens. And then I saw Stella watching me.

I stole quick glances at Jens for the rest of the set. When it was over, he disappeared. We stayed until the last song. Lance drove me home first and Scotty walked me to the back door. We'd almost reached the steps when Scotty drew me around the side of the house, away from view.

"I've been wanting to do this all night." He leaned down and kissed me, his hands pulling the back of my neck. It was a hard, awkward kiss and his teeth knocked against mine. "I'm about as good at kissing as I am at dancing," he apologized when I pulled back.

"No. It was perfect," I lied.

"You're just being nice."

"It was my first kiss," I said, wanting to rub the back of my neck where he'd pulled on it.

He looked pleased. "I'm so glad I was your first. A pretty girl like you, I thought you'd have lots of boyfriends by now."

"Of course not, Scotty. You're the first boy I've ever dated."

"This is going to be a great year, Lorraine. I don't care about all the crowds watching me play basketball; I only care if you're there. Promise me you'll make it to my games."

"Sure. If I can."

He gave me another quick kiss. "It just takes practice," he said. "I intend to practice a lot. And I'm not referring to basketball." He smiled and led me to the door.

I watched him get in the car and waved as they pulled away. I was meant to be Scotty's girl. We attended the same church, we both had one sibling—Scotty had a younger sister—and we'd known each other since we were kids. He was kind and considerate, and so handsome that the sight of him left me weak in the knees. I was lucky to be Scotty's girl.

But I couldn't stop thinking about Jens.

I went inside. Daddy was still waiting up for me; a copy of the *Farmer's Almanac* lay open on his lap.

"Shouldn't you be asleep?" I asked.

"I wanted to make sure you made it home okay. And usually it's the parents who say that."

I wondered if Daddy knew we'd been kissing. "I saw Jens. He was playing the saxophone with the band and working in the kitchen."

"I'll be! You don't say! Günther said that other prisoners work in processing plants and nurseries, but that's the first I've heard of one playing at the Surf."

"I'm sure they don't advertise it. It was probably just this one time. The regular band member took ill."

"How'd he do?"

"He's good. Really good. I've never heard anyone play like that."

"As good as your singing?"

"Daddy," I said, embarrassed. "You can't compare the two."

"Günther said they may be shipped out soon."

I froze. "Shipped out? Why?"

"They're being sent to England. They move the prisoners around, I guess. I could still use their help. I have some late corn to pick." He paused and looked around. "Don't tell your mother, but I'm gonna miss those guys."

"Even Helmut?"

"Well, maybe not him so much. But it's going to be awful quiet around the farm. I guess I got used to them being here."

"Me, too," I squeaked out, then turned to go to my room. My throat was dry and my hands were shaking.

"So, did you have a good time?" Daddy asked from behind.

As I walked up the stairs, I could only nod, not wanting him to see the tears in my eyes.

Twenty-one

✦

1944

A prisoner escaped last night," Daddy whispered to me the next morning at the kitchen table.

"Who was it?"

"Norman didn't say. Someone dug under five fences and squeezed out. They searched Algona but didn't find him. Now the FBI and Iowa State Patrol are joining in the search."

"You don't think it's anyone we know, do you?"

He shook his head. "Norman would have told me. Where would a POW go? We're in the middle of the country out here."

I shrugged, relieved it wasn't Jens who'd escaped.

Daddy let out a small laugh. "They're tightening security for all the prisoners now. I guess that means Norman will have to start carrying his gun again."

As he put on his cap Daddy said, "Don't tell your mother."

"No. Of course not."

I remembered Lance's words about visiting the farmer's daughter. The words tasted like bitter tea in my mouth.

✦

Later I found Günther sitting away from the others, reading a local newspaper.

"I heard Jens play at the Surf Ballroom last night," I said.

"He is a gifted musician. But he misses the farm."

"It's not the same without him here," I said.

"You have feelings for him." It was a statement, not a question.

So he'd noticed. Did they all know? Did Daddy know? I nodded, too afraid to say it out loud. Did my feelings make me a Nazi sympathizer?

Günther turned a page of the newspaper to the picture of a local boy, Jerry Ashland, who'd died when his ship was sunk by torpedoes. He belonged to our church and was only a year older than Pete. Mom had broken down at the news of his death.

Günther pointed at the picture. "A German newspaper would have only shown the dead enemy," he said. "When the war is over, and I believe it will be soon, and the Allies win, much will change in my homeland. The future will be bleak, and my country will need to be rebuilt. I tell only you this, no one else, because it is a dangerous point of view to acknowledge the impending collapse of the Third Reich."

He looked over at Helmut, who was eating a piece of fried chicken. Günther lowered his voice. "Many of my fellow prisoners feel the same but do not say anything." He nodded at Helmut. "Men like him will fall apart when we lose. That is as it should be. Each day during the drive here, he points at a large farmhouse, telling us it will be his when Germany wins the war. But last week we watched films that showed the concentration camps. Some say it is American propaganda, but it fills me with shame."

I took a bit of satisfaction in thinking of overconfident Helmut reduced to a broken man. It would serve him right.

Günther continued. "I know Jens must return to Germany, but I also know that he cares much for you. He has spoken of returning here after the war."

He smiled and touched my cheek.

His words filled me with hope. Hope that this wretched war would soon be over, and hope that Jens felt the same way I felt about him. But on the way back to the house I remembered that Jens had seen me dancing with Scotty. Why would he return if he thought I was in love with someone else? I had to let him know how I felt about him. Before he left. But how? I couldn't go to the Surf anytime soon, and even if I managed to go there, I might not have a chance to see or talk to him. He might never play there again.

My hand patted Pete's letter, which I'd been carrying around in my pocket since it arrived. Here was my answer. I could write a letter and send it with Günther. The idea was risky. What if a prison guard intercepted the letter? What would they make of an Iowa girl professing her love to a German POW? I'd have to be careful. I could trust only Günther to make sure Jens received it.

I waited until bedtime, after Mom and Daddy had gone to bed and I could hear Daddy's snoring through their closed bedroom door. Hopefully, Mom wouldn't be roaming the hall tonight. Still, I didn't risk turning on the light. I went to the window and opened the drapes, writing in the faint light of a full moon that shone in on the ledge.

Dear Jens,

I heard that you might be moved to England. I will miss you. I know I'm not supposed to feel this way but I do. And if you decide to come back to Iowa after the war is over, please know that I will wait for you.

Love,
Lorraine

I wanted to write more but didn't dare. Besides, it took the better part of an hour just to get those words out. I'd started with "sincerely," then moved to "regards," then finally wrote "love." But it still seemed lacking so I added a line at the end: *See you soon.*

The next day I folded the letter three times and carried it deep in my pocket when I brought their afternoon snack. I felt like a spy, like a traitor to my brother, to Jerry Ashland who was buried at the bottom of the ocean, and to all the boys who'd died fighting.

As I left the house and walked to the fields my heart pounded with each step. Petunia let out a low moo as though warning me to stop. The corn stalks were like darkened streets where Lance Dugan and his cohorts could be waiting at any turn to jump out at me and confiscate my letter. They'd march me through town like I'd seen in the newsreel, and people would shout and throw things at me and demand that I be strung up in the bandshell for everyone to see.

I was shaking by the time I reached the worksite. The men were picking corn by hand and tossing the husks into the wagon that the horses pulled, inching forward a few feet when Daddy commanded the horses, or when he pulled on their reins because they were stubborn.

The men stopped working when they saw me. Even though it was a cool, windy October day, they looked tired and sweaty.

"Just in time," Daddy said, wiping his brow off on his shirt sleeve. The men attacked the basket of food and settled down for their break. Daddy and Ludwig talked machines while Jakob sat chatting with Norman, who now ate from the basket of food along with his prisoners. Norman even lent a hand with the corn picking now and then. If anyone had changed these past few months, it was him. He joked with Jakob, and had even bought a football for Ludwig to take back with him to Germany. I wondered if their friendship would extend past the war.

I found Günther sitting alone, as usual, with a piece of Mom's bread and a book. He was reading *War and Peace* in English.

I almost turned back, but then I thought of how I might never see Jens again. What if something happened to him? How could I live the rest of my life if I didn't let him know how I felt?

I waited for Günther to look up. "I need your help," I said quietly.

I glanced around to make sure no one was watching, especially Helmut. My hand patted the letter in my pocket but I couldn't bring myself to take it out. "It's dangerous," I told him. "It's a lot to ask. You can say no. I'll understand."

His eyebrows shot up as though he didn't really believe me.

My trembling hand lifted the envelope from my pocket with Jens's name on it.

He took it silently and put it in his book. "I see nothing dangerous," he said calmly. "Now, *Fräulein,* I must get back to my reading."

I stood there a moment longer, waiting perhaps for lightning to strike me. But Günther didn't look back up. No one had seen. The walk back felt lighter, as though the letter had weighed me down. I had expected something to go wrong. But Günther's calm voice had been reassuring.

Still, I shivered and crossed my arms in front of me. It struck me that I had started something that could change my life. I had professed my love to a German soldier. In writing. Now I had to wait for Jens to write back.

The next day at school was painfully long. Was it too soon to expect a reply?

Scotty walked with me between classes. "Can you make the bonfire on Friday?"

"I don't know."

"Say you'll come," he begged. "I can't go without my girl at my side."

"Sure," I said, thinking that it might seem suspicious if I turned him down.

Later Stella asked me if I was still interested in singing with her cousin's friend's band.

"They're playing here again next month," she said. "I could ask if they'd let you sing one song." I knew this was her way of apologizing for telling Lance about the POWs.

"I want to more than anything," I told her, "but Mom won't let me go to the Surf now without a chaperone or date to accompany me."

"But we used to go stag all the time."

"Pete was with us. I guess that made it okay."

"Then just get Scotty to take you."

"I'll think about it," I said. I wanted to sing more than anything, but somehow it felt like I'd be using Scotty now.

The bus ride home took forever. Even though I lived closer to town than most farm kids, we still made a dozen stops between school and our driveway. There were only a few students left on the bus when it reached our farm.

I ran down the long gravel road through dry leaves that crunched beneath my shoes. I couldn't wait to get into the fields. The late afternoon sunlight was already waning, making Daddy's work days shorter. Soon I wouldn't have to bring an afternoon basket; they'd be quitting earlier. Or they'd be shipped out. I'd miss seeing the men.

✦

The first thing I noticed when I came around the side of the house was Grandma Kindred's black Chevy. She lived near Charles City and seldom drove her car this far. I didn't see Daddy until I was almost at the back door, until I had nearly stepped on him. Why wasn't he out in the field? Daddy sat on the steps, his head down, grasping a letter. My stomach lurched.

He looked up when he saw me. His eyes were puffy and red. Daddy never cried.

It couldn't be my letter in his hand. It couldn't be a letter from Jens, either. Daddy would be angry, but he wouldn't cry. Then I realized it wasn't a letter. The yellowish paper was small, the size of a telegram.

I froze.

"No," I whispered. "Not Pete."

I stopped and took a step backward, wanting to undo this moment.

"Lorraine," he said, his voice cracking.

"No!" I screamed. "He's coming home!"

Daddy stood up. He grabbed me and held me tight.

"He's coming home," Daddy said. "Just not like we planned."

"It's a mistake," I insisted. "I heard that happened once, that they told a family their son had died but they had the wrong boy. It was a mix-up. Pete would never die. He was careful. He wouldn't leave us."

"No," Daddy said, shaking his head, "Not a mistake. The Battle of Aachen."

"Where's Mom?" I had to see Mom.

"Grandma Kindred is inside with her now. She was alone when the telegram was delivered. I can't imagine her having to see that car come down the driveway, having to answer the knock on the door and know what that man was holding in his hand. I wish I'd been here with her." Daddy's voice cracked and he put a hand on his forehead.

I broke away and ran inside. The radio sat at its usual spot on the table but it wasn't turned on. It was eerily quiet.

"Mom!"

Grandma Kindred came around the corner. "She's resting upstairs," she said quietly. Grandma gave me a tight hug. She was a small, stout woman who barely came up to my shoulder.

"I can't believe he's gone," she said, crying into my coat. "Not our Petey."

I stood there in shock, a statue. I let my grandmother hug me even though I wanted to run away.

"Mom can't handle this," I finally said.

"I know this is going to tear her apart, but she's an Iowan. We Iowans have a lot of gumption. And we'll help her through it."

My chest was so tight I thought it might explode. All I wanted to do was crawl under a rock and die.

Grandma patted her eyes dry. "Would you like something to eat, sweetie?"

I shook my head no. I wanted to get away from Grandma's stifling pity, but Daddy came into the kitchen just then.

"I shouldn't have let him go," he said, his voice ragged.

"He'd have found a way," Grandma said, patting his back.

There was truth to Daddy's words. Mom had warned us. She'd said Daddy had picked duty and honor over his son's life. Maybe Daddy should have tried harder to stop Pete from enlisting.

Would Mom blame him for Pete's death now?

Grandma picked up a dishrag and started scrubbing the counter, which was already clean. "I wish this damn war was over. I'm ready to kill every one of those Germans myself."

Her words were like an ice pick. Was I just as complicit as Daddy? I'd professed my love to a German soldier.

"Father O'Connor is on his way," Grandma said. "He'll bring us consolation and lead us in prayer."

I didn't want consolation. I ran out the back door, away from Daddy and Mom and Pete's room with his record player and blue chenille bedspread and all his things that were waiting for him just as he'd left them. Because no one had touched them, and now Peter would never touch them again. I ran past the barn and the horses and our cows and chickens, past the creek. I ran until I felt my lungs would burst.

But I couldn't escape. Pete was all around me, in the barn playing hide and seek, in the creek catching crawdads. There was no place to go. I collapsed beside a fencepost and finally let the tears flow.

Twenty-two

✦

1944

There's enough food to feed a battalion of men," Grandma said as she came back from the kitchen. "You can tell how much Pete was loved." Despite the rationing that was going on, people were generous with their food.

I couldn't eat. Neither could Mom or Daddy. I guessed the food must be for everyone else.

I hadn't known I could feel this empty inside. I wondered if it was how Mom felt. She was hard to read because her face was void of almost any expression. Daddy and Grandma were taking care of everything.

Usually a person was laid out in a casket in the family home for viewing before the funeral, but we didn't even have a body to bury. So we just put up a picture of him. His remains were buried somewhere in Belgium. I had to find it on Pete's globe; I traced the distance between us with my finger, like Mom had done months ago.

"I baptized Pete Kindred as a baby," Father O'Connor said during the funeral service at St. Patrick's Church. "And I know that even though we all share in your sorrow, his death isn't defeat, but victory. We should be proud of his sacrifice and the sacrifices of all our boys."

I glanced up as the choir sang. Every member there had signed a card for me with their condolences. Miss Berkland had tears running down her face.

"That was the most stirring sermon I've ever heard," Daddy told Father O'Connor. "And I've been attending St. Patrick's for more than thirty-five years."

Mom said nothing.

Afterward, people crowded into our farmhouse.

Daddy spoke to everyone: the men who talked weather and farming because it was too painful to talk death, the women who worried over him and related their own stories of death and loss. They said that at least Pete hadn't suffered like so many of the other boys, and Daddy agreed with them, as though that was some kind of comfort. Daddy talked until his voice became hoarse. He shook hands and accepted hugs until his leathery face looked drawn and exhausted.

"He was one of the good ones," Mom's cousin Viola said, putting her hand on Mom's shoulder. Mom plastered a mournful smile on her face and said "Thank you for coming," but mostly just sat on the sofa and held my hand, as though I was a lifeline to her other child.

Everyone said Pete was a hero. He'd been on the outskirts of Aachen with his platoon as they worked their way into the city, crossing a field. He'd been responding to a fellow soldier who'd been hit. But as he went through a break in the fence, he'd stepped on a buried mine, which killed him and another man behind him.

A single misstep. Two lives gone in an instant.

"That don't make him any less a hero," Daddy said in front of everyone, and they all agreed. "He fought bravely for his country and was attempting to save his fellow soldier."

That doesn't make him any less dead, I thought, and stopped myself before I said it out loud.

Mom didn't say anything. But she stared hard at Daddy as though he'd planted that mine himself. I hadn't heard her say but two words to him since the telegram had come four days ago.

Now I caught Daddy staring out the living room window at the fields, a pained expression on his face. Who would take over the farm now? The future had been ripped out from under him. All those plans gone, along with my brother's life.

Scotty and his parents stopped by. Scotty squeezed my hand and stood by me protectively. The room was intolerably warm with all those bodies, and I felt as though I'd suffocate right there in the living room with Mom on one side and Scotty on the other.

Finally, I couldn't take any more. I excused myself and went upstairs, where I changed out of my dress into rolled-up jeans and loafers and a heavy sweater. Pete's door was closed, but at night I kept watch from my room, waiting for it to open and for Pete to stick his head out and motion to me to come over and listen to some new record he'd bought. He wouldn't let me touch it, though. No messy fingerprints on his precious vinyl records. It struck me how none of this mattered to him any longer, that perhaps it hadn't mattered to him for a while. Is that why he'd written and told me I could have his record player? Had he had a premonition that he wouldn't be coming back?

The house was heavy with grief. I had to get away. I snuck down the stairs, ducked outside, got on my bicycle, and pedaled as fast as I could. It was cold enough to see my breath and I hadn't worn a coat, but I pedaled harder, the memories keeping pace. Everything reminded me of Pete; even the bike I was riding was a hand-me-down that Pete used to ride.

I was near the main highway and my shoes were caked with gravel dust. I stopped and looked around, feeling the soreness work its way up my legs as I stood still. I was surprised at the pain, at feeling anything except the emptiness. There was nowhere to go so I turned around and pedaled back, pushing my legs even as my calves ached. When I returned my legs felt like rubber but my heart still felt like stone.

The sun was setting, a fiery red too bright for this sad day. Everything about this day felt wrong. We weren't alone in our sorrow, so many other people had gone through this, but it felt different now that it was our family. All hope had gone out of our lives. I hated war and Hitler and I hated the fact that people couldn't live in peace with one another. But mostly I hated Pete for leaving me.

As I went to put my bike in the barn, a sudden noise startled me. It wasn't the cats or the horses or our cows. It was whispery and sounded human.

"Lorraine."

I approached the barn cautiously. I was almost inside when a hand reached out and grabbed me.

I tried to scream but the hand clamped over my mouth and pulled me away from the light.

"It's me. Jens."

He removed his hand and stepped back. Jens wore a jacket over his work clothes, one with a dark green collar and shoulder straps. He had a musty, burnt-wood smell to him.

"Jens. What are you doing here?"

"I escaped."

"What? Why?"

"Do not worry. I am going back to camp. But I had to see you. To tell you I am sorry for your brother."

"You escaped to say you're sorry?"

He nodded. "And to ask you. Please do not hate me."

"Hate you? No." I hated myself. I'd refused to give in to the notion that Pete could die. I should have prayed harder. I should have written to Pete more. I should have told him how much I loved him.

I looked at Jens and started crying. He held me, letting me bury my face in his jacket as my tears dripped onto his collar.

"So, so sorry," he whispered, rocking me as I cried.

He held me for a long time, until I finally ran out of tears and could only manage small shudders of sobs. He handed me a handkerchief and I wiped my eyes and nose.

"How did you escape?"

"I hopped on back of truck that was leaving. Hid under tarp. No one saw me."

"How will you get back inside?"

"If I walk up to gate, I think they will let me in."

"But you'll get in trouble."

Jens shrugged. "I do not care."

"Günther said you're leaving soon."

"Ya." His eyes were sad.

"When?"

He shook his head. "Soon."

We were quiet for a while, listening to the sound of the wind creaking through the slats in the barn and the scurrying of cats among the haystacks.

"Jens, I don't want you to go."

His hand rested on my face. "I do not want to leave you."

"Please do something for me?" I asked.

"Anything," he said.

I was tired of pain and emptiness. I wanted to feel again. And there was only one person my body responded to.

"Kiss me," I said.

He kissed me then. His lips were soft on mine, a whisper-kiss. It was delicate, as though he was afraid of hurting me. He pulled back and looked at me.

"Günther give me your letter. You must not wait for me. You must go to university. You must find happiness." His eyes searched mine. "I will never forget you."

I held his face in my hands and felt his lips against my fingers. I kissed him then. A long kiss of passion. A kiss he would remember so that he'd find his way back to me someday.

"I won't forget you, either," I said, gripping his neck, and I kissed him again. He pushed me back against the door and our kisses became more urgent. My throat ached with longing. I pressed into him and felt his body shudder. He kissed my neck and his hand was under my blouse, cupping my breast. Then, suddenly, he pulled away.

I reached out to him, but he kept my arms back. He was breathing raggedly; his face was flushed.

"No," he said, but I could see that he wanted this as much as I did. He was shaking with desire.

"Jens," I said. "We may never see each other again." This was reason enough for me.

He took a deep breath and exhaled, letting go of my arms. "Not this way," he finally said.

"I want this," I said, even as I wondered if people were missing me inside. Jens ran his long fingers through my hair, caressing individual strands as though memorizing them.

"I love you, *mein Schatz,*" he said softly, and I understood that he was going to leave me, that he wouldn't be coming back to this farm, which already felt empty and desolate because Pete was gone.

Jens kissed me again, but it was a leaving kiss, one that held sorrow and loss. He stepped away. "I must go back." He pressed a picture into my hand. It showed him bending over in our field, stripped down to his T-shirt and pants, his blond hair reflecting the light and the dog tag dangling from his neck.

"Norman took picture and give it to me. I give it to you so you can remember me. Remember that I love you."

He touched my face and forced out a sad smile. Then he left.

Twenty-three

✦

2007

I'm looking through the old photo album when Daisy arrives.

"I'm double-parked," she says. "Aren't you ready yet?"

I continue to flip through the worn pages, trancelike and mesmerized, and am reminded of a line an author had quoted at a library talk Sid and I had attended: "Memories are poetic truths that blur the line between reality and fantasy." After speaking to that man at the dance last night, I'd hoped that seeing these old photos would help me distinguish what was true and put the past to rest. I was sure there was a picture of Jimmy Dorsey here somewhere.

"I was going through these while waiting." I finally look up from the floor, a stack of albums beside me.

"Why did you start this when you have an appointment?" She unfolds her arms and picks up one of the albums. "These are ancient."

The pictures are mounted on black paper with the dates written underneath.

"They're pictures from my youth, thank you very much. Old, not ancient."

"Who's this guy in uniform?"

"My brother Pete. You've seen pictures of him before, haven't you?"

"I don't remember. He looks so young."

"He was young."

"Is this you, Mom?" Daisy holds a picture of me in front of a microphone. "Where was this taken?"

"The Surf."

"I didn't know you sang there."

The words are on my tongue, the cutting reply that she doesn't know because she's never been interested in my past, but I swallow them down.

"Why did you quit singing?"

I shrug. "I was too busy. I made a choice, I guess. I'll put these away later," I say, grabbing a sweater. Daisy looks as though she wants to protest. She never leaves her house in the tiniest bit of disarray. But I stand at the door and she sighs and follows me out.

The tests are exhausting. The cardiologist assures me he'll call with the results, but I hear Daisy talking to him in the hallway. It makes me feel like an invalid when she takes it upon herself to have private conversations about my health without consulting me. I know she's worried after losing her father just last year, so I let it pass.

After Daisy drops me back at home, I'm too tired to clean up. Instead, I take a short nap on the sofa, surrounded by black-and-white photos of people who are long gone.

I wake up feeling confused, as though I was dreaming and my dream slipped away before my mind could make sense of it. Something about the Surf.

I have a nagging headache that sleeping during the day often gives me. I hope fresh air and a change of scenery will provide some relief, and find myself driving back to the ballroom. I can't help but feel drawn to the place.

It's dusk when I arrive. The front door is unlocked and the lights are on, but I don't see anyone else around. I peek in the outer office. I can hear voices coming from another door inside; it appears as though they're in a meeting.

People in North Iowa have always loved to dance. The White Pier Dance Hall was the first ballroom to be set up in 1911 and offered dime dances, but it was destroyed by a tornado. The Surf took its place until 1947, when it burned down, and the rebuilt Surf has lasted almost sixty years. I have no doubt it will outlast me.

I wander down one of the hallways filled top to bottom with pictures on both sides. Most of them are signed photos from musicians recognizing the Surf or one of its managers throughout the years. A young-looking Lawrence Welk, the Clooney sisters, Glenn Miller. All the great musicians have played on this stage. How lucky I've been to see so many of them.

One picture is of the original building with old jalopies parked out front. On the corner of the building is a sign: *Beer—Eats. Decker's.* My mouth waters at the memory of their delicious hamburgers. Did they really taste better back then or is it just the nostalgia?

I come to the picture of Jimmy Dorsey and stop. I have to make sure it was really him. I run my finger along the glass over his handwriting:

> *To Alvin*
> *Sincerely,*
> *Jimmy Dorsey*

He has that same twinkle in his eye that makes me grin now as I think of dancing with him. This place makes me feel young, as though the air is charged with an energy that I can't identify.

What was it that strange man said to me the last time I was here, that the magic is part of all of us, that it's in our blood? Is that why the Surf has lasted so long?

"Skippy."

I jump. A sudden chill runs up my arms. I haven't heard that voice in over sixty years and yet I still recognize it.

I turn and he's standing beside me in his dress uniform with the woolen shirt, black tie, and black belt that fastens over the jacket, one that he doesn't quite fill out. His cap sits straight over his dark hair. He's so young and thin, with the same crooked smile as Daddy.

"Aren't you going to say hi to your big brother?"

"Pete," I croak, tears filling my eyes.

He reaches over and wipes a tear rolling down my cheek. "Hey, don't go getting all mushy on me now."

I put my hand on his, resting it on my cheek. "Either you're real or I'm having one hell of a hallucination."

"Little sister learned to cuss," he says, raising his eyebrows. "It's me. In the flesh." He winks at his joke.

"I can't believe it." I shake my head. "I've missed you so much."

"I miss you too, Skippy. You're looking good."

I let out a short laugh. "I'm old, Pete."

"And you've aged well. Living has been good for you."

"You were so young when you died," I say, my voice filled with sadness. "So many things you didn't get to see or do."

He tilts his head. "My timeline was different than yours. Doesn't mean I didn't have a good life, though."

I have a sudden revelation. "I thought of you today and here you are," I say. "That's why you're here."

He shakes his head. "It doesn't work that way, Skippy. I'm not here because you summoned me."

"Why are you here?" Although I don't really care what the reason is. My big brother is standing in front of me.

"Come on," he says, and takes my arm. He leads me down the hallway to another large room, the one that used to be a restaurant. The Surfside Six Café sold hamburgers, French fries, and old-fashioned malts. Now it's an empty room, a museum of sorts, dedicated to rock and roll. There are guitars on the wall and memorabilia, and hundreds of pictures, including a large tribute to the legends who died in the plane crash after the famous Winter Dance Party of 1959.

"Time stands still here," he says as we walk past the phone that Buddy Holly used to call his wife the night he died.

"I suppose it does." I want to freeze time and stay here with him.

He gives me a slight push. "Do you remember when I first learned to dance? How I used you as my guinea pig?"

"You were horrible," I say.

"I didn't want to bring you to the Surf," he says. "I didn't want the other girls to think you were my date."

"Then why did you let me tag along?"

"Because you could dance and you made me look good. I wasn't as self-conscious about asking them to dance after I'd twirled around the floor with you."

"Lucky you had good looks or no girls would have ever danced with you."

He twirls me around. I laugh as he catches me.

"See? I learned a few things without your help."

"Oh, God! I've missed this!" I feel the sudden pang of regret for all those years we lost, all the experiences we didn't get to share.

"No tears, Skippy. Your big brother is here to help. Don't say I never did anything for you."

"Help? I don't understand."

"How come you never listened to my record player?"

"It was too painful," I say, thinking of how the player is still stored in a box in the back of my closet. "It was yours."

"Darn tootin' it was mine. But I left it to you, Skippy. Now it's an artifact in your own miniature museum."

"My museum? That makes me feel even older than I am."

He laughs. "You always cracked me up." Then he frowns. "But I meant for you to listen to my records and remember me."

"As if I could ever forget you, Pete."

"To hide who a person was and what they loved is the same as forgetting. Still, I forgive you, sis. And you'll figure things out."

"I'm not even sure what I'm supposed to figure out," I say. "I don't understand any of this."

He takes both my hands in his. "Don't fret about it. It'll come. I gotta go now."

"No! Don't leave me."

He nods toward the office. "Meeting's over. I don't want them wondering what a World War Two soldier is doing wandering around the place."

"But I still don't understand," I object.

"You will. I have faith in you. You're the smart one, remember?"

"Please," I beg him. "Stay with me a little longer."

"I'll promise you a dance," he says. "Next time. Hey. Who's in that picture?" He points at the wall.

I glance away for just a second. "What picture?"

When I turn around he's gone.

"You tricky Pete," I say, my eyes filling again.

I cry all the way home.

✦

I lock the door behind me when I get home, a city thing. We never locked our door on the farm. It's dark out and I'm exhausted, but I can't go to bed. I don't want to dream, not when my whole life has become one, when I'm having trouble discerning what's real or not.

I end up looking through the old photo albums again, studying Pete's face. I look at pictures of us swimming at the lake, standing in front of our barn, which seemed old even when we were young. I come across a picture of our whole family on Pete's birthday. The last picture of us all together.

Mom and I are standing in front, and Pete and Daddy are behind us. We're all dressed in our Sunday best, Mom and I in sleeveless dresses and the two men in suits. Mom has a round hat on her head, one with a bow on the front. Pete has his hand on my shoulder and he's flashing a tolerant smile, as though we're keeping him from something more important. He enlisted the next day.

I search my closet and find Pete's old record player. I wipe off a layer of dust from the tan lid and open it. The vinyl record still sits on the turntable, the same one Pete had played before he'd left. I locate the plug and fit it into the socket, wondering if it will even work after all these years. Then I turn the switch.

Dick Robertson's voice sputters and comes to life with the static haziness of bygone technology. I lean back and listen to the scratchy song, feeling melancholic for my youth. I dread being alone every day, getting older and more out of touch with the world, becoming a walking relic.

Life was so much easier back then. At least that's how I remember it.

Twenty-four

✦

November, 1944

They're gone," Daddy said in a low voice so that Mom wouldn't hear us, even though she'd barely left her bed since the funeral. "Shipped out to England. The camp offered us replacements, but I told 'em no."

"It wouldn't be the same," I said. The men hadn't been back since we'd had the news about Pete. The farm was eerily quiet without them. Even the animals seemed restless.

Grandma Kindred, who was readying herself to leave after helping out for a couple of weeks, made a *tsk* sound. "Good riddance. I never did feel comfortable with them on this land."

Daddy and I shared a silent look. We both knew differently.

Grandma pointed upward. "Besides, I think having to see those men every day would upset Gladys more than necessary."

Whereas she hadn't slept before, Mom barely did anything now except sleep. The blue star in our window was replaced with a gold one, and all the shades were drawn. Anyone who passed by our house would see the mark of death.

Mom became thin and pale and had to be reminded to do basic things such as wash herself and eat and drink. Without Grandma, I'd have to take over the household chores until Mom recovered.

"I wish she'd just yell at me," Daddy finally said. "Anything is better than this damn silence."

"People deal with grief in different ways," Grandma said. "She's still in shock."

"She's always been this way," Daddy responded. "But losing Pete"—he shook his head and wiped at his nose—"this is too much. She might just curl up into her shell and never come back out. I don't want to lose her, too."

"We won't, Daddy," I said, although I had no idea how to stop that from happening. Pete was the only one who had ever been able to get through to Mom. I could barely get her to eat. Despite coming from hardscrabble farm stock, Mom wasn't a strong woman, but she was a stubborn one.

"It might be time to call Doc Cornelius," Grandma said as she picked up her purse and coat. Whatever we did, it was clear that Mom was our responsibility now.

"We'll make sure she eats," Daddy said as Grandma walked out the door. As though food could cure her.

As soon as Grandma had left, Mom took up stalking around the house all night and sleeping during the day. I could hear her footsteps pacing in the hallway. Some mornings I'd find her asleep on Pete's bed.

Two weeks after Grandma left, Daddy finally called the doctor. I led him up to her room and knocked softly, opening the door a crack.

"Mom, Dr. Cornelius is here to see you."

"Go away," she said and pulled the blanket up to her nose.

"Remember that I told you he was coming?" I said, feeling embarrassed by her behavior.

"I don't need a doctor," she said. But I knew otherwise. Yesterday I'd noticed her ribcage through her nightgown, how the gown swallowed her like a bird peeking out from an oversized nest.

Doctor Cornelius entered the room and instructed me to open the shades. "I may need your help in getting her undressed," he whispered.

The room smelled like sweat and, if there was an odor associated with it, sadness.

He sat his black bag down and pulled up the chair that Daddy's flannel shirt was draped across. Mom looked fearful, but when Doc Cornelius asked her to let him listen to her heart, she lowered the blanket. He nodded at me then. "You can wait in the hallway."

I paced outside the door, listening. At one point I heard Mom crying, and the doctor softly hushing her. When he finally opened the door to leave, he gave me a bottle of tranquilizers. "Make sure she only takes one at night."

He paused on the steps. "And don't leave them out where she can get them."

✦

In December, when Pete's friend Mike Schmitt died in the Battle of the Bulge, I didn't think my heart could feel any more pain. Would the war last forever or until there weren't any boys left?

The darkness of winter surrounded the farm and our lives. Pete's room was closed up, a mausoleum of everything Pete, of our lives before. For the first time we didn't put up a Christmas tree. Instead, we attended Midnight Mass and had a quiet supper of oyster stew that Daddy and I made afterward as we listened to Christmas music on the radio.

Mom didn't cry at the news of Mike's death. In fact, I hadn't seen Mom cry since Pete's death. She just became a blank surface. Daddy spent more time out in the barn, coming in late and sleeping on the couch. I went back and forth between feeling sorry for Mom and being angry with her. She still had a husband and a daughter. Weren't we worth living for?

I did my best to study and keep up with chores at home as well as most of Mom's duties. I was still dating Scotty. The basketball team was having their best season ever, thanks to him, and he signed a letter of intent to play for the Hawkeyes. I went to his games and we dated on weekends. I let him kiss me, but it all felt lackluster, as though I was an imitation of myself. Maybe it's because I was thinking of Jens. Or perhaps it was grief. But at least I was trying.

Dating Scotty became another chore, and soon I felt overwhelmed. One February day after school I met up with him and told him I couldn't see him anymore. The wind was brisk and the sky threatened snow. He shoved his head down into his coat.

I looked away so I didn't have to see his disappointment, or worse, relief. "I have to help take care of Mom," I explained. "She's had such a hard time since Pete died."

I turned to leave but Scotty stepped in front of me. "You don't have to break up with me. I'll still wait for you," he said.

"No. Don't do that. I, I just can't handle a boyfriend right now. Please understand, Scotty." I hurried to the bus as the wind whisked me away. When I found my seat, I looked out the window. Scotty was still there on the sidewalk, his head down, shivering in his letter jacket.

✦

Two weeks later at lunch I overheard Lance brag that he and two other guys had visited the POW camp and left messages for the prisoners on the poles surrounding the camp. He laughed when he told how the prisoners had had to repaint the poles. It was like spreading butter, the way he harnessed them in with his dramatic voice.

"Hey, retard," Lance said, turning his attention to Tommy Moser, a closer target than the POWs. "I think I hear a toilet bowl calling your name."

I tried to ignore his comments, to take the higher ground, but something inside me snapped. I stomped over to his table. "It takes a lot of courage to torment other people, doesn't it, Lance? A sweet boy who never did anything to you, and prisoners of war who are locked up."

Lance eyed me as though he was sizing me up. "You know, Lorraine, you always walk around like you're better than everybody else just because you can carry a tune and you got that Rita Hayworth look about you. But you shouldn't be holding your nose up in the air so high. You're right. I don't know anything about those Jerrys. But you do, don't you?"

Heat flooded my face. "What do you mean?"

"You were more than friends with those Krauts . . . at least, that's what I heard."

My courage faltered and I settled my gaze on the rest of Lance's lunch: the remaining half of his hard-boiled egg, which I could smell from where I stood, and two frosted gingersnaps, the store-bought kind that few of us could afford.

When I looked back up at him, he was smiling. "Stella told me about your Nazi saxophone player."

The room felt hot. My mind raced. She'd promised! Stella went home for lunch every day, so I couldn't confront her now.

Scotty was sitting at the next table. We hadn't spoken since our breakup, but when our eyes met, I saw that he knew, too.

"Guess I was right about the farmer's daughter after all," Lance remarked, and my hands curled into fists. But Scotty was on his feet, already advancing on Lance.

"Shut up," Scotty said, yanking Lance up by the front of his shirt.

"I was just thinking of you," Lance said. "She threw you off for some Jerry."

Scotty pulled Lance up to his tiptoes. "I said, *shut up*! Now apologize to her."

Lance put his hands out in retreat as a crowd gathered. The vice principal was hurrying across the lunchroom toward us.

"Sorry," Lance said, giving me a curt nod.

Scotty let go of him. The air stilled and I felt the eyes of my classmates on me. I glanced down at the forgotten lunches. The room smelled of milk and bologna. I wanted to crawl under the table.

Someone took my arm. "Come on," Betty Lou said, pulling me away. I held my head up and my gaze steady as the crowd parted for us, and let her guide me back to my table. Betty Lou sat down next to me.

"Lance is so mean," she said, as she patted my arm. Other students were still staring at me, keeping their distance.

"Thank you," I said, my voice breaking. I didn't trust myself to say anything more. I looked down at my half-eaten biscuit. My stomach lurched, and I thought I might throw up.

"Excuse me," I said, and I got up and ran to the bathroom. I drank water out of the faucet and stared at my reflection, telling myself that it would be okay. Everyone knew Lance was a jerk.

But inside I felt like a melting puddle of shame. Scotty knew about Jens. I wondered if I could ever look Scotty in the face again.

Three girls entered the bathroom, their chatter immediately ending when they saw me. I dried my hands and went to class, taking a seat next to Betty Lou.

"Are you okay?" she asked, smiling at me reassuringly. She hadn't heard from her brother in over a month.

I nodded, then opened my book. I kept my head down, and books became my refuge for the rest of the day.

Twenty-five

✦

1945

Lance exaggerated the whole story. You know I'd never hurt you, Lorraine, especially after what happened to Pete. You don't know how terrible I feel. If I'd been there, I'd have hit Lance myself."

She'd apologized at least ten times, explaining how she'd gotten drunk and hadn't meant to tell him, but it had spilled out.

"I've told everyone that Lance is a jerk and I'm not speaking to him," Stella added, though she didn't say she was breaking up with him.

Stella had been my best friend since first grade. We hadn't been as close in the months since Pete died, as I was keeping to myself more. Breaking up with Scotty had taken a toll on my popularity at school. And Lance's accusations didn't help, either. I wasn't ready to throw away our friendship, even if she had betrayed me.

I looked over at Stella, at her unfinished homework that lay sprawled across her desk. She'd been a good student before she started dating Lance. It seemed he was a bad influence on her. I remembered how much she'd liked Scotty last year before I started dating him. "You should date Scotty instead. You have my permission."

Stella rolled her eyes. "I know Lance isn't much to look at, and he can be obnoxious." She sighed. "But Scotty's still hooked on you. You broke his heart, you know."

"I didn't mean to."

"I know things have been hard with your mom, but you don't want to let him get away. Believe me, if I had a chance with him, I'd snap him up in a heartbeat."

Stella thought I was a fool. Maybe I was. I had told myself that breaking up with Scotty had nothing to do with Jens. But I couldn't forget the way Jens had made me feel, the way I still felt when I thought of him. And even though everyone would say I was wrong, I knew that Jens was a good person, no matter what side of the war he was on.

"You don't have to settle just because we're at war," I told Stella.

"Yes I do. All the good ones are dead." Her eyes widened. "I'm so sorry, Lorraine."

"No. You're right. They are." I just hoped Jens wasn't among the dead.

"Well, other than your brother Pete, you can't do any better in this town than Scotty Bishop. Remember that."

She was right, of course. Scotty was a class act. I hadn't told Mom we'd broken up, not that she'd notice. Mom was a shell of her former self. The tranquilizers helped her sleep at night, but she hadn't improved much otherwise. She'd wander about during the day and night, barely speaking two words to us, and she'd given up on most of her basic duties. The only task she performed daily was to walk to the mailbox, as though she still expected a letter from Pete to arrive.

What did arrive on a rainy April day was a letter, along with a Silver Star Medal for Pete's gallantry in battle. Dad hung the star-shaped medal with its red-white-and-blue ribbon on the fireplace mantel next to Pete's picture, but the medal went missing a few days later.

When Daddy inquired about it, Mom stuck out her jaw and said, "I couldn't stand to look at that thing, a daily reminder of my son's death.

I don't understand how that's something to be proud of." The one thing Mom was holding on to tightly was her anger over Pete's enlistment, which she continued to blame Daddy for. Daddy didn't mention the medal again. On May eighth we celebrated VE Day. The war in Europe was over. Businesses closed and classes were dismissed. Residents gathered in the city park to celebrate and to dedicate their efforts to the war against Japan. There was even a special celebration dance at the Surf, but I didn't attend. I wondered what would happen to Jens now. Would he be released? Or would he be kept in a prison camp until the Japanese were defeated?

Daddy adjusted the bill of his cap on his way out to the fields the next day. "Things are going to get better now that the war's over. It's a damned shame President Roosevelt didn't live to see it happen. Greatest president in history, and he died pursuing victory for his country."

I turned away and busied myself at the sink, afraid he might hear what I was thinking, that it was a damned shame Pete hadn't lived to see it happen, either.

I took the newspaper up to Mom's bedroom after Daddy left. "The war is over," I said, showing her the headlines. Mom looked at me, the first time in a week she'd made eye contact. Then she turned around and stared out the window. "Six months too late," she whispered.

✦

Daddy stood outside the room pacing the hallway until the doctor came out.

"Well?" he asked, as though Doc Cornelius would be able to make Mom instantly better.

The doctor shook his head. "We might try electroshock treatment. That's had some good results for nervous breakdowns."

"No," Daddy said. "I won't allow you to hook her up and run a current through her."

"She needs to find a way to keep busy," Doc Cornelius said. "Something to help her get interested in life again."

"She has lots to do. That's not the problem," Daddy said.

"She doesn't *do* anything," I said, then felt my face grow hot. Mom would never want me to reveal that.

Doc Cornelius cleared his throat. "If she doesn't get better, you should bring her to the hospital in Mason City."

Daddy stuck his hands in his pockets and shook his head. "No. I'm not sticking her in the crazy ward."

The doctor put his hand on Daddy's shoulder. "I understand, but she's becoming very weak."

"We'll figure out something," Daddy said with resolution. "We'll make her better."

We woke Mom up the next morning and got her dressed and fed, but I came home from school to find her in the same chair as when I'd left in the morning.

"At least she's getting up," Daddy said.

"For what? What does she do all day?" I asked. "She doesn't clean or do laundry or feed the animals or cook. She sits there staring at the walls except when the mail comes. She's rotting away, Daddy."

"She's getting out of bed," he said. "We'll take it one day at a time."

But days turned into weeks. One morning I was cleaning the kitchen when I found a torn-up recipe card in the drawer. I put the pieces together like a puzzle. It was a recipe for chocolate macaroon cake, Pete's favorite. My anger erupted. All the vicious words I could think of worked their way up my throat.

I stomped up to my parents' room and pulled the covers off my mother. "Get up!"

Mom groped around for the covers and rolled into a ball.

"Get up, Mom. Pete wouldn't want you to do this."

"Pete isn't here anymore," Mom said.

"Well, if he *was* here, he'd be ashamed of you. And since you're not going to do anything except wallow in self-pity, I'll just go clean out his room."

I marched over to Pete's room and opened the door. The curtains were drawn and the room had a musty smell, but everything was the same. His record player sat on the walnut dresser, the same as it had ten months ago with his collection of records. And above the dresser was the mirror, which reflected my mother's horrified face behind me. I went to the window and started opening the shades. Mom grabbed my arm; her strength surprised me.

"No!" Mom screamed. "Don't touch anything!"

"Then you start acting like you're supposed to," I said in a threatening tone. "Or else you'll wake up one day and this shrine will have disappeared."

"You wouldn't!"

"I would!"

I saw the anguish in my mother's eyes. *Finally* I'd gotten a reaction. If I had to shock her into reality, I was willing to do so.

Mom pressed her lips together. "I'll get up. Leave his room alone."

I wanted Mom to say she was sorry, to say that her daughter and husband were important to her and worth living for, but there was no apology.

Mom tried after that. She stayed out of her bed for entire days at a time. She went to the annual Memorial Day parade with us and spoke to some of her old friends. She planted a garden, even though it was late in the season, and spent most of her days in her floppy hat tending to the vegetables. The outdoor sun did her good, and she developed a healthy tan and put up pints of her strawberry-rhubarb jam. She started cooking again. Even though she was still a ghost of the mom I remembered, life gained some sense of normalcy.

Twenty-six

✦

2007

I sit across from my daughter and son-in-law in a booth at Perkins and stare down at the oversized plate in front of me. Eggs over easy, toast, hash browns, and bacon. Our monthly Sunday brunches have been a staple of our lives for the last ten years, interrupted only by Daisy and Harry's busy summer schedules, and have resumed today.

Daisy holds up her fork. "So where did you go the other day after I dropped you off from your appointment? I thought you were going to take a nap."

"I did. Then after I woke up, I went for a drive."

"Where in God's name did you go?"

"Around the lake. Do you remember how we used to do that when you were little? We'd go for a Sunday drive around the lake after mass, look at all the fancy houses, see who was out fishing, then we'd stop at the state park and you and your father would try to skip rocks across the water. Afterward, we'd get ice cream at that little shop, I forget the name of it now; it went out of business. That used to be the thing to do on Sunday afternoons. Cheap entertainment, I guess."

"Right. But you weren't home after dark when I called. There isn't anything to see at night, is there?"

Daisy is very perceptive. In my opinion, an outright lie is worse than a sin of omission, so I shrug my shoulders and look down at my runny eggs.

Her eyes narrow. "You're keeping something from me."

"You know what, honey?" Harry says as he motions to the waitress for more coffee. "Maybe you should lay off those pills."

"Don't try to distract me."

I look up. "What pills?"

Daisy waves her fork in the air. "With work and going through menopause, I needed *something* to help me make it through the day."

"You told me they helped you with anxiety," Harry says, which earns a glare from my daughter. He stands up. "I'm going to the restroom."

Daisy picks at her fruit like she's mining for gold. "Everyone I know takes something," she says defensively, as though she's talking to her fruit.

"I think it's great that you're getting therapy."

"Who said anything about therapy? My doctor gave me the pills."

"Oh. I just assumed."

"How is your food tasting?" a young girl with a long ponytail asks as she pours more coffee in our cups.

Daisy pushes her fruit plate away. "I'm full, thanks."

As soon as the girl leaves, Daisy says, "The honeydew melon tasted like brick. It's obviously not ripe. And last time the plate had raspberries."

"Why don't you try some of my hash browns?" I suggest.

Daisy recoils. "Do you know how many carbs are in that?"

"You're just as thin, if not thinner, than you were ten years ago."

"And I intend to stay that way," Daisy says, sipping her coffee.

"How *do* you make it through the day?" I ask her. "You barely eat and you work so hard. You need to take care of yourself. I worry about you."

"I'm fine, Mother."

"I thought you were cutting back on your design business."

Daisy takes out her phone and reads her messages while she talks. "I plan to. But we've been really busy. Did I tell you I'm doing the mayor's house? It's right on the lake—a huge, older home that we're going to update."

Daisy continues to pay attention to her phone. I watch as other restaurant patrons interact and chat. I think of my own mother. I've been noticing the similarities with Daisy recently. Like my mother, she's moody, demanding, and often impatient.

"Maybe you *should* see a therapist," I say.

Her eyes widen and she sets her phone aside. "Why do you think I need to see a therapist?"

"Well, if you need pills for anxiety, it might help to also talk to a therapist. My own mother had sort of a nervous breakdown—they didn't really have a diagnosis for it back then. Maybe it's hereditary."

"I'm not having a breakdown! I'm stressed, is all. I have a lot on my plate," she says.

"Then maybe you should take some time off."

"Why? I enjoy my work. What causes me stress is trying to balance work and all my other commitments."

"What other commitments?"

Daisy stares at me, as though it's obvious.

I feel a sudden anger. "Seeing as how I'm one of your commitments, I guess you're trying to make me feel as though I'm a burden."

"How can you say that? Is this because I didn't spend time looking through those old albums with you?"

"No," I insist. "Although, truthfully, you don't seem to enjoy spending time with me." There. It's finally out in the open.

Daisy rolls her eyes. "You're overreacting."

We've been this way for so long that it's become normal. My strained relationship with my own mother left an imprint on my heart, which is why I've ended up tiptoeing around Daisy's moodiness.

I don't want to sound like my mother, to spout words that could just as easily have come from her mouth, but right now it feels unavoidable. I am her daughter, after all. "Someday I'll be gone, you know."

Daisy looks at me and I can see the challenge in her eyes, still there after all these years. She picks up her phone. "Is that a threat or a promise?"

Afraid I'll make some comment I'll later regret, I break eye contact and study a bulletin board across from our table. I notice an advertisement for the Grotto of the Redemption. Nearby attractions are listed, including the world's largest Cheeto, a bed and breakfast in Algona, and a POW museum.

My heart races. I'd forgotten about the museum. I'd heard that it had opened in Algona to preserve historical data and artifacts from World War II and the POW camp that had existed there at one time. I'd wanted to take Sid there, but he'd been too sick by then. I stare at the flyer as though it's a magical parchment.

I've never been as religious as Daddy was. I tried, but I often felt as though my prayers went unanswered. But lately, since I've been seeing ghosts . . . well, I have to admit that there's much I don't understand. And who knows what I'd see at a POW museum?

Harry returns just then and sees me looking at the flyer. "Do you want to visit the Grotto? We haven't been there in years."

"Actually, I want to visit the POW museum in Algona."

"What POW museum? I didn't even know we had POWs in Iowa. Why would you want to go there?" he asks.

"During World War Two we had a group of POWs work on our farm when I was young."

"Really? That's fascinating."

"Don't encourage her," I hear Daisy mutter. "We don't want her traipsing all over Iowa and passing out again."

"It only happened once," I say. "Do you constantly have to throw that back in my face? And I'm right here in front of you. I can hear you. I'm not deaf."

"I'm only thinking of you, Mother."

"No. You're thinking of one of your commitments," I say, then immediately regret it.

Daisy glares at me.

Harry, sensing the tension between us, sits down and motions to the waitress. "Check, please. And I'll take that pie to go."

Twenty-seven

✦

December, 1945

On a cold December day in my senior year of high school, Daddy called to me from the back porch. Mom was in the living room listening to the radio, where Fibber McGee and Molly were debating whether to have a white Christmas tree or a green one. I wondered why Daddy hadn't joined us.

"I found this in the mail this morning," he whispered, handing me a small white envelope, "although if your mother had known what it was, she would have destroyed it."

My hands fumbled to open the envelope, my heart racing with possibilities. Was it a letter from Jens?

In August, Japan had surrendered. Scotty had left for college. So had Lance Dugan. Stella had started our senior year with a promise ring on her finger. Even as the anniversary of Pete's death passed, I still hadn't heard anything from Jens or any of the POWs who'd worked on our farm. I knew they were likely in England now, and that they might not be free yet. The camp in Algona still had prisoners, even though the war had ended months ago. I had read in the newspaper that the United States was planning to turn over many of its POWs to France to be used in coal mines and reconstruction. Other reports said they'd be sent to England before being returned to Germany.

The letter wasn't from Jens or any of the POWs. It was an invitation to visit the prison camp. Some of the POWs had spent the last year constructing a nativity scene, and it would be presented to the public at a special dedication ceremony.

"Do you want to go?" I asked Daddy.

He nodded.

"What about Mom?"

"No," he said. "She can't handle it. I'm not sure she'll ever be able to put this past her and forgive."

He didn't say who she needed to forgive.

"I'll go with you," I said, handing it back. Daddy tucked the letter inside his coat pocket. "I was hoping it was a letter from one of the men."

"I wish we knew what happened to our boys," he said. Daddy only called them "our boys" in front of me. "I reckon Helmut is torn to pieces about Germany's defeat. I heard that after VE Day, seven of the Algona POWs went insane."

"Maybe we could call the camp," I suggested.

"I miss them too, Lorraine, but I don't think we should call. It's for the best. Were you very fond of that young man, Jens?"

I looked down at the oval rag rug that covered the cracked linoleum, one of many rugs that Mom had made in our house, each woven as tightly as Mom herself. I remembered how Lance had accused me in front of the whole school of being a Nazi lover. "No, Daddy. I mean, we were just friends. I was curious, is all."

"Good. I mean, after all that's happened, with your mother and Pete and all . . ."

I turned away. "Can I take the car into town? I'm supposed to help Miss Berkland with the children's choir."

Daddy paused, as if he wanted to say something more. "Sure," he finally said. "Just be careful with that clutch."

Last fall I'd started helping with the children's choir at church. I'd barely been able to handle Mom's constant moodiness, and this had been something to get me out of the house. I loved how the little kids called me "Miss Kindred."

I drove to St. Patrick's Church. As I entered, I could hear the children singing upstairs; their voices comforted me as I knelt and prayed. I hadn't done much praying since Pete had died. I wasn't sure God was listening to me anymore. But I put my head in my hands and prayed for the safety of Jens and the other men. I prayed that Jens would somehow find his way back to me. And I prayed that Mom would find a way to forgive— not only those responsible for Pete's death, but Daddy, too.

"You're just in time," Miss Berkland said when I went up to the balcony. "I told the children how you have a solo in the school concert next week. They want you to sing for them."

I looked at the three rows of children, ranging in age from seven to ten. They were all girls except for the four boys at the back, but Timmy Miller had a higher voice than most of the girls. They treated me like a local celebrity, all because I was Miss Berkland's star performer.

"I don't think I could do a good job today," I told her, feeling suddenly depressed at the thought of how this holiday would be the second one without Pete.

"Nonsense, Lorraine. You shouldn't ever take your gift for granted. God gave it to you, and it's your responsibility to use it. Especially at this time of year."

"I just don't feel like singing."

Holidays were the worst. The memories were stronger, too painful. I dreaded how Mom would take it this year, if she'd withdraw again. Or would she simply refuse to celebrate? That would be fine with me. Except for my solo at the Christmas concert, I didn't have much to look forward to. No one had invited me to any holiday parties. Other than Stella and a few friends, the other students at school were polite but standoffish. I'd come to realize that it wasn't the accusation of being a Nazi sympathizer that had made them so cool toward me. It was the fact that I'd broken up with Scotty Bishop.

"Perhaps the children can help you get in the mood. They'll sing with you."

The children cheered their support. Miss Berkland played the intro to "Jingle Bells." Their high voices sang out, *"Dashing through the snow, in a one-horse open sleigh. O'er the fields we go, laughing all the way."*

I looked at their happy faces, their mouths open wide like they'd been taught. I slowly joined in on the chorus. My voice faltered at first, then grew strong and clear as the song progressed. By the time we'd made it through the second verse and chorus, I was lost in the words and melody. *"Oh! What fun it is to ride in a one-horse open sleigh."*

The children clapped afterward, except for Timmy, who was picking his nose. Miss Berkland nodded at me to curtsy like I would on stage. I bent one leg behind me and pulled my skirt out wide, reveling in the joy that came when I performed. It wasn't the clapping or the recognition; singing just did that to me. Hitting the notes just right, making that sound belt out the way it did; I marveled that I had it in me. Singing sent pricks of goose bumps up my arms.

✦

A week before Christmas, Daddy and I drove to the camp. From far off we could see the searchlights skating back and forth across the stark land surrounding the camp. Three miles away were the city limits of Algona, which was slightly smaller in size than our own town, and not touristy. But they had a Gamble Store, and the paths of the Chicago,

Northwestern, Milwaukee, and St. Paul railroads intersected there. When we reached the gate, I stared up at the intimidating guard towers and winced at the barbed-wire fencing. I couldn't imagine Jens living in this place.

An armed guard met us at the gate.

"I need to see your credentials," he said.

Daddy nervously presented his driver's license and the letter we'd received. We were then directed to a parking area outside the gates. We'd have to walk through the gate to an area between two rows of high barbed-wire fences for half a mile in the cold night air.

We went arm in arm toward a compound, noticing others walking in hushed silence ahead of us. The frozen grass crunched beneath our shoes, and our breaths left little icy contrails. Then the group ahead of us abruptly stopped. We huddled in the open like a herd of cattle, barbed-wire fences on either side of us.

The sound of boots marching in the distance drew our eyes toward the inner fence. A few coughs, and heavy breathing that belonged to the POWs. We couldn't see anyone in the dark, but we sensed their presence. We stood still, waiting. Then we heard a pitch pipe, followed by voices singing in the dark.

> *Stille Nacht, heilige Nacht,*
> *Alles schläft; Einsam wacht.*

I recognized the familiar melody right away, as did everyone else. As they sang, a slow beam of light cut through the darkness. In front of us was the crèche, which contained the Holy Family surrounded by shepherds and sheep. They were large figurines, almost life-size, made of clay from the soil of the camp and painted. The scene was magnificent, a work of beauty that spoke of their commitment to perfection.

The crowd let out a collective "ah" of appreciation. We hadn't expected it to be so big or so intricate.

I looked at the shadowy men standing in formation, their voices rising above the barbed wire. They were thousands of miles from home, isolated, a beaten army, waiting to return to a ravaged country. And yet they sang with spirit and dignity on a remote Iowan hillside. And they'd made this gift for us.

Soon we joined in, singing the English version of "Silent Night" alongside their German version. Daddy squeezed my arm. When I looked at him, I saw tears running down the sides of his face.

More songs were sung, followed by a short prayer. Then the lights faded and the men returned to their confinement. We turned back, facing a bitter north wind. My legs felt stiff with cold by the time we made it to our car. But inside, my heart was on fire.

Twenty-eight

✦

2007

I visit the Surf during the day. Tourists with cameras are inside, watching a video on a large screen that details the history of the Surf and the bands that played here.

I explore the greenroom next to the stage, where performers used to wait before shows. The walls are filled with signatures of great performers. I stroll the hallway to the right of the lobby, which is covered from top to bottom with pictures.

I buy a commemorative magazine at the gift shop and read trivia about the Surf. I learn that a radio DJ took rolls of pictures of Buddy Holly the night he performed here, and when he went to get them developed, they were all blank. Ritchie Valens had flipped a coin for the third seat on the ill-fated plane and said it was the first time he'd ever won anything. And Waylon Jennings had given his seat to the feverish Big Bopper, then teased Buddy Holly, saying he hoped the plane crashed, a comment that haunted him for years. The Surf had been a landmark before they played here, but their deaths made it a rock-and-roll legend.

I don't see the person I long to see, the man I miss so dearly. I drive home disappointed. When I turn into the driveway of my condominium, Harry is standing out front waiting for me.

I grab a tissue and look at my face in the rearview mirror. It's blotchy and tired-looking. I get out of the car, dabbing at my eyes.

"Are you okay?" he asks.

"Yes. Um, allergies," I say as I blow my nose. "What are you doing here, Harry?"

"You didn't answer your phone, and Daisy was worried."

Harry follows me into the building, up the elevator, and waits for me to get inside. I pick up the phone from the counter, where it's still plugged into the charger. It lets out a little beep, but I have no idea what that means.

"She left you six messages," he says.

Oh, is that what the beeping means? "I forgot to bring it with me," I say apologetically.

"Where were you?"

"I went for a drive."

"You know Daisy doesn't like it when she can't get ahold of you."

I fold my arms. "Daisy shouldn't worry so much."

He frowns at me as though he can tell there's something wrong, which isn't too hard because I look a mess.

"She worries because she cares," Harry says. "She can't handle losing anyone else right now. She'd probably become a basket case. Or more of a basket case than she is already."

He smiles at that last part.

I nod. "Daisy was our miracle child. I didn't have her until I was in my thirties. I'd had two miscarriages beforehand, and we didn't think we'd be able to have children. We spoiled her rotten. We couldn't help it." I pat Harry's arm. "But she turned out okay, despite her overindulgent parents. I shouldn't complain about having someone worry about me. I'm lucky to have people care about me enough to be concerned. Thanks for stopping by to check on me."

He's reluctant to leave. "While I'm here, have you given any more thought to the fire that burned down the original Surf? Any memories surfacing? I'm just wondering because I was finally able to track down two witnesses who were at the fire back then, and one of them's a firefighter. I learned a lot from them."

"Oh?" Goose bumps prick my arms.

"And it's funny how your name seems to keep popping up."

"My name?"

"Yes. The firefighter said that you actually helped the Fox family during the fire."

I purse my lips, which are trembling. The words are close to forcing their way out. I want to tell Harry everything. It would be a relief to have someone to confide in.

I'm just not sure the right someone is Harry.

"I do remember that it was a night of panic," I say, cautious about what I tell him. "They evacuated nearby houses in case the fire spread. So everyone was pitching in, carrying furniture out of homes, trying to help them save whatever they needed. To top it off, some thief stole two hundred dollars out of Mrs. Fox's purse, which had been thrown in a dresser drawer during all the excitement."

Harry takes a notepad out of his pocket and starts scribbling. "So when did you arrive at the fire? It must have been soon after it started."

"I don't really know."

He looks up at me. "But you remember the two hundred dollars?"

I poke my head with my index finger. "Who knows how this old mind works?"

"The fire started late, early in the morning. Were you out with friends? Do you remember why you were out that late? Did you go to the dance that night?"

"Well, I'm sure I was out with my friends. But none who are still alive," I quickly add. "I think it was a Saturday night."

Harry nods. "Technically, Sunday morning. April twentieth. Hitler's birthday."

I put my hand to my throat. "Really? I didn't know that fact."

"Yeah. And the year was 1947, shortly after the end of World War Two. From what I've read in old newspaper accounts, there was some kind of explosion right before the fire was discovered. Kind of makes a person wonder."

"I guess so."

"That's the thing," he continues, the excitement building in his voice. "I think there was more to that fire than they knew. For one thing, Mr. Fox had recently sold the Surf to a company in Chicago. And another one of Mr. Fox's properties, the Terp Ballroom in Austin, Minnesota, was nearly destroyed by a fire in 1945. Not to mention that he changed his name from Carl Fuchs to Carl Fox."

I didn't know that. The things Harry has found out! I put up a hand. "Mr. Fox loved this community. He would never do anything to destroy it."

"I'm not saying he did. But, two suspicious fires in less than two years? That adds up to something."

"I don't think you should jump to conclusions, Harry. You have to remember, we didn't have fire alarms and sprinkler systems back then. A little kitchen fire could easily spread."

"You're right. I'm getting ahead of myself. I have to concentrate on one fire at a time."

"Well, I'm really tired. It's been a long day." I yawn, hoping he'll take the hint.

"There's one other thing," he says. "I found a report that listed the injuries. There was only one. And guess who it was?"

My voice sounds far away. "Who?"

"Lance Dugan, who happens to be our mayor's uncle."

I keep my face frozen. "Lance Dugan?"

He nods. "Seems he was injured by flying debris. But shortly after that, Lance went out east. I mentioned it to Daisy and she said she doesn't want me asking Chad or his uncle a bunch of questions, stirring up dirt right before an election. And Lance has cancer. But I'd really like to talk to him. He's one of the few remaining survivors, and it doesn't sound like he'll be around long."

I should have known Harry would find out about Lance's injuries.

Harry closes his notebook. "The thing is, Daisy said you know Lance Dugan."

"We went to school together. A very long time ago."

"I wondered if you'd be willing to go with me to talk to him?"

"But Daisy said . . ."

"I was hoping you could go as a concerned friend. And if the subject of the fire comes up, well then."

"Oh, Harry. I barely know him."

"Just think about it," he presses. "I really need your help."

"Okay," I say. He walks out and I close the door behind him. I'm terrified by the thought of talking to Lance and the things he could tell Harry.

I go fix myself a cup of tea. I doubt I'll be able to sleep at all tonight.

Twenty-nine

✦

2007

Lance Dugan lives in a new senior community home, the kind that brags a putting green, fitness studio, spa, and library. It also provides nursing care at all levels and looks out over a lush golf course.

"This place is nice," Harry says as we pass the landscaped walkway. "Almost makes you forget you're in a nursing home."

"This isn't like any nursing home I've ever been in," I say, thinking of how hard it had been to keep Sid at home that last year, even with hospice care. "This must cost a fortune."

"Well, he can afford it, I guess."

I stop in front of the entrance. "What if Daisy finds out we're here?"

"So what? You're just visiting a friend, remember?"

"But what can he tell you that you don't already know?"

"There was a report of an explosion, but the wiring had been recently checked, so I doubt that was the problem. A friend of mine has architectural software that can re-create the fire based on what we already know. I had him run it with the old evidence on file, and the way the fire spread, something big must have caused it. And maybe Lance remembers seeing or hearing something that he didn't report. They didn't ask him back then because he was injured, and as far as I can tell, there was no follow-up questioning."

"Why is this so important to you?"

Harry opens the door for me. "I don't know exactly. My parents used to tell me about the original Surf ballroom, how the lights glistened on the water, and how they wished it hadn't been rebuilt away from the lakeshore. I have a sense about these things, and something doesn't feel right about this fire. Too many contradictions."

We walk into an expansive lobby. Behind it is a restaurant-style dining room where we're told we'll find Lance.

The director, a woman with sharp eyes and a kind smile, takes us aside before we meet with him. "He gets confused easily," she says. "Don't be too concerned if he isn't able to remember you."

"We understand," I say nervously, "but I hope we don't upset Lance."

"Oh, no. He loves visitors. I'm afraid he doesn't have many. He's a bit cantankerous. Some people get that way with age."

Harry whispers to me as we follow her to the dining room. "Chad's wife refuses to visit him because he's such a mean old coot. Chad doesn't like him either, but he's the only relative Lance has."

Lance's wheelchair is pulled up to a mahogany table decorated with a vase of fresh daisies. He has oxygen nubs in his nostrils and he's bent over, fumbling with a straw, trying to get a drink of water. An aide attempts to help him, but Lance pushes him away with his papery hands, knocking the glass as he does so and spilling some of the water.

"May I help?" I ask. I take the napkin next to him and soak up the spill.

Lance's expression changes from annoyance to puzzlement. "Who are you?"

The director flashes a benevolent smile. "Lance, this is Lorraine Deters and her son-in-law Harry O'Donnell. Lorraine went to school with you and wanted to visit."

"School?" He stares at me, as though the word is foreign to him.

"Well, I'll let you talk. I'll be in my office if you need anything."

Lance barks at his aide, a young man with long hair who stands off to the side. "Leave us. I can't talk with your suffocating presence."

The aide, who I remember seeing at the hospital with Lance, shrugs off the insult and smiles at us. "I'll be in the other room. Let me know if Mr. Dugan needs help. Or causes trouble."

"You don't know anything about trouble," Lance yells after him.

I glance at Harry. I can see he's questioning whether we should have come.

It's that odd time between breakfast and lunch, and we're alone in the dining room. Garlicky smells seep from the kitchen. Spaghetti, I'd guess. Or lasagna.

Lance fiddles with the nubs in his nostrils. "I smoked two packs a day for fifty years. The cancer is putting me in my grave, and I'd still kill for a cigarette. You don't have one, do you?"

"No. I don't smoke."

"That's a damn shame. They won't let me have any."

Harry shakes his head and mutters, "He'd blow himself up."

"Lance, I don't know if you remember me," I say.

"I saw you at the hospital. I'm not as feeble-minded as they make me out to be."

"Yes. We went to school together. I was a few years younger than you."

"I left this town years ago. Went to college out east, you know. Got a Cadillac Coupe de Ville for graduation. One of the first ever made." He spits into a handkerchief. "Then I married a girl from out east. Didn't last long. Still, I never thought I'd come back here."

"Well, it hasn't changed all that much since you left."

He looks over at me. "Everything changes. You say we went to school together?"

"My name was Lorraine Kindred back then."

"Did we date?"

"No. You dated my friend Stella."

"Doesn't ring a bell. Was she a looker?"

I shrug.

"No," Lance says, and he leans back a bit in his chair. "Not school. I remember you from the Surf."

Harry straightens up and pulls a small notebook from his front pocket. "Speaking of the Surf, Mr. Dugan, I wondered if I could ask you a few questions about the fire."

"Fire?"

"The fire at the Surf Ballroom. The one that burned down in 1947. There are few people left who remember it."

Lance touches the scar on the side of his face. His eyes are panicked, as though he's seeing the fire again. I remember that fear, the nightmares that haunted me for months afterward.

"Do you remember that night, Mr. Dugan?" Harry asks. "You were there."

I hold my breath.

"I was there," Lance says, and a puzzled expression replaces the panicked one. He looks at me clearly for the first time, as if he's in the midst of remembering.

Harry persists. "Is the fire where you got that scar? Do you remember it?"

"How did I get out?" Lance asks me.

I purse my lips together.

"No, you weren't inside," Harry says, "You were hit by debris."

"I couldn't get out," Lance says. "There was smoke everywhere. I couldn't breathe. It was so hot. Thought I was a goner."

"You were inside?" Harry asks. "But they didn't report anyone inside. Do you know how the fire started?"

Lance coughs into his handkerchief and looks around. "Where's my lunch?"

Harry sounds frustrated. "Do you remember anything about the fire? What part of the building it might have started in? Anything at all about that night?"

Lance starts coughing more intensely, a spasming type of cough that brings his aide running.

I offer Lance a drink of water, but he's coughing too hard to take any.

"It's okay," his aide tells us. "This is a common occurrence. Lance, let's get you back upstairs to rest awhile."

We take the hint and leave.

"I'm sorry, Harry. He wasn't much help," I say as we walk to the parking lot.

"Did you see his eyes when I mentioned the fire? He was terrified."

"Well, he was injured in that fire."

Harry shakes his head. "It's more than that. He said twice that he was inside. And you know what? His injuries were consistent with someone who was inside a burning building, not standing outside. He knows something. If I can just figure out a way to get him to tell me."

I pray he never does.

Thirty

✦

1946

One day that winter Miss Berkland stopped me on my way to lunch. She was wearing a tight skirt and sweater set that made her bulky figure look even larger. But her eyes held a contagious excitement. "I met with a former colleague of mine this weekend who told me about the wonderful music program at St. Olaf College in Northfield, Minnesota. I mentioned you since you're my best student, and he's interested in having you apply there."

"College?" I had thought about singing with a big band, not attending college. "I don't think my father can afford to send me to college."

Miss Berkland kept talking as though she hadn't heard me. "I know it's a Lutheran college, but there's a wonderful Catholic church in town and a Catholic student association. And the best part is that you could get a scholarship!"

"What kind of scholarship?"

"A singing scholarship, of course," she said, as though it should be clear to me.

"I'm not sure my parents would allow me to attend," I finally said.

"Then we'll have to convince them." She squeezed my arm and left beaming, as though it was all settled.

I hadn't given much thought to my dream of becoming a singer lately, not with all that had been going on. Would I be content, left on the farm with Mom for the rest of my life? I only knew that whatever my future held, I wished that Jens could be part of it. The war had been over for a while now, but I still hadn't heard from him. Not a single word, not even a note to let me know he'd made it home. I began to wonder if I'd exaggerated what had happened between us; if I was a diversion he'd forgot about as soon as he left our country.

A few weeks later Miss Berkland approached me again about college. "You'll need to audition. And I have the perfect song for you. It's a new Rodgers and Hammerstein number called 'You'll Never Walk Alone.' Gorgeous melody that runs from the base of the voice to the top, and can really showcase your range. We can start practicing next week."

I hadn't encouraged her. But Miss Berkland couldn't be dissuaded. I still didn't have any real plans for after high school and, somehow, the idea took hold of me. I wanted to get away from home, and getting an education seemed more important now that the war was over. It might provide an opportunity for something other than farm life.

We practiced for several months and in the spring Miss Berkland drove me to Northfield herself to visit the campus and attend the audition. I hadn't told my parents the purpose of our visit, just that I was accompanying my favorite teacher. I reasoned that I might not get in, so why bring it up? Plus, I knew that Daddy couldn't afford college. He'd just taken out a loan to buy a hay loader, and he'd had to hire help since Pete was no longer around.

Miss Berkland turned onto the road leading to the campus, and the manicured lawns and limestone buildings came into view. It was like a picture postcard.

We first met with Miss Hilleboe, Dean of Women Students, a thin, serious-looking woman who impressed upon me that "college is a privilege, doubly so when so many are denied the opportunity. And opportunities always imply responsibilities." Her eyes fixed on me as though sizing me up. "I recommend a rigorous program of self-discipline and training to fully develop your intellectual capabilities.

"Above everything else," she went on, "there must be continued growth in spiritual vision and power, an inner strength that comes from the fear and love of God Himself."

I wasn't sure I could live up to all that.

"Isn't she wonderful?" Miss Berkland said afterward. "And she teaches Latin, too."

"She's so smart," I said, feeling more than overwhelmed.

Miss Berkland patted my arm. "You'll do very well here, Lorraine. As she said, it's a rare opportunity."

After eating our bag lunches in the shade of a tall oak, we found the building where I'd be auditioning. There were four other girls there, all vying for a spot in the prestigious choir. We would be performing for Mr. Olaf Christiansen, a younger version of the founder and director, Dr. Melius Christiansen, who had recently retired. Judging by his expression as he listened to the other girls sing before me, he wasn't someone who was easily impressed. And the other girls all sounded far more talented than me.

I put a hand on my unsettled stomach as I sat with Miss Berkland in the audience, a nervous wreck.

Finally my name was called. "Oh, dear. You look as white as a sheet," Miss Berkland said. "Take a deep breath and hold it for ten seconds."

I did as I was instructed.

"Now let it out. Feel better?"

I gave a slight nod.

"Chin up. You can do this," she said, giving my hand a squeeze before taking her place at the piano where she would accompany me.

My voice trembled. I sounded nervous, but Miss Berkland kept smiling at me and I concentrated on the words and melody. As the song progressed I felt better and my voice didn't warble. I finished strong.

"Lovely," Mr. Christiansen said, and he nodded encouragingly.

As we drove home, Miss Berkland was ecstatic. "He said lovely!"

I said a wistful goodbye to the picturesque campus. I knew the odds of getting a scholarship were stacked against me.

The beginning of summer was uneventful. I spent time at the beach with Betty Lou, whose brother was finally home, and went to a couple of dances with Stella when Lance was out of town. Stella cried on my shoulder, telling me that she didn't think Lance had been faithful to her while he was away at college. I consoled her as best I could, knowing she was probably right.

Then one morning Miss Berkland called and asked me to meet her at school. I found her in the empty choir room that held so many memories for me. She was beaming. "Lorraine, you may want to sit down. Because I have wonderful news."

"News about what?"

"About St. Olaf. About your audition."

"Are you saying that I was accepted?"

"Yes! With a full scholarship, no less! I'm so excited for you!"

"How?! What did he say?"

"He said a voice like yours is a rare gem. One that should be nurtured."

"I can't believe it! I didn't expect this at all."

She hugged me and I walked giddily through the rest of the day, repeating the words "rare gem" over and over in my head. It wasn't until later that I started to worry. How would Mom and Daddy cope without me? And then there was Jens. Part of me wanted to go on with my life, like Jens had told me. The other part worried that he wouldn't be able to find me if I left. I still held on to a sliver of hope that he was alive and hadn't forgotten me.

That night I finally worked up the nerve to tell Mom and Daddy about the scholarship. "It's not that far away. I'll be able to take the train or bus up from Mason City and come home once in a while to help out."

"Honey, I'm proud of you," Daddy said, smiling.

I looked at Mom. "What do you think?" I asked her.

Mom put down the cross-stitch she was working on. "It costs too much."

"I got a scholarship."

"There are other costs. Who's going to help around here? Your father can't do all the chores and the fieldwork, too. We'll have to hire someone else. And why do you need to go to school to learn how to sing?"

"She's smart. She should get a good education. We'll find a way," Daddy said. "Don't you worry about it, Lorraine. You're gonna be the first Kindred to go to college."

"Well?" I asked Mom, my voice edgy. "Daddy said I should go." I wanted her to be more like Daddy, to say it was okay so I wouldn't feel so bad about leaving. I knew it would be extra work for them, but I wanted her to be excited for me, not make me feel guilty. Why couldn't she ever support me?

"You asked my opinion. I told you. If you want to be selfish and think only of yourself, then go ahead and leave."

That September I went anyway.

Thirty-one

✦

December, 1946

G oing home for Christmas?"

    I nodded at the elderly woman across from me on the train. "My first time home since leaving for college."

"You must be excited to see your family."

I nodded. I felt as though I'd been gone for years. Life at St. Olaf was a completely different world. My teachers were strict and expected so much from me. I'd made a new group of friends, ones who valued the same things I did, who saw singing as more than just a waste of time. I also came to realize that it took more than talent to succeed, that it took hard work, too.

The train slowed and I spotted Daddy at the station. He was dressed in his Sunday suit and he had a huge smile on his face. I waved at him, my eyes tearing up just at the sight of him.

"I've missed you," he said, wrapping me in his arms when I got off. He smelled of Old Spice. I took a deep sniff, and a flood of memories overwhelmed me. Christmases past. Cousin Viola's wedding. Easter Sunday.

He ran a hand across the ends of my hair. I'd cut it in college so that it hit my shoulders in a bob.

"I didn't expect this," he said.

"I can't always look like a little farm girl, Daddy. This is how all the girls style their hair."

"You look all grown-up."

"Where's Mom?" I asked, already guessing she hadn't come.

"She's cooking dinner," he said.

I raised my eyebrows. "What are we having?"

"You just wait and see. She's been doing fine these past few months. Mrs. Harbinger came out to see her and got her involved in the church circle, and she's almost like her old self again."

It was disconcerting in a way, that Mom had gotten better only after I left. I *wanted* her to be better, but it reinforced the feeling I'd always had that I was somehow the cause of her sickness.

"Well, I'm going on and on," Daddy said, and I realized I hadn't been following the conversation. "How are you? How was your first semester away from home?"

"I made some friends. And school is great, but hard work. Our choir took a trip to Minneapolis. I've never seen such a big city!"

Daddy took my suitcase and led me to the dark blue Pontiac he'd just bought. I put my arm through his as we breathed out cold wisps of air.

"No snow?" I said. "We have lots of it up in Northfield."

"Forecast is for snow tomorrow. I guess it was waiting for you to come home," he said.

"Oh, Daddy," I said, and laughed.

"It's good to have you home." He patted my hand. "Christmas is always the hardest."

"I know." I wondered if it would ever get any easier. It had been two years since Pete had died.

"No special boy yet?" Daddy asked me on the drive home.

"School is hard, Daddy. I have to study a lot."

"I'm sure you still see the opposite sex every now and then?"

I fingered the armrest. "No special boy yet."

"That's good, because it's part of the surprise."

"What surprise?" I wasn't in the mood for a surprise. I was looking forward to quiet family time.

"There are two, actually." He cleared his throat. "I'm not supposed to tell, but I think you deserve advance warning. Scotty Bishop called. He's in town and wants to see you."

"Scotty Bishop? Why does he want to see me?" I hadn't heard from him since he'd graduated.

"I don't know, but there's a Christmas dance tomorrow night at the Surf. Your mother told him you'd be there." He looked over at me. "I know she shouldn't have done that without asking you, but it's the first thing she's been really excited about in ages."

Poor Mom was still trying to marry off her daughter. "That's okay, Daddy. I'll go."

"Really?"

"Sure. Why not?"

"I'm glad you don't mind. You're a good egg, kiddo," Daddy said.

"So what's the other surprise?"

"The other surprise I couldn't tell your mother about." He reached into his coat pocket and pulled out a letter. "It's from Günther. I received it a few weeks ago. I made it to the mailbox before your mother. Good thing I did."

"That's wonderful!" I removed the letter from the envelope and tried to read in the ribbons of light that flashed across the window, hoping for news of Jens.

Dear Mr. Kindred,

I hope you and your wife and Lorraine are doing well. We were all happy that the war was over, but we were still held prisoner in England. Helmut was sent to France, where his job was to dig out the unexploded bombs left behind by the Luftwaffe, even though it was against the Geneva Convention. That is unfortunately how Helmut met his end.

I was recently released from the prison camp and have made my way back to Hamburg. I'd heard about the bombings but it does not prepare you for the devastation, of seeing whole neighborhoods reduced to rubble. Half of the city is gone. Many people are dead or have left the city. There is very little food and no law or order to speak of. My family survived, but our home was demolished. So now we must rebuild.

Ludwig has it worse than me. His town was bombed and his home is gone. He still searches for his family, not knowing if they escaped the bombing. To not know their fate is far worse than being in a prison camp. I only pray he sees his wife and daughter again.

I know your family suffered an unspeakable loss, too. War disrupts all lives and we must ensure that this perverse absurdity does not destroy mankind again. It is only through peace that we will progress as humans.

The one bright spot in this whole experience was meeting you and your family. Your kindness and generosity reminds me that there is hope for this world. The days spent on your farm were ones that I will cherish till my dying days. We were not treated as prisoners there, but as human beings. Your fields were a respite from the war. I will never forget the taste of your wife's fresh biscuits. My mouth waters now as I remember them. But I thank you most for being my friend when you could more easily have been my enemy.

Günther

Poor Ludwig. I remembered the photo he'd carried around of his daughter.

There was no mention of Jens. Günther knew how I felt about him. I'd taken his picture with me to college; I'd even slept with it under my pillow a few times.

"It sounds terrible over there," I told Daddy. "So much suffering."

"I've been sending some care packages to Germany," Daddy said. "Shoes, socks, sweaters, and candy for the children. Basic things."

"You're a good egg yourself, Daddy." I hugged his arm. "And it makes me realize how lucky we are."

He turned on the radio to a Christmas tune. Perry Como was singing "I'll Be Home for Christmas." The song choked me up and I hugged Daddy's arm again.

"It's gonna be a good Christmas this year," he reassured me.

I smiled but my hand clutched Günther's letter more tightly. It felt like proof that Jens no longer cared for me. Günther would have mentioned him otherwise.

We drove past the airport that had just opened between Mason City and Clear Lake. "Things are changing. Someday you might fly home instead of taking the bus," Daddy said.

Things *were* changing. When I saw Mom, it was as though someone had taken a paintbrush to her hair and painted streaks of gray where the brown used to be. I wondered if it was the new medication Doc Cornelius had given her. I'd only been gone four months. Still, she was more animated than she had been since Pete left for the war. She actually fussed over me and admired my hair. Mom had made bread pudding. She'd remembered it was my favorite. Even though I was eighteen and had been on my own for four months, I reveled in her attention. I let a little hope slip in that maybe we could be a family again.

The next night Daddy dropped me off at the dance. I had second thoughts as I got out of the car. I was doing this for Mom, I reminded myself. I wore a red dress with a black belt and a red bow in my hair. Once inside, I wished I'd called Stella to meet me. The last I'd heard she was working the cosmetics counter at a department store in Mason City, helping to support her family. I didn't know if she was still dating Lance. We hadn't kept in touch.

A huge Christmas tree adorned the lobby of the Surf. The mood was festive and I couldn't help but feel excited. I hadn't seen Scotty in a year and a half, since he'd left for college. I'd read newspaper articles about him, though. He was a starter on the basketball team, excelling in his studies, and had brought a great deal of pride to his hometown. I was sure he was engaged to some cheerleader by now.

I stood in the lobby, not quite ready to go into the ballroom, and watched the dancers during a slow waltz. Men in uniform dotted the ballroom floor like sprinkles on a Christmas cookie. They came home slowly, individually, not as a group. Other than family gatherings celebrating their return home, there'd been no formal acknowledgment of the sacrifice they'd made for their country. But at least they were home. For now that was enough, when so many hadn't made it back.

"Lorraine."

I turned around. Scotty Bishop stood in front of me, more dashing than I'd remembered. He wore a black suit with a red bow tie, and I noticed that he'd filled out a bit in the chest.

"You look beautiful," he said, his brown eyes brightening. I couldn't hold his gaze. It had been a mistake to come.

"It's been a long time," I managed to reply. "I've kept up with your basketball career. You're in the newspaper all the time."

"Not really a career," he said, shrugging. "More of a diversion from studies. I'll be graduating in another year and a half with a degree in business."

Even with all the attention he received, Scotty had somehow managed to maintain a humble attitude.

"Well, you've certainly made your hometown proud," I told him.

He exchanged nods with a man who limped past us in uniform. "Not as proud as guys like that."

Scotty was just as I remembered him, but even more appealing.

"Would you care to dance?" he asked me.

Maybe it was being back at the Surf. Maybe it was all the Christmas finery, the sheen of light that bounced off the frozen lake outside the window. But at that moment, taking Scotty's arm felt right.

"I'd love to," I said, and he guided me to the crowded dance floor. A waltz was playing and Scotty held me close. I felt comfortable in his arms. I recalled how stiff we'd been with each other when we were in high school. The awkwardness was gone now, replaced by a mature confidence.

"You've been practicing," I kidded him.

"I'm not tripping over myself now," he said. "I've been working on it when I can find a partner."

"Any girl would be happy to practice with you," I said, remembering how every girl in high school had had a crush on him. I doubted that had changed in college.

His eyes held mine. "Not every girl."

I looked away.

"I've been meaning to ask you this for a while," he said after a silence. "And if it's too personal, I understand. But that night at the Surf when we double-dated with Lance and Stella, well . . . that saxophonist worked on your farm, didn't he?"

I nodded, not meeting his eyes. "He was from the POW camp."

"I could see the attention you gave him that night. You couldn't take your eyes off him. Is he the reason you broke up with me?"

I finally looked at Scotty. He deserved the truth, and he deserved to have me look him in the eye when I told him. "Yes," I admitted softly. "At least partly."

He nodded. "I had a feeling. What happened to him?"

"He was sent to England two years ago. I never heard from him again."

Scotty continued to waltz me around the floor. The song was a sad one that made me think of all that had transpired these last two years.

"You know," Scotty said. "My coach has a saying about teams we've lost to before. How the past is water under the bridge and every game is a chance to start fresh again."

I tilted my face up at him. "What do you mean?"

"Not to brag, but I've had plenty of dates in college. But I never forgot about you, Lorraine. I know you had a tough time with your brother's death and your mom being sick and all. I don't blame you for breaking up with me. What I'm saying is that I was kind of hoping we could start fresh. Of course, that's presuming you're not seeing anyone else right now?"

"I'm not dating anyone," I said. "But I'm studying at St. Olaf College in Minnesota. And you're still a student at the University of Iowa. There's a lot of distance between us."

"I didn't say it'd be easy," he said, twirling me around. "But if a clod-hopper like me can master this dance, then I think we should give it another chance."

I thought of Günther's letter, of how he'd talked of rebuilding. I hadn't entirely given up hope of seeing Jens again, but I realized that he was probably in Germany rebuilding his life. It was time to rebuild my life, too. After all, Jens hadn't written in two years. Maybe it was time to let go of childhood dreams and face reality.

It was definitely time to stop sleeping with his picture under my pillow.

The music changed to an upbeat tune, and Scotty held out his hand to me. "What do you say, Lorraine?"

I took his hand and smiled at him. "I'd like that."

Thirty-two

✦

2007

I direct Daisy to Mom and Daddy's spot in the Clear Lake cemetery. Although Daisy has been here numerous times with me, she still has trouble finding the headstone, parallel to the Abraham Lincoln statue and facing an overgrown pine tree. Next to the stone is a marker for Pete, noting his division and where he died in service, even though his remains are still buried in Europe.

Sid is buried on the other side of the cemetery, in the newer section. His headstone also contains my name and date of birth, with a hyphen awaiting my death.

"Why the sudden interest in visiting the cemetery today?" Daisy asks as she gets out of the car, carrying the pot of red geraniums I'd bought.

"I won't always be around to help you find your grandparents' tombstone. It would be nice if you could locate it on your own."

She follows me over the uneven ground to the granite stones. We place the geraniums in front of my parents', and the single white lily I'm carrying in front of Pete's. A spray of orange and purple rosebuds sits on the floor in the backseat of Daisy's car, waiting to be placed in front of Sid's grave.

Daisy stands back, fanning herself in the hot sun. "I could find it if I had to. But you realize, it's not going to be a hobby of mine to visit. I don't especially like hanging around dead people. I've only been to Daddy's gravesite once since the funeral."

"I think it's very peaceful here."

She adjusts her wide-framed sunglasses on her face. "Sorry if I don't share your fascination. Why bother with real flowers? They'll wilt in the sun. You should have gotten artificial ones."

"They have no scent," I object.

"And who's going to be smelling them? The guy who mows the grass?"

"I know it seems silly, but it's important to me. When most of the people you know are in a cemetery, you might care about things like that, too."

"Don't count on it."

My attention is drawn to an old, faded tombstone that looks to be made of limestone. I've never noticed it before. The stone is pressed flat against the ground, neglected, overgrown with grass and dirt, the name illegible. I fight back the urge to go clean it up. Daisy doesn't have all day to spend here; she's already mentioned twice that she has a meeting tonight to prepare for.

I gaze off toward the other side where Sid's tombstone waits. Will that be our fate, too? Abandonment? Or pity?

"I remember Grandpa Kindred," Daisy says as she kneels and traces his name with her finger. "He could always make me laugh."

"He doted on you," I say, kneeling next to her. I remember how happy he'd been at her birth. "When you were born he appeared at the door of my hospital room with a huge bouquet of daisies. We hadn't decided on your name yet, and, well, you've heard this story a million times, I know."

"Yes, I have. But it's a good one, as stories go."

"When was the last time you laughed?" I ask.

"What?"

"You said that Grandpa Kindred used to make you laugh. Harry mentioned that you don't laugh much anymore."

"He said that? Are you two plotting behind my back?"

"No, of course not. He's just worried about you. And you sound like my mom when you talk like that."

Daisy reads the dates on the tombstone. "She died before I was born. . . . Wait! It's the anniversary of her death. Why didn't you mention that was the reason you wanted to come here today?"

"I don't know. Maybe because we didn't always get along well."

"But you said she had some mental health issues? Which you tried to tack on me?"

"That's not what happened, Daisy. I only mentioned it because you sometimes seem"—I resist using the term *wound up tight*—"stressed, as you call it. My mom was like that. I felt as though she was always on the verge of a nervous breakdown. And when she lost her only son in the war, she fell apart."

"But she still had you and Grandpa."

"Pete was her favorite. She couldn't stand losing him. And we weren't enough, I guess. The doctor wanted to use electroshock therapy on her, but Daddy wouldn't let him."

Daisy recoils. "How awful!"

"That was standard practice back then."

A light, refreshing breeze washes over us, and I let out a deep sigh. It's quiet except for the trill of the birds. We're the only ones in the cemetery.

"I *haven't* laughed in a long time," Daisy confesses as she fingers the grass, and I can see creases in her forehead. "Harry laughs all the time. He laughs at silly things, like the cat when she's chasing the ball. How can he laugh after seeing such horrible accidents as a fireman?"

"Laughter is a coping skill. It helps alleviate the pain."

"Did your mother laugh?" She has a worried look on her face, as if she might be a candidate for shock treatment simply because of genetics.

I shake my head. "No. But she was more fragile than you," I reassure her. "She never recovered after Pete's death. And I always felt responsible for making her happy. It took me years to realize that you can't make someone else happy. You can't give what you don't have."

Daisy flips her glasses up for a moment to look in my eyes. "You were unhappy?"

"I was then. I've since learned that it didn't matter how much I sacrificed, I'd never be able to make up for Pete's death. But I always wished we'd had a better relationship, and that's why I come every year on the anniversary of her death. I guess I'm still searching for some sort of reconciliation."

Daisy helps me up and takes my arm. "Let's go visit Dad's grave and then have lunch. I'm even going to let you pick this time." She pauses and adds, "as long as it isn't fast food."

Thirty-three

✦

1946

Scotty wooed me all during Christmas break. We went to the Surf almost every night, dancing until we nearly dropped from exhaustion. Mom adored Scotty, and Daddy was impressed when he brought him a bag of fresh walnuts, which were still being rationed.

"These are impossible to get," Daddy had said, running his fingers through the nuts as if they were diamonds.

One night, Scotty drove his dad's Ford Coupe onto the frozen lake and let me drive. I turned the steering wheel and pushed down on the gas, spinning the car around in circles until we were dizzy. We made out in his car under a moon that was larger than the lake itself. Scotty was a better kisser than I remembered.

"You have to come to dinner at my house tomorrow night," Scotty said as he drove me home. "My parents and my sister Kate want to properly meet you."

"Sure," I said.

The next evening, Scotty brought me to his family's elegant home that sat on a hill overlooking the south side of the lake. He showed me the short dock they'd put up at the bottom of the hill, where they fished during the summer.

Back at the house, his kid sister commented on my wide-legged trousers and belted sweater.

"You look just like Lauren Bacall in the movie *The Big Sleep*," Kate said, and begged her mother to buy her a pair of trousers, too.

We popped corn and sat in front of a roaring fire listening to Abbott and Costello. Scotty and I played Chinese checkers with Kate. I had met Scotty's family years ago—after all, Clear Lake wasn't a huge town—but I'd never really gotten to know them.

They reminded me of my own family in happier times. Kate was fifteen, the same age I'd been when Pete had gone off to war. Now that I was eighteen, the war years seemed like such a long time ago.

"You've won them over. Especially Kate," Scotty told me later. "They all love you."

"They're so nice," I said appreciatively. I could see myself belonging to this family, spending holidays and long summer vacations together.

As 1946 was about to end, everything in my life was finally making sense. I felt content. I had a wonderful boyfriend, my college studies, two caring parents, and I loved Scotty's family. What more could I ask for?

"You and Scotty have been seeing a lot of each other," Mom commented. "I'm glad you didn't fall for one of those big-city boys. Scotty has good roots."

As if big-city boys didn't? But Mom was interested in me again, so I didn't risk upsetting her.

Then one day Miss Berkland surprised me with a special gift. "The Lynn Kerns Orchestra is playing at the Surf on New Year's Eve. They've agreed to let you sing a song with them."

Me? Singing at the Surf? It was almost too much to take in! I rushed home to tell Mom and Daddy.

"We'll have to come and see you," Daddy said, "although tickets on New Year's Eve might be hard to come by."

Mom pursed her lips. "Do you really think Scotty is going to be impressed with you because of your singing voice? He wants a wife, not Dinah Shore."

"Scotty will be excited to see me sing," I said, hoping that it was true.

"Well, I'm not going out on a busy night like that. I'm getting a cough, and that cold air isn't good for me."

Daddy protested but Mom wouldn't give in. Her rejection stung. I felt fifteen again, when Mom had forbidden me to sing at the Governor's Ball. I told Daddy to stay home, that he should be with Mom and I'd be too nervous with them watching me anyway.

On New Year's Eve Scotty picked me up. I wore a new dress, a daring black-and-white off-the-shoulder gown that swept the tops of my feet and flared out at the bottom.

"Our last night together," he said, pulling me close in the car, and I already felt the hole of his absence. He had to go back to school for basketball practice, and I had one week left before I returned to school. It was bittersweet; we'd discovered each other again in just a few weeks.

At the Surf Miss Berkland introduced me to Mr. Kerns, the band leader.

"You aren't singing until the second set, so just enjoy yourself until then," he told me.

I sat with Scotty in the booth he'd reserved for us. We cuddled on the same side as I tried to contain my nerves. I'd sung with my choir at college, but this was different. This was my dream come true.

"I'm going to miss you," Scotty whispered into my ear.

"Easter break," I reminded him. "And you'll write every week. Promise me."

"I promise." He smiled and held me closer.

Someone bumped into our table, and we turned to see Lance Dugan, who peered at us through bloodshot eyes, his tie already loosened and his suit coat unbuttoned. One chubby hand held a bottle of beer, while the other held the hand of a girl I didn't know.

"Bishop!" Lance shouted. "You old dog! How's your hoop shot?"

"I'm a starter on the team, if that's what you mean. How's Columbia?"

Lance settled into the opposite side of the booth, dragging the girl down with him and spilling his drink. He took out a cigarette and lit it.

"It's overrun with GIs, but they're starting to cut back and filter out the undesirables. New York is a bang. You'll have to come visit me." Lance gave me one of his leering appraisals. "The farmer's daughter," he said, nodding. "Old habits die hard, I see."

"I see that you've moved on," I said, glaring at him and nodding toward his date, a girl who looked to be as drunk as Lance. Her makeup was already smeared, and her bun half-toppled from her head.

"Let's just say the big city has broadened my horizons," he said, puffing out a stream of white smoke.

"From what I've heard, you've been broadening them while keeping a foothold here." He'd been a two-timing jerk ever since he'd given Stella that ring.

"You've always been a little Red Hot, just like your hair color," Lance said, leaning across the table. "That's a compliment, by the way."

"Excuse me," I said, "I need to go to the ladies' room."

Scotty stood and let me out of the booth, giving my hand a reassuring squeeze.

"I'll come too," said Lance's date, whom he hadn't even bothered to introduce. She stumbled after me through the crowd, but I didn't wait for her. If she fell flat on her face, I wouldn't have cared. I hurried to the ladies' room, where I fixed my hair and applied a bit of powder to my nose.

The music was in full swing when I returned to the crowded ballroom. I was relieved to see only Scotty at the booth.

He stood when I came back, his hands fidgeting inside his jacket pocket.

"I'm glad you got rid of them," I said, scooting into the booth.

Scotty sat next to me. He stopped and glanced around nervously.

"What is it, Scotty?"

He looked straight at me. "I'm no good at this stuff."

"What stuff?"

He took my hand. "I don't know if this is the right time or place, but I just can't wait any longer or I'll burst. These last few weeks have been the best ones of my life. I'm leaving tomorrow and you're going back next week, and I know it seems kind of sudden, but I've known you since you were a little girl with red pigtails. I'm crazy about you, Lorraine. I always have been. I'm going to graduate in another year and I've already got lots of job offers. Heck, I have some from businesses just ten miles away in Mason City. So even though I don't have a lot to offer right now, I think I have a bright future ahead of me. And I only want to share it with one person. You."

I held my breath as he took out a small ring from his jacket pocket. The tiny diamond caught the light and sparkled like a miniature star.

"You would make me the happiest man in the world if you married me," he said, holding the ring out to me.

I put out my hand and let him slip the ring on my finger. It was too large, so he took it off and wrapped a piece of napkin around the bottom of the band, then put it back on my finger. I stared down at it, unable to speak. This was so sudden. And I had to sing in just a few minutes!

"Does this mean you'll marry me?" he asked.

My heart remembered another love, one so passionate that it had consumed my whole being. But that had been a lifetime ago. I'd been just a girl then, and it had been wartime. Things were different now, I told myself. I was too old to be pining away like a schoolgirl. I remembered how Stella had told me I was a fool to let Scotty Bishop get away from me. Now I had another chance. That alone was a miracle.

"Yes," I finally said after a long pause, "I'll marry you."

Scotty took my hand and kissed me. "I promise I'll make you happy, darling."

He was so excited that when the music ended, he raised my arm into the air and yelled, "We're engaged!" Everyone cheered.

We danced and toasted our good fortune. Lance Dugan sent a bottle of champagne to our table. I'd never tasted it before and could only take a few sips of the bubbly.

"I don't want to be tipsy when I sing," I said.

"You'll sound like an angel no matter what," Scotty said, kissing me again.

The band was winding down for the break when I excused myself to get ready for my performance. I worked my way toward the stage, noting that the band was dressed in matching white jackets and black bow ties, and my black-and-white dress fit in perfectly. The bandleader was leading the two rows of musicians in an upbeat tempo, his dark hair parted in the middle and a huge smile on his round face as he turned occasionally to the audience.

And that's when I spotted him. In the second row on the end. He was the same as I remembered, except even more handsome in his white jacket instead of the work clothes he'd worn on our farm. His dimple became pronounced when he blew on the saxophone.

I froze, unable to move. How was it possible? Here, of all places. Now, of all times.

I stood in front of the stage, feeling dizzy and sick to my stomach.

The music wound down and the bandleader announced a short break. The band shuffled offstage, and I stumbled after them, hardly aware of what I was doing. I only knew I had to see him up close, to make sure he wasn't a figment of my imagination. Perhaps he just looked like Jens. It had been several years, after all. Maybe the champagne was getting to me.

The door to the dressing room was ajar. The men were enjoying their own New Year's celebration with drinks provided by the club's manager.

"Happy New Year, fellows!" One of them lifted his glass into the air.

"Thank you, Mr. Fox!" another man said, which was followed by laughter.

The door abruptly opened further as one of the musicians exited the room. He stopped when he saw me.

"No autographs right now, sweetheart. The band is on break."

"I wasn't . . ."

"She's our singer." Mr. Kerns motioned me in. "This is Lorraine Kindred," he said, introducing me to the band.

I could only look at one person. Jens took in my long dress and my hair and I could see in his eyes the hint of recognition. Of perhaps something more.

"Jens?" I said in a high voice.

"You two know each other?" Mr. Kerns asked.

"Yes," Jens said.

I was a statue, unable to speak or move. I couldn't believe he was sitting right in front of me after all this time.

"Jens," I repeated, my brain failing me.

"Give us a moment," Jens said, taking my arm and leading me behind the stage. It was cold and dark; there was a small leak of winter air coming from an opening. Jens was thinner than before, but he hadn't changed much other than that. His eyes still held the same determined look they'd had when he was learning English.

"Lorraine," he said, finally acknowledging it was me in a tone I couldn't quite decipher. "It is good to see you."

Good to see me? Was that all he could say after all this time? I'd always expected a different reunion. He would scoop me into his arms and kiss me and tell me how much he'd missed me. Not this awkward, polite restraint.

"What are you doing here?" My voice sounded strange.

"I came to United States two months ago," he said. "Mr. Kerns sponsored me. He gave me job in the band."

"Two months," I repeated. He'd been here for two months. He'd never even contacted me. "You're here. I thought you . . ." I couldn't finish. My throat closed up. Had I been nothing more than a diversion during his prison camp days? What a fool I'd been all this time. I wanted to yell at him, to hit him for what he'd done to me. Those wasted years. Wasted tears!

"You thought what?" he asked, his voice breaking at the end as he shifted his weight and looked at his feet.

I swallowed the lump in my throat. "I thought you'd come visit us. I mean, after all my father did for you," I said, my voice growing angry.

He paused for a long moment, and when he looked up at me I saw a glint of pain in his eyes. "I did."

"What?"

"First thing when I came to this country was go to your house. Your mother told me you were going to marry another man. She said go away. I wasn't welcome at your farm."

I gasped. "She said that? That wasn't true! She lied!"

He glanced down at the ring on my finger. The proof of his words caught the light and sparkled.

"She did?" he asked.

I clutched my stomach, feeling suddenly sick.

"We need to get back. Your number is up next," Jens said, guiding me toward the stage.

How could I possibly sing now?

✦

I couldn't breathe. The bandleader was introducing me, but all I could think of was the boy sitting behind me, his instrument resting in his lap.

The song I would be singing was about love and loss, and forgotten promises. I couldn't sing that song now, not with Jens sitting behind me.

I walked onto the stage, and the band started playing. I opened my mouth, but nothing came out. I backed away from the microphone, shaking my head.

Miss Berkland was near the front of the crowd, nodding at me in encouragement, but all I could think of was how the lights were too bright and the room too hot. Everything was blurry. This was no longer a dream, but a nightmare. I didn't want to look at anyone: not at Miss Berkland, who was surely regretting helping me. Not at Scotty, who couldn't understand what I was feeling. And especially not at Jens, who thought I had betrayed him.

The music started again, but it was too late. I couldn't sing. I couldn't even breathe. I ran off the stage, barely aware of what I was doing.

If the band continued playing, I couldn't hear it. I could only hear the pounding of my heart as I ran out the door into the parking lot.

Scotty came out shortly afterward with my coat in his arms. "I shouldn't have proposed right before your debut. I'm afraid I caused you too much excitement. You looked overcome."

"We need to leave, Scotty," I said, feeling more lightheaded than before.

"Don't feel bad, sweetheart," he said as he wrapped my coat around me. "Forget about singing. We haven't told our folks yet! We have to wake them and share the good news!"

He waved at a few well-wishers as we walked to his car. It was just after midnight.

"They're going to be so happy," Scotty said as he opened the car door for me. "Just like we are."

Thirty-four

✦

January, 1947

I couldn't confront Mom. Not when Scotty and I showed up at home with news of our engagement. But I was so angry with her. She'd sent Jens away. She'd told him I was engaged to another man, and now I actually *was* engaged to another man. I felt tricked and manipulated. But mostly I felt helpless. What could I do? I had to see Jens, if only to explain. Just the thought of him sent shivers down my arms, and with those shivers, memories of how I'd felt around him quickly rushed back.

Scotty left for school the next day with the promise to call every week.

"Basketball will be over soon and so will school. We'll be together again before you know it." He kissed me long and hard.

That night I held my hands behind my back to keep from fidgeting as I told Mom that I was going to the Surf again. "Stella wants to go," I explained before Mom could object. "I haven't seen her in ages."

I asked Daddy to drop me off on his way into town. I wore a simple sweater-and-skirt set and arrived early, before the band had even set up. Last night's celebration still hung thick in the air. Stale cigarette and alcohol fumes seemed to be embedded in the walls. All the booths were empty. I found one near the back and sat down to wait.

My mouth was dry and my stomach grumbled. I hadn't slept last night and had eaten only a few soda crackers. I had no idea what I would say to Jens. I just had to see him, to know what had happened to him these past two years.

I was alone except for some men who were setting up on the stage. Then I saw him. His shoes clicked across the hardwood floor, and he flashed a friendly wave to the men onstage. He was dressed in a flannel shirt and jeans, with a panama hat on his head.

I stood up, wondering if I should wait until he wasn't busy, wondering what I could possibly say to him. His eyes swept the room and then he saw me. He stopped. I gave a pathetic wave and plastered a fake smile on my face.

I thought for a moment that he was going to ignore me. We were both older. I was engaged to another man. Maybe too much time had passed. But he walked over and slid into the booth across from me. My heart thumped and my palms were sweaty. I didn't know what to expect. I had to take short breaths to calm myself.

"Hi," he said.

"Hi."

"How are you feeling?"

"Foolish," I replied, then added, "I've wanted to sing here my whole life. But I blew it."

"You will have another chance. Do not give up."

I nodded, not feeling particularly encouraged.

"Do you want something to drink?"

"No thanks," I said, although having something to hold on to would have helped my quivering hands. "Your English has really improved."

"I have continued to study and practice. Being in English-speaking country for two years helped."

I remembered Günther's letter. "Right. You were in England after you left Algona. How was it there?"

"Not as good. Very hard work. A different kind of cold. Less to eat. We did not get any pay for our work there. People were not as nice as Iowa people."

"I'm sorry about my mom," I said. "She's never gotten over losing Pete. She shouldn't have said those things to you."

"I understand. Günther said that loss hardens hearts. He helped me. He was still in prison camp when I was released. I don't know where he is, or the other men who worked on the farm."

"Daddy got a letter from Günther. He's back in Hamburg. I can get his address for you."

"I would like that. I want to thank him."

"Helmut died when a land mine exploded. I don't know about Jakob. Ludwig's hometown was bombed. He is searching for his wife and daughter," I went on.

He shook his head. "Poor fellow."

"There's always hope," I said.

"He lived in Pforzheim. Nothing left of city."

Ludwig had already survived the war and two prison camps. His wife and daughter had kept him going. They couldn't be dead. But then again, I had been wrong about Pete. I'd been certain he would come home. Instead he became a statistic, a casualty of what would be hailed as a victorious battle.

An awkward silence followed. I thought of that first day I'd met Jens in the fields on the farm, of his persistence in talking to me despite how I continued to ignore him. And now we were both free to talk, or touch, or take that walk, or dance . . .

The band was warming up with a slow tune. "Dance with me?" It was the first time I'd ever asked a boy to dance.

He hesitated. "Okay." He stood and held out his hand. I got up and moved toward him. He took my hand in his. I shivered as he put his arm around me on the empty dance floor. We moved slowly, not talking, just taking in the feel of being this close, of it being permitted this time.

"When we danced so long ago," he said, "I thought it would be the only time I ever danced with you."

"Is that why you told me not to wait for you?"

"Yes. I did not want to cause more grief."

"You never wrote to me. I had no idea if you were dead or alive."

Jens stopped dancing and furrowed his brows. "But I did write. Many times. You did not reply."

"I didn't get any letters. . . ." I closed my eyes and winced. Mom always insisted on getting the mail herself. "My mom must have intercepted them."

"I thought you did not want to hear from me anymore. Maybe to ask you to wait was selfish."

"But I did wait."

His finger touched the ring on my hand. "You don't have to explain. I understand." His voice held pain.

"No," I insisted. "You don't understand. I waited and waited. I thought you didn't care for me anymore."

"Time has not changed how I feel about you," he said, looking me in the eyes. "But I have no right now. Perhaps I never have right. I was enemy of your country."

I remembered the shame I'd felt when Lance Dugan accused me of having feelings for a POW. How we had let everyone else tell us our feelings were wrong.

"You were never my enemy," I said.

The band was playing Bing Crosby's song, "I'll Be Seeing You."

Jens smiled. "I remember this song."

He pulled me close, gently brushing his lips across my ear. Every part of my body lit up, like his kiss was electric. The floor was ours alone, as though the Surf had locked its doors so we could have this dance.

Jens sighed. "Who is your betrothed? Your school boyfriend?"

"Yes," I said, wishing I could just forget about Scotty right now, pretend that the last few weeks hadn't happened, that I wasn't engaged, so Jens could kiss me and I could kiss him back.

The song ended too soon. I wanted to keep dancing like this forever, just the two of us.

Jens still held on to me. I looked into his soft eyes. "I wish. . . ." I couldn't finish the thought. I didn't want him to leave me. Then my ring pinched my finger beneath his hand. I was about to move away when his lips covered mine, a sudden kiss that I'd dreamt about for two years but was still unprepared for. It was a kiss of longing and regret, a kiss that melted the years and the pain. It was our own private armistice.

When he finally lifted his head, I could barely breathe. "You came back," I said, trembling. "I thought you'd marry a German girl and forget all about me."

"Never," he said.

People were now starting to arrive.

"Can you get away for a while?" I asked.

He nodded. "I can get someone to cover."

Jens borrowed a band member's car and we drove to Mason City, ten miles away. I sat in the passenger seat, still tasting his kiss, trying to make small talk about his band. Just last night I'd sat next to Scotty and agreed to marry him, and now I'd thrown all common sense out the window. But I couldn't stop myself, any more than I could stop a speeding train. We found a small café that was nearly empty and slid into a private booth.

I still felt as though we were on uneven ground, as though our future was tipping one way or the other and I couldn't tell which way it would go. Two years apart had made us strangers again.

"Tell me about what happened after you left," I asked him. "Tell me about England."

Jens took out a cigarette, but then started to put it away. "Sorry. I know you do not like. Hard habit to stop, especially when nervous."

"It's okay," I said. "You can smoke." Daddy still had his Lucky Strikes in the evening on the front porch. He called it his daily vice.

Jens lit his cigarette and blew out white curls as he told me about life in the prison camp in England. I felt as though he was keeping a lot from me, though. His voice sounded different than when he spoke of our farm.

"Memories of you and farm made prison camp bearable. The British hated us. Our rations were cut. It was difficult time. Some POWs were sent to France. After I was released from the camp in England I returned home. But my home was gone. My mother sold it and move in with her sister. So I stay there with them, but they don't have much room. Then last year she died."

"What about your brothers?"

"They died in the war. I was the only one to return."

"Oh, Jens. I'm so sorry." So much loss. So many lives ruined. And Jens had no one. I was lucky to still have my parents.

"Ya. There was nothing left for me there. I did farm work to save up money to come back here. And I wrote Mr. Kerns to sponsor me. He heard me play in the camp band. Tell me I can play anytime with his band."

"You're doing what you always wanted to do," I said. "You're playing in a band."

It seemed the stuff of fairy tales, that Jens would make his way back here.

"And you go to the university?" he asked.

I told Jens about school and the choir, about how Mom had arranged for me to see Scotty just a few weeks ago and how I'd lost hope of ever seeing Jens, and that that was why I'd started dating Scotty again. I'd thought I needed to move on.

"Things would have been different if I'd gotten your letters," I said.

"Or perhaps you would have tired of waiting for me," he said. "Two years. When I was in England I was not sure I would see you again. I dreamed of freedom, of being outside those barbed wires."

I thought of Scotty, of how dependable and kind he was. How, yesterday, it would have been easy to plan a life together. I hadn't even known whether Jens was still alive.

"I thought I was happy until I saw you again," I said.

"I did not come back to make you unhappy."

"I know. But you're here. I can't just forget about you."

He reached across the table and took my hands. "So what are you going to do? Your mother does not approve, I know." There was a bitterness in his voice.

I shook my head. Two years was a long time. I barely knew Jens now, didn't know what he'd been through, or how it had affected him. I had changed, too. I wasn't a kid anymore. "I need time to think," I said.

The café owner was sweeping the floor, piling the vinyl-backed chairs on top of the tables. It was getting late. Jens paid the bill.

"What accent is that?" the man asked as Jens handed him the money.

Jens flinched. "German, sir."

The man narrowed his eyes. "That's what I thought." He pushed the money back across the counter toward Jens. "I don't need your business and I don't want to see either of you in my place again. Understand?"

My throat tightened. Jens nodded and pulled me out the door, leaving the money on the counter.

He drove me home slowly, as though he feared this was the last time he'd see me. His band was going to play one more night at the Surf before leaving for South Dakota. I was still in awe that he was here next to me. I couldn't think about Scotty or my parents or school. Everything fell away, now that Jens was back. I sat close to him and he put his arm around me.

Jens opened my car door for me and walked me up the narrow path Daddy had shoveled last week. I knew I couldn't invite him in, so we huddled near the back steps. Neither of us wanted this night to end.

Jens pointed at the apple tree in the distance, its crooked, bare limbs reaching up out of the snow in stark contrast to its hardy summer bloom.

"I remember our dance beneath tree," he said. "We made promise not to forget."

"These last two years I've sat under that same tree and thought of that dance," I confessed. "It should have bushy leaves and be full of fruit."

"In winter? That would be miracle."

"No less a miracle than you being here with me right now."

"No miracle." Jens shook his head. "Determination."

My voice broke. "I'm sorry, Jens. Somewhere along the way I lost hope that we'd ever see each other again."

"But we are together now." He leaned over and kissed me. His lips were warm and the kiss was soft. It was like opening the barn door on a hot day, feeling a rush of cool air sweep through me. He pulled back and opened his mouth, but before he could speak, I grabbed his coat and drew him closer. I kissed him as though I couldn't get enough of him, as though I'd been starved these years without him.

When we finally pulled apart, our heavy breathing formed tiny swirling clouds in the winter air.

"I never forgot you," I said, desperate to convince him.

Jens's brows furrowed. He pointed up at the stars, which seemed twice as bright on this clear, cold night.

"When I was in prison camp and could not sleep, I look up at stars and think of this farm, of you under same tree, under same stars over Clear Lake. And I was happy. No matter what happened to me. No matter if we never see one another again. You give that to me."

I looked down. I had given him something to hang on to during those two years and he was thanking me for it, even as I'd moved on with my life. I still felt ashamed.

Jens had memorized the constellations and he pointed them out, saying the names in both German and English. "*Kassiopeia* looks like the letter W. I think the name is similar in English."

I followed the line of his finger in the sky. "I wonder what the name means?"

"*Kassiopeia* was beautiful woman, but vain. When Poseidon sent a monster to her land, she sacrificed her daughter Andromeda. But before the monster ate the princess, Perseus saved her and she became his wife."

His blue eyes focused on mine with such intensity that I was certain he was talking about us. I tilted my head. "Andromeda was lucky to have someone love her so much."

His face, already flushed from the cold, went from pink to crimson. "*Perseus* was lucky. He only had to save her from a monster, not fiancé."

"Jens . . ."

"I give you time," he said quickly, then let out a frustrated breath, "but I have only one day left to make up for two years."

I put a finger to his lips. "Two years have done nothing to change how I feel about you. I know things aren't easy, but please be patient. I don't want to lose you again."

He slipped his hand around my neck and tilted my chin up. He kissed me, a hot, passionate kiss that took my breath away. "You won't lose me," he said. "I promise, *mein Shatz*."

"My treasure," I repeated. He'd called me that when he was a POW, when speaking like that had held danger for us both. There was still risk involved, I reminded myself. Just a different kind of risk.

We held on to each other until our fingers and toes were numb. "We still have tomorrow night," I said, reluctantly opening the door.

Jens kissed my hand. "Until tomorrow, my fair Andromeda," he whispered.

I watched him leave through the windowpane etched in ice. My blood warmed at the thought of his kiss.

I started up the stairs when I heard a noise. I turned. Mom was sitting on the sofa in the dark. She was still having trouble sleeping, and spent many nights going up and down the creaking stairs. By the look on her face, I could tell she'd been watching us.

"You're an engaged woman now," she said. "I don't know what college life is like, but that's not appropriate behavior here in Iowa. Do you want Scotty knowing that you're kissing boys behind his back?"

There was no denying what Mom had seen. I was tired of tiptoeing around her. I had claimed my own life in college; it was time to claim it at home.

"I was with Jens."

"Who?"

"The boy you sent away when he came to see me," I said accusingly.

She sucked in a breath. "You mean the Nazi?"

"He's not a Nazi."

Her lips puckered up. "He's a German."

"You say that like it's a nasty word, like you don't know plenty of Germans right in our own town. He said he wrote to me. What did you do with his letters?"

"I burned them."

How easily she admitted it, as though I had no rights or considerations. "How could you?"

"Because I needed to protect you, Lorraine. Do I need to remind you that he was in a prison camp, and an enemy of our country? Why would I want my teenage daughter to correspond with someone like that? And it's unacceptable to see him now. You will *not* throw away a marriage proposal from Scotty Bishop! I won't let you disgrace our family in such a way. Have you forgotten what happened to your own brother?"

"I'll never forget Pete. But the war is over, Mom."

"Do you really think people will forget what they did? You think he could be accepted here or anyplace else? He's an outsider, Lorraine." She stood and crossed her arms. "And as far as I'm concerned, he's as responsible for Pete's death as the one who buried that mine."

"No, Mom. He's not. He's just a boy who was caught up in the war, and your hate isn't going to make him something else. And I didn't say I wasn't going to marry Scotty. But you had no right to keep Jens from me."

"I had every right!" she spat out. "They took my son. I wasn't going to let them get my daughter, too. That boy should never have come back."

"Well, he's here now. And you can't keep him from me." I turned and ran up the stairs, leaving my mother behind.

Thirty-five

✦

January, 1947

The next morning Mom waited until Daddy went to the barn to start in on me. "Do you realize what you're doing, Lorraine? First it was college, and now this? You love Scotty. How can you do this to him?"

"I haven't done anything," I said, but I knew that wasn't true. And I didn't want to hurt him.

"You have a future with Scotty. Can you say the same with this other fellow? What can he offer you?"

I put up a hand. "Scotty and I are fine, Mom. Stop worrying so much."

"Of course I worry. This is a small town, Lorraine. It won't take long for word to get around if you take up with that man."

She was right, of course. I planned to see Jens again that very night. And I didn't want Scotty to hear rumors about me. I didn't know what I wanted.

When I got ready to go out that evening, Mom stood in front of the door. "Where do you think you're going?"

"It's okay," I reassured her. "I just have to talk to him one last time."

She raised her eyebrows as though she didn't believe me. "You start brewing trouble and you know what you'll get?"

"Mom, please . . ."

"Pregnant and alone for the rest of your life. Think about your choices."

I walked around her and out the door.

She hadn't told Daddy, who must have sensed the tension between us and retreated to the barn to milk the cows. That was his way. Leave things be. Don't discuss unpleasantness. Perhaps Mom was right when she said that he lived with his head buried in the sand.

One thing I knew for certain was that Mom would never forgive me if I broke off my engagement with Scotty.

And so much of what she had said made sense. As much as I hated to admit it, when seen through her eyes, it would seem she *was* protecting me by burning those letters. Scotty was a wonderful man. I knew he'd make me happy. And yet, all of that was background noise in my head when I was with Jens.

"Are you okay?" Jens asked when he saw me. I wore a blue dress; the shade nearly matched the color of Jens's eyes.

I scooted next to him in the booth he'd reserved. Number 110, the number of days he'd spent in the Algona POW camp, he told me. He took my cold hand and filled it with his warmth. I knew it was reckless of me, this public display, especially after Mom's words of caution. But I couldn't help it.

"Fine," I replied, although I was anything but. "My mother knows about you. She's not very happy."

"I am sorry. I do not want to cause problem between you."

"The problem between me and my mother *is* my mother," I replied.

"Sound like German mother," he said.

"Remember when you escaped from camp to come see me? Did you get in trouble when you returned?"

"Yes," he said. "I was sentenced to fourteen days in the camp jail. Just bread and water. But it was worth it."

"Well, my mom can't be any worse than that." Or could she?

I hadn't expected things would be easy. I had a mother whose favorite child had died, and now that she was taking an interest in her only daughter, she felt I'd betrayed her.

I spent part of the evening standing at the side of the stage, watching the band play. During the break, Jens and I went back to the booth.

"You're so talented," I told him as we sat down. "I could watch you play every night."

"And I could listen to you sing every night," he said. I'd only sung for him a couple of times when he'd been working at the farm, so his compliment all these years later meant the world to me.

He hugged me, but his arm quickly dropped to his side. Standing in front of our table was Lance Dugan with a girl at his side, a different girl than he'd been with the other night. He was in much the same shape as last time, perhaps more drunk.

"Well, if it isn't the pot calling the kettle black," Lance said, staggering and lifting his drink in the air. "After I sent you and Scott a bottle of champagne the other night to celebrate your engagement, the minute his back is turned, you're taking up with a musician?"

"My personal affairs are none of your business, Lance."

"You always did act like a prima donna."

"And you've always acted like a fathead."

Lance let out a short laugh and turned to Jens. "Hey, buddy, you're messing with another man's fiancée."

Jens stood up. "Leave her alone."

Lance backed up a second, unsteady on his feet. "Is that a German accent? Aren't you in the wrong country? Didn't we just beat your sorry ass into the ground?"

"I spent the war in a prison camp," Jens admitted.

"Lucky bastard." Then Lance's face registered the information. "Oh! Were you one of *those* POWs? The ones who spent all that time with the farmer's daughter? Tell me, is she really a red-hot lover?"

Jens swung, striking Lance squarely in the jaw and sending him sprawling across the maple hardwood floor along with his drink.

I had never seen Jens angry before, but in a flash his anger disappeared.

"I'm sorry if I hurt you," he said, extending a hand to Lance. "But you must respect Lorraine."

"Keep your filthy Kraut hands off me," Lance yelled while his date tried to help him stand.

I quickly guided Jens back to the stage, away from the scene where people were gathering to see Lance Dugan lying flat on the floor. "Lance Dugan isn't someone you want to make an enemy."

Jens smirked. "He was drunk. Maybe he won't remember."

"No one in this town has ever stood up to Lance Dugan before. You can count on one thing. He won't forget."

I could also count on him to tell Scotty what he'd seen.

✦

After the ballroom had emptied at the end of the night, I found Jens as he was putting away his saxophone.

"Can I try?" I asked, wondering how he managed to make such beautiful sounds come out of that instrument.

He wiped off the mouthpiece and handed it to me. "Sure."

Jens showed me how to hold it with my left hand on top and right hand on the bottom.

"Curl lips," he said as I put it up to my mouth.

"Now blow."

A loud squeaking sound pierced the air. Jens covered his ears with his hands.

"Sorry." I handed back the instrument.

"Maybe you should stick to singing."

I winced, thinking of how I'd failed miserably just a few nights before on this stage.

"You will sing here again," he said, reading the look on my face.

We lingered in the dark lobby after the equipment had been packed and loaded.

"Two years, and hardest part is leaving now," Jens said, taking my hands in his and kissing them. "Our band will play at Prom Ballroom in St. Paul next month. Is near your school?"

"It's not too far. I'll come see you."

He smiled. "That will make me very happy."

I handed him a piece of paper with my school address.

"I will write to you," he promised. He kissed my hands again. "Until next month."

I wiped from my cheeks the tears that I'd tried to hold back. Two years of separation had been erased in two days. The feelings I had for Jens were stronger than ever. I loved this man; I loved his accent and the way he listened to me, as though every word I said was important. I loved how I could make his eyes shine with joy. And I loved how every nerve in my body responded to his touch.

I sniffed, not wanting to leave. One month was nothing, a drop in the bucket after two years apart. But it felt like an eternity right now. "I'm not sure I can let you go, Jens."

We kissed for a long time in the darkened lobby, until Mr. Fox came up behind us and I had to leave.

✦

Five days at home seemed interminably long since Mom was barely talking to me, a bitter reminder of how much I craved my life back at school. I decided that I would reach Scotty before Lance talked to him. But I wasn't sure what to tell him.

While Daddy was out at the barn, I walked up behind Mom. She was sitting on our green sofa cross-stitching a doily, staring out the window at the wind whipping the snow into textured patterns across the fields.

The needle worked confidently in her hands, an automatic motion that barely required her attention. That alone was a testament to her recovery. Her skin was still pale, though her eyes were sharp.

"Mom, can we talk?"

I saw her shoulders tense up.

I sat across from her in Daddy's easy chair and folded my hands in my lap.

Mom didn't look at me; instead her eyes went to her cross-stitch. Patterns of dainty pink flowers were taking shape on the white fabric. "Is this about that boy?"

"Yes," I admitted.

Mom's face twisted up. "There's nothing to talk about. You have a choice to make, and I hope to God you make the right one. Don't betray Scotty and bring shame to our family by taking up with that war criminal."

The only noise in the room was the sound of thread being pulled through the fabric and the ticking of the grandfather clock, a dark monstrosity that Mom had inherited from her parents.

"I'm sorry, Mom. I'd hoped things would be different now that the war was over."

Mom stopped stitching and stared at me. "Different? How long has this been going on? Were you taking up with that boy behind my back the whole time he worked here? While your brother was dying for his country?"

I wanted to tell her it wasn't like that. She was making it out to sound like something horrible. But I realized that in her eyes, it *was* horrible.

"I suspected as much," she spat. "Well, you've never been one to listen to good sense. You ignore everything I tell you. But if you don't do the right thing now, you're no longer welcome in this house."

She was going to kick me out? Did Scotty warrant more loyalty than her own daughter? I had no idea her hate could run that deep. I finally found my voice. "I'm going to take the bus to Iowa City to see Scotty. And I don't know if I'll be engaged when I come back. If you want to disown me for that, so be it."

As I went to pack a bag, my indignation cut through sudden hot tears. I'd hoped that Jens would have a new start here. But there were people like Mom, who couldn't find any forgiveness in their hearts, and people like Lance, who couldn't accept someone who was different.

Even if I broke my engagement to Scotty, did Jens and I have any hope of a future together? If we did, it didn't appear that we would have one here.

Thirty-six

✦

1947

I bought a bus ticket for the ten o'clock departure, then walked over to the high school. I found Miss Berkland in the music room, preparing for her next class.

"I'm so sorry about the other night, Miss Berkland," I said.

She held up her hand. "Every performer deals with stage fright, Lorraine. You should have had a chance to practice on stage before the audience arrived. I feel responsible for putting you in that position. You'll get better with practice. I know it."

"To be honest, Miss Berkland, it wasn't the audience. It was the band."

"The band? I don't understand."

I couldn't hold in the tears any longer. My heart felt as though it would break. I collapsed into a chair and buried my face in my hands.

Miss Berkland hurried over and patted my shoulder.

"Come now, Lorraine. It can't be as bad as all that."

I told her everything: about how I'd fallen in love with Jens during the war, and how Scotty had proposed to me right before the performance. I told her how awful I'd felt that I hadn't been able to sing, and how my mother was so fragile and yet so unbending, and how it scared me to cross her. Of how Mom would never accept my singing or Jens.

When I finished talking I was afraid to look at Miss Berkland, fearing that I'd see hatred or disappointment. I stared at the floor while she handed me a handkerchief and I wiped my eyes. Her voice was soft. "You must understand one thing, Lorraine. Our hearts aren't like our voices. They're not instruments that can be trained with discipline or practice. Our hearts have a voice of their own."

Miss Berkland looked out the window for a moment, then cleared her throat and continued. "When I was young, I also fell in love with a saxophonist. He was playing for a band that we went to hear."

I couldn't hide my surprise. I looked up at her. She'd never mentioned a boyfriend before.

"Yes, I was young once like you," she said, reading my expression. "He played for a jazz band, and he was a very good man and so talented, but he wasn't someone I was allowed to date," she said.

"Why not?"

Miss Berkland walked over and closed the door before continuing. "This may shock you, and I have to ask that you never tell another living soul what I'm about to say."

"Of course. I promise." I couldn't imagine Miss Berkland having anything to tell me that might shock me.

"He was a man of color, a Negro, and there were strict laws regarding such relationships. But the law didn't mean anything to my heart. I only knew how I felt about him and how he made me feel."

My mouth fell open. Miss Berkland had always seemed like such a prudish woman, not the kind who'd do anything against societal norms. "You fell in love with a colored man?" We only had but two colored people in our community.

"Yes. We were playing an extended gig in Chicago at the time. I was young, your age. And he was so handsome and played music that spoke to my soul. We were very much in love."

"What happened?"

Her voice took on a bitter tone. "Someone wrote to my father. When he found out, he came and dragged me back home. My boyfriend's name was Sly, and I didn't want him to go to jail, which he could have if my father had pursued matters. That ended my singing career. I wound up teaching school instead of following my ambition. I gave up everything, because—well, I don't really know why I did it, except that I didn't want to bring shame to my family. That's not what we Iowa girls are supposed to do, is it?"

I thought of everything she had given up, of how my decision to follow my heart could bring a similar shame upon my family.

She clasped her hands together. "I suppose that's why I pushed you so hard, Lorraine."

"I'm so sorry, Miss Berkland."

"Don't be sorry for me. I love teaching, and life could be a lot worse. I don't imagine it would have gotten any easier if we'd stayed together. I have plenty of regrets, but I have a lot to be thankful for, too."

I felt utterly confused. "I don't know what to do," I confessed. "I have a bus ticket to Iowa City. I was going to tell Scotty about Jens, but . . ."

"You're worried you'll ruin your life and shame your family?"

I nodded. When I was with Jens I couldn't deny my longing, but I didn't want to have to choose between him and my family.

"I can't tell you what to do. That's a decision you have to make yourself. There's nothing wrong with sacrifice if that's what you want, but letting yourself get trapped into a life you don't want isn't what I'd wish on anyone." She had tears at the corners of her own eyes, and I handed back the damp handkerchief, which she used to dab at her eyes. "You only have one life, Lorraine. And you only have one heart."

She hugged me, and I collected myself before I walked to the bus station. The long ride gave me lots of time to think, but I was no closer to a decision when I arrived in Iowa City than I had been when I left. I walked around, admiring the sprawling campus that was so much larger than the small site that St. Olaf occupied. It was getting late; the buildings were casting longer shadows, and the air was blowing in an icy stroke that swept through the streets.

I found Scotty at practice, and waited outside the gym until he came out. My fingers and legs were nearly frozen.

Scotty almost walked past me with his teammates. "Lorraine? What are you doing here?" He scooped me up, but then his eyes narrowed. "Is something wrong?"

The look on his face was too much for me. "I just had to see you," I lied.

His face held a perplexed smile. "I just left you three days ago!"

I started shivering uncontrollably. Scotty put his arm around me. "Let's get you someplace warm."

He took me to a large brick house with four white pillars in front, the Kappa Alpha Theta sorority house, where a friend of his gave me a hot cup of tea and offered to put me up for the night. The girls all knew Scotty, and it was evident in the way they fell over themselves to help me that they adored him.

It was difficult to find a place to talk without someone listening in, but Scotty managed to locate a small study that was empty.

"Now," he said, sitting next to me and taking my hands in his oversized ones, which made mine practically disappear. "What's this all about?"

His expression was kind and full of concern. The last thing I wanted was to cause him pain, but who knew what Lance would tell him?

My voice was a whisper. "My German soldier is back." His face dropped and I imagined his heart shattering into a million pieces. "I saw him playing at the Surf."

"I thought we were going to get married," he said. "I thought you were happy with me."

"I was," I insisted. "I am. I'm only telling you because . . ." How could I say that I was only telling him because I was afraid he'd find out through Lance? "I don't want to keep secrets from you."

"Oh, sweetheart," he said. "I thought for a minute that . . . well, you don't still have feelings for him, do you?"

I had to look away before answering. "I accepted your ring, Scotty," I said with too much conviction.

"Yes, you did. I love you, Lorraine, and I'm not about to give you up. I'll fight for you if I have to." He held me and I felt safe in his arms, knowing we still had a future together.

"I know you cared for him, but that was a long time ago," Scotty said, as though he was trying to convince me. "Things have changed. He can't just reappear in your life like that."

I felt him pull away, but his face brightened. "Let's get married this summer!"

"But . . . what about my scholarship?"

"They have a music department here. Maybe you can still take classes, or just be with me. I know it will be hard," he said, his voice gaining strength, "and we won't have much money. But you'll be able to go to my home games. You don't know how much it would mean to me to see your face in the crowd, and the important thing is we'll be together."

"I don't know," I said hesitantly. "I love school and choir. I love singing."

"Please, Lorraine. This is how it's supposed to be for two people in love. Not hundreds of miles away from each other."

His words made sense. If we got married sooner, I'd have less time to think about Jens, to let myself be confused and indecisive. I knew that a future with Scotty would be less of a struggle than any hardships Jens and I would face.

"I can't bear the thought of another year apart from you," he said, bringing me close again.

"Okay," I finally said, although it all seemed so sudden.

The next day Scotty kissed me at the bus door in front of everyone, and promised to call in a week. I smiled as if nothing was wrong, as if I could forget Jens, how his kiss had ignited a fire within me.

A former soldier who'd lost a leg rode in the front of the bus. He still wore his uniform, which was patched at the elbows and had a hole in the knee of his good leg. The other pant leg hung limply across the seat, a mark of what he'd lost. It had been almost two years since the war had ended, but the scars—some visible, others not—were a reminder of all we'd suffered as a nation.

Still, it seemed that most people were hopeful and happy. And now that my family had begun to reclaim some of that hope, I wasn't sure I could make a choice that might tear us apart.

The ride back to Clear Lake was long and uncomfortable. I would be leaving to go back to school soon, and I was so conflicted.

Mom forgave me when she saw the ring still on my finger, but I felt a cold indifference toward her. I didn't mention our summer wedding plans. I didn't want to give her the satisfaction. And I was glad she didn't come with Daddy when he took me to the train station.

"You gonna tell me what's eating the two of you?" he asked before I boarded the train.

Poor Daddy, always the last to know.

"It's Scotty," I confessed, the tears coming again. "I wasn't sure I could marry him. I know you really like him."

Daddy hugged me tight. "Of course I like him, but I don't have to marry him. I take it this is why you made the trip to Iowa City?"

I nodded and sniffed.

"Does he treat you good?"

"Yes, Daddy."

He looked thinner than before, and the lines on his face had deepened. "Well, I only want what's best for you, honey. If he's not the one, you'll find someone who's right for you."

"Mom told me if I broke up with him I wasn't welcome at home anymore."

He shook his head. "Oh, Lorraine. Don't pay her any mind. You know how she gets. She just wants the best for you. She'll get over it," he reassured me. "You still plan on coming home for Easter break."

The whistle blew and I had to go, so he patted my back and helped me on the train. He stayed and waved until the train left.

Would Daddy understand if I told him about Jens? If I told him what Mom had said to Jens when he came to our house, how she'd destroyed his letters? Would it drive a wedge between my parents, or between Daddy and me?

Since Pete's death our family had been like one of the few remaining cornstalks that still stood in the fields, fragile and bent under the weight of the snow. And now I might be responsible for adding more weight on top of it. The guilt pressed heavily on me as the train pulled out of the station. What would happen if I broke up with Scotty?

I knew the answer. The cornstalk would snap off and break entirely.

Thirty-seven

✦

1947

I stared down at the two envelopes in my hand that had been waiting for me upon my return to school—one from Jens and one from Scotty. I leaned against the cold windowsill in my room, reading quickly before my roommate Bernice returned from dinner. She was a shy girl who was studying to be a home economics teacher. Swatches of colored material lay strewn across her bed.

My breath puffed out in white swirls on the cold glass. I read Jens's letter first. His choppy writing was interspersed with German when he didn't know the English translation.

Dearest Lorraine,

War is schrecklich-horrible, but it performed one act of kind-ness, to bring us together.

I have felt this fate many times in my life. An meinem Geburts-tag, my ten year of birth, my father trade a sheep for saxophone after we hear great American jazz musician Sidney Bechet play during fair in Leer, near my hometown. Despite small obstacles,

no money for lessons, I learned to play. And it was by way of
saxophone that I find a sponsor to bring me back to you. When I
play I am back in Ostfriesland in my hometown again, the one of
my youth before the war. And now it also make me think of you.

I stopped reading to wipe a tear from my cheek. I could hear it in his playing, how Jens transformed music, how it became more than notes and
rhythm, how it spoke to him and became part of his soul.

Jens had saved me, just as I had saved him. The love we'd shared had
helped me survive the unspeakable loss of my brother.

Jens wrote of how much he missed me, how he couldn't wait to see
me in a month. I'd gone to Iowa City with just one thought: to tell Scotty
that the German soldier I loved was back. But I'd returned with an engagement ring still on my finger.

"Oh, Jens," I whispered, my tears blurring the blue ink. "You should
have come back sooner."

Then I read Scotty's letter.

Dear Lorraine,

    We're on the road again. I'm writing this on the bus on our
way to Wisconsin. Hope you're still rooting for this Hawkeye,
because he's crazy about you and can't wait to see you at Easter
break. Two months seems like forever. I'm so glad we moved up
the wedding, although I have to admit that it will be hard to get
any homework done when my beautiful wife is here. But I'm so
happy just thinking of how you'll be there every night when I
come home. I'm already the envy of every guy on the team who's
seen your picture. And they don't even know what a swell girl
you are!

    Coach Harrison is walking the aisle so I better end this and

get busy with homework. Miss you and love you, future
Mrs. Bishop—you'd better get used to answering to that, by the
way.

Scotty

I put the two letters side by side, as though I could play a game of eenie, meenie, miney, mo to determine the rest of my life. Which path would I choose?

I hid one letter in my dresser drawer and laid the other on top.

That night I stayed up late after Bernice was asleep. I wrote letter after letter, but kept tearing them up until the wastebasket overflowed with white scraps. I spent hours searching for the right words and finally realized there weren't any that would make it less painful for either of us. I settled on the truth.

Dear Jens,

Seeing you last week was both exhilarating and confusing. I'd given up any hope that we might meet again. We shared a special connection during the war and I will never forget the love we shared. But I can't let those two nights of nostalgia distract me from the commitment I made to Scotty. We plan to wed this summer.

I'm happy you've made a new life for yourself in the US, and I know you'll do well. Please understand. This is the hardest decision of my life.

Lorraine

My hand trembled the next day as I dropped the letter in the mail. Had I made the right choice? Being separated for two years had only strengthened my feelings for Jens. There were still so many obstacles.

Even though the war was over, Mom would never accept Jens. The war had put us on opposite sides, and Pete's death had cemented that division.

And then there was kind and dependable Scotty, who would provide a stable life for me. We shared a common history, and if Jens had never returned I'd have been perfectly content with him.

These thoughts did nothing to stop my blood from running cold at the thought of never seeing Jens again. I tried to concentrate on school. A new semester had begun. In addition to classes in voice, harmony, and music appreciation, I had signed up for freshman composition, biology, and a religion class titled The Life of Christ. That, combined with choir practices, kept me busy and distracted.

A week later I received another letter from Jens. This one had an Eau Claire, Wisconsin, postmark. I carried it in my pocket like a hidden jewel during class, kept patting my pocket to make sure it was still there. In the waning hours of the afternoon I found a private spot in a corner of the library and read his letter at least ten times.

Dearest Lorraine,

   Your letter was very difficult to read. Perhaps if you receive my letters while I was away things could be different. But that is in the past and I know I must accept your decision. I wish you and Scotty happiness. You know that I will love you always. This will never change.

Jens

Tucked inside the letter was a ticket to the Prom Ballroom in St. Paul where Jens and his band would be playing in two weeks. On the ticket he wrote, *If you change your mind.*

I studied the ticket. How easily I could take the bus up to St. Paul, perhaps book a room at a women's hotel, the kind where unmarried girls stayed. I'd go to the Prom Ballroom and surprise Jens. I'd watch him play and take in the sights of the city. And then what?

Just the mere thought of seeing him again made my heart race. It was like holding my palm over a candle, when all I could feel was the warmth, and not the hot lick of the flame burning my hand.

I closed my eyes and kissed the ticket, then dropped it in the trash before I could change my mind.

Thirty-eight

✦

1947

I looked at myself in the mirror. I'd worn the blue dress to church this morning, but before that the last time I'd worn it had been with Jens at the Surf. I didn't need something that would dredge up memories of him while I was at Scotty's house. He was on my mind enough as it was. I shook it off and tossed it on the bed with two other dresses I'd already dismissed.

"Lorraine, are you ready yet?" Mom's voice carried up the stairs. "Why don't you just wear what you had on in church this morning?"

"I spilled jam on it," I lied.

I took a deep breath to calm my nerves. When Scotty's mom had invited us to Easter dinner, she'd said it would be the perfect opportunity to get to know our family better. The idea had caused a stone to take up residence in my stomach, weighing me down.

I finally settled for a pleated green-and-blue plaid skirt and a button-down white blouse with a wide bow at the neck. I tied back my thick reddish locks with a green ribbon. I'd lost weight the last few months, and my face had a sharper look to it. Would Scotty still like what he saw?

I hurried down the stairs and grabbed my coat. Mom and Daddy were waiting in the car.

Mom had on her new pink pillbox hat over tightly woven curls. She'd insisted on a visit to the beauty shop. I couldn't remember the last time she'd made an effort to look nice.

"My daughter is marrying Scotty Bishop, you know," she'd babbled to Rosie Griffiths, who was combing out her faded brown hair. Rosie was four years older than me; her husband was in the navy, stationed somewhere in the Pacific.

"It's the talk of the town," Rosie said, encouraging Mom. "I remember Scotty from high school. He played on the varsity team as a sophomore, and was such a tall, skinny kid back then."

I'd sat rigidly on a hard bench, staring at a Cream of Wheat ad in *LIFE* magazine while inhaling the ammonia fumes in the salon, trying not to listen to Mom's endless prattle, and all the while the stone in my stomach grew.

"He's still tall, but he's filled out nicely," Mom said.

"I know lots of girls who are heartbroken right now," Rosie added, and Mom's face lit up in the mirror with pride.

"What kind of pie are you making?" I'd asked Mom, trying to derail the conversation.

"You know I always make chocolate pie. It's my specialty."

Afterward, even though Mom looked exhausted, she'd made me drive to Lundberg's to try on dresses for the dinner. I'd tried on three, none of which I liked, then made a visit to the cosmetics counter to see Stella, who acted more excited about the upcoming dinner than me. Our friendship had been rekindled by my recent engagement. Marriage was our common ground, even though Stella wasn't dating anyone.

Now Mom tightened her death grip on the chocolate pie balanced on her lap, trying not to get her white gloves soiled in the process. "Don't take the corners so fast," she shouted at Daddy. "I didn't spend all yesterday afternoon making this pie to have it end up on the floor of our car."

Daddy rolled his eyes at me through the rearview mirror, but slowed down a bit.

I picked at the pleats in my skirt, feeling a rush of panic at my attire. I should have tried harder to find something suitable at Lundberg's. I looked more like a schoolgirl than a fiancée.

As we parked in front of Scotty's lakeside home, I watched Daddy's eyes follow the columns of white pillars up to the tall overhanging roof.

"Looks like the kind of place where you need to wipe your shoes before you go in," he remarked, then wiped a hand across his suit and straightened his tie. I had a sudden urge to go back home.

I hadn't seen Scotty since Christmas, when I'd told him about Jens and we'd moved up the wedding date. We'd written a few times, spoken on the phone once.

I'd barely gotten out of the car before Scotty swept out the door. His dark hair was shorter, and he had on a blue sweater vest with a white shirt and tie over dark slacks. He flashed his debonair smile that made me feel like I was back in high school again, when having his attention had been a dream come true. He scooped me into his strong arms, twirling me around. The cold air took my breath away, or was it the handsome man who held me? He smelled of Barbasol, and I took in his scent as he set me down.

"I've missed you so much, Lorraine," he whispered. "You look like a million dollars."

He kissed me right there in front of Mom and Daddy. He tasted like peppermint and I kissed him back, letting my lips linger on his, feeling the warmth and comfort of his body against mine. I was so relieved at his enthusiasm that I almost forgot we weren't alone. I finally pulled back, slightly embarrassed by my display. "Scotty," I said, motioning toward my parents.

"Sorry, Mr. and Mrs. Kindred," Scotty apologized, shaking Mom and Daddy's hands. "It's been hard being so far away from Lorraine."

"Seeing as how we're going to be family, you can call me Buck," Daddy said, giving him a firm handshake.

Mom nodded. "We're thrilled to be here, Scotty, and you can call me Mom."

I thought I saw a grimace on Scotty's face at that remark, but maybe it was me.

Succulent turkey smells wafted out the open door, and Scotty led us into the living room where his parents were waiting. Mr. Bishop stood near the fireplace, and Mrs. Bishop and Scotty's sister Kate awaited us at the entrance. Blue floral chairs faced a beige sofa, separated by a glass oval table on which sat a large vase filled with white lilies. A Steinway grand piano occupied a place of honor near the windows, but Scotty had confessed that no one played it. Kate had taken lessons when she was young, but gave them up.

Scotty took care of the introductions. I watched as Mom with her fresh curls, holding the chocolate pie, and Dad in his Sunday suit, his hair plastered with Brylcreem, were both greeted warmly.

Mr. Bishop picked up a bottle of champagne, neatly wrapped in a white napkin. He winked at me, every bit as charming as his son, even with his receding hairline and portly appearance. Mrs. Bishop, in an elegant cream-colored suit, her dark hair piled in a neat bun on her head, held a tray of crystal glasses, while Kate busied herself hanging up our coats and hats in the hall.

"Thought we'd toast the young couple first," boomed Mr. Bishop. "So much to celebrate, don't you think?" He popped the cork and poured the sparkling liquid into the glasses.

"Oh, my goodness, yes," agreed Mom, and I hid a smile. Mom was a teetotaler. She was out of her element here and flustered, but she bravely sipped from the flute pressed into her hand.

"To the happy couple," said Daddy gamely.

It was the first time I'd been offered an alcoholic drink in front of my parents. We raised our glasses and there was a satisfaction in being treated like an adult. I sipped the champagne, which left a bitter aftertaste and reminded me of the last time I'd drunk it, the night Scotty had proposed at the Surf. The night I'd seen Jens again. My hand shook a little and I steadied it. We stood around in an awkward circle until bubbles flew up Mom's nose and she sneezed. But at least it broke the ice and everyone laughed.

After they'd raved over Mom's chocolate pie and Mrs. Bishop had asked for the recipe, we were ushered into the dining room. An enormous turkey, already carved, sat in the middle of a sideboard, surrounded by steaming dishes filled with sweet potatoes, vegetables, stuffing, gravy, and fresh biscuits. Next to them was a stack of elegant green floral china plates that I recognized from Mrs. Bishop's display hutch the last time I had visited. We were to help ourselves and then settle around the gleaming mahogany dining table. There were place cards showing us where to sit. I relaxed when I saw my name next to Scotty's.

Indistinct voices and the splashing of water into pots and pans echoed from behind a closed door. It was then that Mom must have realized Mrs. Bishop had help in the kitchen. She shot Dad a glance and motioned to the kitchen with her head, a smile of satisfaction plastered on her face. It was as if her thoughts were written on her forehead. *Lorraine has made a good match.*

I sat next to Scotty and looked up at the sparkling chandelier that spun a pattern of light across the table.

Mr. Bishop led the blessing. "Dear Lord, we give thanks for this food and for our families, especially our children who have brought us together today. May the happiness we've known as their parents be multiplied a hundredfold in their lives. We thank God for peace on earth, for our friends, and for the bounty we are about to receive on this Easter Sunday."

As I mumbled "Amen" along with everyone else, I felt a sudden ache for my brother. The last two Easters had been so hard with an empty chair at the table. But the wedding was helping us move on. Mom was complimenting Mrs. Bishop on the tableware, and Daddy was ruminating about when the ice on the lake would break up.

"How many points did you score in the last game, Scotty?" Mr. Bishop asked as he refilled my glass with champagne, even though it was just half empty.

"Six, but Coach Harrison took me out when we were ten points ahead and let some of the graduating seniors play."

The conversation flowed along with the champagne, and I began to relax. Things were going well.

"I hear Brad Thistle's little brother is playing center guard next year," Scotty told Kate as he helped himself to a second helping of turkey. "They'll have a tough time beating Algona."

"No team is ever going to be as good as when you were playing," Kate said. "And no one is ever going to sing the school song as good as Lorraine did at graduation."

I looked at Kate with renewed appreciation. No one had mentioned my singing since that terrible embarrassment at the Surf a few months ago.

I listened to the voices surrounding me, thinking that this was how my life was supposed to be, at the side of Scotty Bishop. I took a generous sip of champagne, feeling safe in the glow of Scotty's love.

"I had a terrible time finding material, what with the shortage still going on," I heard Mom say to Mrs. Bishop. "So when I found a roll of ivory satin I bought it on the spot. Who knows when they'll get more in? And if I do say so myself, the dress looks gorgeous on her. I can't wait for her to wear it."

"They're such a good-looking couple," Mrs. Bishop said. "We're so glad that Scotty is marrying one of our own."

I wasn't sure what she meant by that. That I was a local girl, or a Catholic, or from the right family? I knew my parents didn't run in the same social circle, and they'd never hire help for a meal. I thought of Jens, of how we'd forged such an unlikely friendship that crossed so many lines, a friendship that had grown into something more despite our differences; of how even in the midst of this celebration my mind kept turning back toward him, as though I was being guided away by unseen forces.

It was then that I realized Scotty was staring at me. Was my face such an open book? I blinked, trying to hide whatever was giving me away. My heart raced at the thought that Scotty might suspect.

"What is it?" I whispered.

"Nothing," Scotty said. "You seemed far away, is all."

His mother's voice rang in, "Did you tell her, Scotty?"

"Tell me what?"

Scotty ducked his head bashfully. "Mom wants to help us out after we're married. Decorate the apartment for us."

"How generous of you!" Mom was beaming.

"Yes, thank you very much," I said, nodding at Mrs. Bishop. They were already paying for part of the cost of the apartment that wasn't covered by Scotty's scholarship. I looked at the white taper candles in the middle of the table, wondering if our apartment would reflect her tastes or mine.

"Well, it won't be as nice as the home you'll have once Scotty graduates, I'm sure. But you'll want something decent for your first year of marriage." She sighed and turned to Mom. "They'll give us some beautiful grandchildren."

I felt my neck grow hot and looked down. Scotty squeezed my hand under the table.

"Perhaps by this time next year we'll be celebrating again," Mom chimed in. "A little one in the nursery."

Maybe I'd drunk too much champagne. The room felt stuffy. Sweat trickled down my spine. I pulled at the collar of my blouse, trying to breathe.

Scotty leaned over. "Lorraine, are you okay?"

"You're not getting ill, are you dear?" Mom asked.

I scooted my chair back, my napkin fluttering to the floor. "I just need some fresh air," I said a bit brusquely.

Scotty fetched our coats.

"I'll go too," Kate said, but Mr. Bishop motioned her back down in her seat. "Let the lovebirds have their privacy," he said.

We escaped out the back toward the lake shore, hand in hand in the twilight. Scotty had calluses on his hands from catching so many basketballs, and I rubbed my fingers against the hard spots. The smiling faces of our families shone through the brightly lit windows, as if plucked from the cover of a *Saturday Evening Post*. The cold air was a respite. I felt as though I could finally exhale, as though I'd been holding my breath for the last hour and a half.

Scotty put his arm around me. "It's the champagne. You felt sick from it the night we got engaged."

I nodded. "I don't have much of a stomach for it, I guess."

"I'm glad for the excuse to finally be alone with you." He pointed at a distant island in the middle of the lake. "Remember how I promised to take you out in the boat this summer? We should have a picnic lunch on the island. It'll be romantic, don't you think?"

"Sure," I mumbled.

"Is something bothering you, Lorraine?"

"Why?" I shivered as a cold wind blew off the lake.

"You haven't really been yourself tonight. Distant, somehow."

"Actually Scotty, there is something." I paused. How could I tell him the truth? That every day that drew closer to the wedding I was panicking just a little bit more, second-guessing my decision. That I still had feelings for another man, a German on the side of the war that had taken my brother. I was desperate to know whether I was doing the right thing in marrying Scotty, desperate to rid myself of this doubt.

"I know what it is." Scotty put his arms around me.

"You do?" My voice hitched. Had Lance told him more than I knew? I looked out across the lake, wondering if the Surf was visible from here, wondering what Scotty knew about Jens. My body tensed beneath his touch.

"Of course I do, silly." Scotty kissed me softly. "We don't have to start a family right away. There are ways, sweetheart, to make sure it doesn't happen till you feel absolutely ready."

He squeezed me until there was no breath left in my body. "Oh, Lorraine, I love you more than anyone else in the whole world."

"I love you too, Scotty." And I meant it. Even the ground felt more firm under my feet when I was with Scotty. He was rock solid, and any girl would be happy with that.

Except maybe a girl who had stars in her eyes.

My gaze turned to the sky and I could see the letter W, a bit crooked, but standing out in the sky as though a spotlight was shining on it.

Thirty-nine

✦

1947

Mom had me read the marriage announcements in the newspaper while she finished the embroidery of my veil, which would extend halfway down my back. I looked at the veins that crisscrossed her pale hands as we sat in wicker chairs on the front porch.

I'd noticed them more when she'd sat next to Scotty's mom, who had such smooth skin. Whereas Mrs. Bishop was active with numerous committees and played bridge twice a week, Mom was always tired, her health precarious. Her eyes were sunken and her face was lined with wrinkles. She looked ten years older than her true age, much older than Mrs. Bishop, who actually had three years on Mom. Mom had never fully recovered from losing Pete. I was hoping the wedding would improve her health as well as her spirit.

Despite her frailty, the needle moved deftly and her stitching held a perfection mine would never possess. The veil would be a masterpiece.

"What happened to your own veil?" I asked.

"It was an old hand-me-down, not fit to pass on. We had a simple church wedding and a private dinner at my parents' home afterward. Nothing like the lavish affair you're having."

Our "lavish affair" was supper for ninety guests in the church basement, catered by Witke's Restaurant.

"Keep reading," Mom commanded me.

"She wore a white slipper-satin gown with a fitted, beaded bodice, and long, pointed sleeves . . ."

Mom sighed. She took in the words like prayers, her eyes closing at particularly touching descriptions of the bride's gown. "Yours is just as beautiful, if I do say so myself. We must find a way to describe it so people will appreciate its beauty."

"Mrs. Bishop wants to post a picture of me in the paper," I told her. My hand-sewn dress was a white ivory satin gown with a scalloped neckline and matching chapel train. It was hanging on my bedroom door, waiting in the garment bag for my wedding in sixty-eight days.

"That's wonderful. But we'll still need a description," Mom said, "one that does it justice. Those newspaper photos don't capture the detail."

"I'll work on it, Mom." I returned to the announcements. "Oh, Dixie Waverly got married," I said. "Do you remember her?"

Mom's hands froze, and she let out a low moan. It was then that I remembered. Pete had dated Dixie a few times.

"It was bound to happen, Mom," I said softly.

But her eyes were already glazing over and she stood, the embroidery slipping from her lap. She leaned against the wall for support, as though the floor had tilted. "She was supposed to marry Pete."

"It's been three years, more than that, since they dated," I said, trying to talk her out of it, as though I was throwing a life preserver to a drowning woman.

Mom put a hand on her head and held it there, her eyes closed.

"Why don't I fix you some tea?" I offered, but she shook her head.

"It's one of my headaches coming on. I need to lie down." Mom made her way inside and up the stairs, using the railing as a crutch.

"I'll get your pills," I called after her. She was retreating into one of her spells, and I was helpless to stop it. And worse, I was supposed to go back to school the next day.

I brought her the pills and water and a warm towel to place on her forehead, and closed the curtains in her room. Then I fixed supper. This was minor, I told myself. She still had my wedding to look forward to. Maybe she'd be better in the morning.

Mom finally came out of her room the next morning when Daddy carried my suitcase to the car.

"Are you okay?"

Mom sighed deeply. "I miss my son. But we have a wedding to plan. I must put on a brave face."

I reached out to hug her goodbye, but she drew back and folded her arms. "Call us when you get there." I tried to hide the hurt I felt, but couldn't help but remember how she used to throw herself in Pete's arms.

"Maybe I should stay," I told Daddy as he started the car. "Until Mom's better."

Daddy looked at me with raised eyebrows. "There's nothing I'd like better than to have you around, especially when she gets this way. But I'll make sure she takes her pills. No sense missing your classes in the meantime."

I got on my bus with Daddy's assurance that he'd call me if she got worse. Over the next two weeks I had three biology quizzes and a paper due in composition. I spent most of my time at the library, and when I wasn't there, I was at choir practice.

I was given my first solo in the year-end concert, something I was looking forward to, since I wouldn't be returning in the fall. Our choir was performing a sixteenth-century hymn entitled "Fairest Lord Jesus," and I would be singing all the stanzas alone except the last one, in which the choir would join me.

I rehearsed every day with Mr. Christiansen before choir practice. He had a typical Scandinavian look, whitish-blond hair and a slender build, and he spoke often and fondly of his Norwegian heritage.

When I trilled a note at the end of the piece, he scolded me.

"Remember," he said, "Your goal is to present sacred music sung beautifully, without distraction, so the listener will be sensitized to the Holy Spirit's message."

I had no reason to suspect that I'd lose my solo if Mr. Christiansen found out I was leaving at the end of the term, but I didn't want to risk it. I kept my engagement ring hidden in my sock drawer and had only confessed my upcoming summer wedding to two close friends on campus. But gossip traveled fast at a small college, and one day I was called in to Miss Hilleboe's office.

"I hear you'll be leaving at the end of the year," she said.

"Oh. Yes. I meant to come and tell you myself," I said. "I'll be getting married this summer."

"Congratulations. I'm sure the choir will miss you. I've heard you have a wonderful voice, a true gift."

"Thank you. I'll miss them, too."

"Will you be matriculating elsewhere?"

"I'm afraid not. My fiancé will be graduating in one year, and I wouldn't be able to finish anyway." I remembered how only just last year she'd impressed upon me the privilege of attending college. She was terribly disappointed in me, I was sure.

"I know that you are the only remaining child of your family, and as a student you have faced new challenges and great responsibilities. I hope this experience is one you'll always cherish."

"I will," I assured her, and fought back tears.

Miss Hilleboe gave a gentle smile. "There's no regret in leaving if it is to follow your heart's desire."

Heart's desire? Was giving up singing and leaving St. Olaf my heart's desire? Was marrying Scotty? "What if you're not sure, Miss Hilleboe?"

She didn't flinch. "Prayer," was her instant reply.

"Oh, yes," I said, thinking that all our prayers hadn't saved my brother from his tragic plight. And no amount of prayer would ever change my mother's heart in regard to Jens.

"Of course, answers to our prayers don't necessarily make things easier," she added.

It was the first thing she'd said that made sense. I gulped back an impulse to blurt out everything. How many freshman girls had crumpled into a ball of tears in Miss Hilleboe's office?

"It also takes fortitude," she said, "a discipline every student at this school possesses." She took a breath as though she was about to say something more on that subject, but then she shook her head. "I wish you the very best in life."

I walked back to my dorm in the sunshine. Overnight, tulips had sprouted and the earth held a damp spring smell. Along the path, day lilies were emerging, and a tree swallow warbled nearby. A group of freshman girls were watching a pickup football game on the grassy knoll in front of Old Main; other students were braving the hills of the campus on bicycles. The world was coming to life again and I felt as though my life was ending. I'd hoped that moving up the wedding would silence my inner doubts. But at night I still dreamt of Jens. And during class I thought of the determined look on his face when I'd tutored him, of how hard he had worked. It seemed whatever activities I took part in, whatever paths I took, all led back to Jens.

When I arrived back at my dorm my roommate Bernice was waiting for me, wringing her hands.

"Lorraine, I need your help. I have to give a talk in front of the entire class on food and nutrition. You're used to being in front of people. How do you do it?"

"There isn't any real trick, Bernice. I'm sure you'll do fine."

"No, I won't. I get the shakes just thinking about it."

Bernice was a short girl with straight brown hair. She never wore jewelry, except for a watch with a silver band that she'd gotten for Christmas. Most of her clothes were handmade. She had on a simple blue skirt she'd sewn, each stitch uniform and straight. She'd made the decorative pillows that were carefully arranged on her bed. Even though her appearance was plain, my roommate had an innate ability to make everything around her beautiful. She also knew how to make a delicious upside-down pineapple cake.

I picked up one of her lacy pillows. "Preparation is the key. I practice a song over and over until I feel confident. You just need to practice your talk until you feel that same confidence that you have in your sewing. I can be your rehearsal audience."

"Oh, thank you. You'd make a wonderful teacher, Lorraine."

"Well, honestly, what I really want to be is a professional singer," I said. Bernice knew how much I loved singing, but I'd never confessed my dream to her before.

Bernice wrinkled her nose. "But don't singers sometimes have to perform in shady establishments? Bars and ballrooms and places like that?"

Our school didn't allow drinking, smoking, or dancing. Plus we weren't allowed to have cars. That didn't stop some classmates from escaping with nearby Carleton College students on weekends to Minneapolis to enjoy those activities.

"Oh, I don't really mind those places," I said. "They have a lot of atmosphere."

"Atmosphere? I'd never have the courage to go into one of those places, not even with an escort."

"But they have great music. You don't know what you're missing. And there are some wonderful ballrooms, perfectly nice establishments."

"My mother says the only nice place to hear music is at church."

"Your mother should get out more."

Bernice crossed her arms. "You're beginning to sound downright scandalous, Lorraine. You'll never land a husband that way."

Bernice evidently hadn't heard the rumors floating around about my engagement. But if having ambition and loving good music made me scandalous, then so be it.

"I've been going to the Surf Ballroom since I was fourteen," I told her.

Bernice's eyes widened. "I don't know what it's like in Iowa, but I've always heard that decent girls don't go to ballrooms."

"I guess things are different where I come from."

Bernice sniffed and picked up her sewing basket. "Obviously."

I'd never considered myself anything but ordinary, but to Bernice I was as shocking as Marlene Dietrich. I tucked away this thought, afraid of how good it made me feel.

As I watched Bernice thread her needle, a small smile crept across my face. Could this be the fortitude Miss Hilleboe spoke of?

Forty

✦

2007

Dr. Baker will be in shortly."

    I nod and stare out the window as a single yellow leaf floats down from a tall oak. It seems foreboding, as I remember a similar sight when I sat here with Sid on a similar fall day two years ago. I knew then that the diagnosis was going to be cancer. Of course, he'd had all the symptoms: blood in his urine, pain, and a general achiness and tiredness that wouldn't go away. Now, as I sit here waiting for my own diagnosis, I wonder if I'm reading too much into that leaf. All I did was pass out once.

    Daisy sits beside me reading a magazine article about a celebrity I've never heard of from one of those reality shows. The office walls are painted a pale blue, and there's a framed charcoal drawing of a dock extending off a still lake. Dr. Baker drew it himself and signed his name in the marshy weeds at the bottom.

    The door opens just then and Dr. Baker enters. He has on a white lab coat over his clothes, and a stethoscope peeks out of his front pocket.

    He shakes my hand and then Daisy's. "Any more fainting spells recently?"

    "None at all," I assure him.

"How about fatigue or confusion?"

I shake my head. Unless you count my conversations with ghosts, I think to myself.

"That's good. Well, I'm not going to beat around the bush. We've always been up front with each other. I have the results of your tests with the cardiologist."

"Oh no, it's bad," Daisy says, gripping the magazine.

"Not really." Dr. Baker looks at me. "You've always had a low heart rate, which is a good thing. But in this case, it's dropped a bit too low, which often happens as we get older, and that's also why you felt light-headed and fainted. Bottom line: you need a pacemaker."

"Are you sure? She only had one episode," Daisy asks.

"One episode is more than you want to have. If her blood pressure dropped too fast, she would do more than just faint. And she *has* complained in the past of fatigue and shortness of breath. Cardiac pacemakers are quite safe, and the people who use them can lead unrestricted lives. You can schedule the procedure in the next few weeks. It will take less than an hour under general anesthesia, and you'll probably spend one night in the hospital."

I'm relieved. I'd expected something worse.

Daisy frowns. "So it's a simple procedure and she'll be fine afterward?"

Dr. Baker smiles. "Well, any time someone is put under anesthesia there are risks. And elderly people are more at risk for bleeding and infection. The heart is located between the lungs, so there is a slight possibility of lung puncture, or pneumothorax. But it's a relatively harmless procedure." He hands me a pamphlet detailing the procedure and what to expect. "You'll be surprised how much more energy you have once a pacemaker is installed."

"More energy? God, I can barely keep up with her now." Daisy stands and is already opening the door.

"I'll be right there," I tell her.

I wait until she's out of earshot. "Are there any other symptoms I should be aware of? Could something like this cause hallucinations?"

"Why? Are you experiencing hallucinations?"

"No. Not me," I say, and let out a small laugh. "I have a friend who has had some recently, and she also has a low heart rate."

"Has your friend been sleeping well?"

"Not really."

"Lack of sleep could cause hallucinations. Does she drink?"

"Oh no, at least I don't think so," I say nervously.

"Well, it's more likely that her prescriptions drugs are causing her symptoms, and without knowing what she's taking, I couldn't really say, although I'd recommend that she gets it checked out. There are many medical conditions besides prescription drugs that could be causing her symptoms, not to mention a host of psychiatric conditions. And an irregular or slow heart rate can cause some confusion, which I suppose could trigger hallucinations."

"Thank you. I'll let her know."

"Anytime," he says, and gives my hand a squeeze. "And if it were you, you'd tell me, right?"

"Of course." I hurry from the room before he sees my lying eyes.

✦

"I'll have to rearrange my schedule so I can spend a couple of days with you afterward," Daisy says on the drive home. She's in business mode, talking fast and making plans.

"That's really not necessary, Daisy. From what I'm reading, it's a very simple procedure, and other than restricting strenuous activities for a few weeks, there shouldn't be any complications."

Her voice becomes soft. "*I'll* feel better if I stay with you," she says. She almost sounds like my little girl again, the one I made peanut butter cookies with and cuddled with under warm blankets on cold winter days.

I look over at her, but she glances away. "To make sure you don't do any strenuous activities, because who knows with you? Remember when I caught you on a chair changing the light bulb? You could have fallen and broken your neck."

Despite her complaints, I catch a moment of emotion in her voice. It's soon gone, replaced by the chilly barrier she constructed long ago.

"You're right. I want you to stay with me for a few days," I reply.

"It's settled then."

"There's something else I'd like to do beforehand," I say. "I want to visit the POW museum in Algona. You don't have to take me if you're busy. But I'd appreciate it if you would."

"Can't that wait until after your surgery?"

"It's not surgery. It's a procedure. But no, it can't wait." I don't say that I've already waited too long.

Daisy grips the steering wheel. "Honestly, Mother. Once you get an idea in your head, you're impossible to live with. It makes me crazy sometimes."

Now *there's* the daughter I know.

Forty-one

✦

1947

Even though I had just been home a few weeks before, and in another month I would be done with school, I took the bus home the third weekend in April. I had heard the desperation in Daddy's voice when we'd spoken on the phone.

"Your mother saw pictures in a magazine of Princess Elizabeth's mother and she started bawling," Daddy had said, and I knew he would be having a smoke in the barn as soon as he hung up the phone. "She said she can't find a decent dress for the wedding, and she can't choose flowers and a cake topping without you here."

Though Mom had eagerly accepted those responsibilities when I'd gotten engaged, I now found myself shopping with her instead of at school studying or practicing for my solo. I chose a simple cross for the cake, adorned by white flowers, and a flower arrangement of red roses and white carnations. Then I drove Mom to Lundberg's where we found a blue chiffon mother-of-the-bride dress that cost twice the amount Mom wanted to spend, but that I finally talked her into buying after mentioning Princess Elizabeth's recent wedding shower.

When she collapsed in her room for a much-needed nap, I stood in the kitchen, staring out the window at the chicken coop, the barn, and the garden, and beyond that, the fields. I knew every path and tree and catch in the brook. I knew where the cats hid their newborn litters, where Daddy threw his cigarette tips, where patches of wild asparagus grew in the ditches.

This was all meant to be Pete's legacy. He was supposed to marry and take over the farm, and he and his wife would move in here with Mom and Daddy. Scotty had no intention of farming, and I'd spent much of my life trying to get away from it, too. What would happen to the farm when Daddy died?

My thoughts were interrupted by a ringing sound. I hurried to the living room, where our black rotary phone was perched on a side table.

"I'm so glad you made it home this weekend!" Stella practically screamed into the phone. I'd missed her excitement, how she was so bubbly all the time.

Stella was to be my maid of honor. I'd asked Scotty's sister Kate to be a bridesmaid.

"A good customer of mine gave me two tickets to the Surf tonight, all because I saved the last tube of Elizabeth Arden lipstick for her—and guess what? Jimmy Dorsey's band is playing! You just have to come with me."

I knew Stella could get a date if she wanted. But she was still pining over Lance, who'd finally broken up with her a month ago.

"It would be nice to have a night out," I confessed.

"Let's get gussied up, then, and dance the night away like we used to in the old days!"

I had second thoughts as soon as I hung up the phone. I'd never seen Jimmy Dorsey's band, but being at the Surf would remind me of a certain blond-haired boy. I'd been trying my hardest to forget him, resisting the urge to write to him, to find out where his band was playing. I didn't even turn on the radio, afraid I'd hear a song that might make me think of him.

I went to my room and found the box I'd hidden deep in my closet, one ear tuned to the hallway to make sure Mom was still asleep. The two letters were buried beneath Scotty's letters in case Mom decided to snoop. I untied the string and felt the weight of the paper in my hand. His words were ingrained in my heart.

As I reread Jens's letters, I thought of our first meeting two and a half years ago, of how our lives would never have crossed if Jens hadn't been captured in Italy, if he hadn't spent three weeks in the belly of a ship and several days riding on a train to the heartland of the United States. If Daddy hadn't called the prison camp. If I hadn't opened my eyes and my heart.

I'd never intended for any of this to happen. I was supposed to be Scotty's girl, had dreamed of him since seventh grade when he'd pulled one of my pigtails as a joke. Scotty was enough of a dream when I was a girl. He was all I could ever want. How could a German boy change all that?

I put a hand on my chest as a sudden pain slid through me. Was this what a broken heart felt like? For the first time in my life, I knew what it must have been like for Mom.

Would I still think of Jens ten, twenty years from now? Or would time fade the memory until I became convinced it was nothing more than a childish crush? Would I become sick with the thought of our lost love, the way Mom became sick when I mentioned Dixie Waverly?

I put the letters back in the box and my eyes filled with wetness. I would have to burn them before I married Scotty.

But not today.

Forty-two

✦

April 19, 1947

I wore a green sleeveless dress that cinched at the waist, high heels, and a shawl. It was an unseasonably warm day for April nineteenth, but the nights still carried threats of frost.

"Stella will give me a ride home," I told Daddy as I opened the car door.

"Give her my regards," Daddy said.

I was meeting Stella early. I waited out front near the ticket booth. Violet Greenwood stood inside the booth chewing gum like it was cud. "You need a ticket?"

"I have one. I'm just waiting for my friend."

She snapped her gum. "Lucky you. We're almost sold out tonight. Jimmy Dorsey's the best."

"So I've heard."

"Lorraine!" Stella hurried toward me and gave me a quick hug. She had her hair up and wore a low-cut white dress with black polka dots. Her deep red lipstick and blood-red nails stood out against the white of her dress, making her appear almost ghostlike under her powdered face.

"You're so skinny," Stella chastised me. "Don't they feed you at that school?"

"Not like at home. And I don't really like to cook. Scotty doesn't know what he's getting himself into."

"You know Scotty doesn't care a lick about whether you cook."

There were only a few other people inside. We found a booth near the side with a good view of the band, whose members were warming up, producing a kaleidoscope of sounds.

"Hold my purse while I run to the bathroom," Stella said.

I watched the band, how each member had his own warm-up routine, a pattern of exercises, some of them playing a single note five or six times before moving on to the next.

I tried not to look at the saxophonists, but I couldn't help it. They were in the front row and I knew that Jimmy Dorsey played saxophone. Still, my throat tightened at the sight of the men holding their instruments, their lips curled around the mouthpieces, their fingers flying up and down the keys.

With the confident look of a bandleader, Jimmy Dorsey sat in the center, wearing a white, single-breasted suit with wide trousers. A neatly folded black kerchief stuck out of the front pocket, and his black bow tie matched the flowers of the small corsage on his lapel. His dark, shiny hair was combed back.

My eyes followed the row of men next to Jimmy to the end, where a blond-haired boy was wiping off his mouthpiece. My heart fluttered and I let out a gasp. Jens? What was he doing here tonight with Jimmy Dorsey's band? I had to pinch myself to make sure I wasn't dreaming.

Stella returned just then. Her eyes were puffy and red. "You'll never guess who I just saw coming in the front door. Lance and some debutante wearing a fur coat like she's full of money and just stepped off the cover of *Harper's*. Honestly, Lorraine, what's he doing here? I thought he was out east."

My heart was still racing. "Do you want to leave?" I asked, and looked up at her.

She nodded. "I know it's terrible of me, but I can't stay and face him." She wiped at her eyes, smearing a line of mascara across her cheek.

I sneaked a glance at the stage. Jens had put down his instrument and left. Had he seen me?

"I'll go with you," I said reluctantly.

She sniffed. "You don't have to go. I hate to make you miss Jimmy Dorsey."

I didn't care a twit about Jimmy Dorsey right now, but my feet were frozen in place. I longed to see Jens one more time. "No, it's all right," I stammered.

As I followed her to the lobby, a small voice inside hoped Jens was here because of me. So foolish. And dangerous. I had no business being here without my fiancé. And yet I walked slowly, hoping for a peek at him, just a glance to know I hadn't lost my mind, that it really was him.

We were almost out the door when someone caught my elbow.

"Where are you going?" His voice was seductive, and I couldn't resist its pull.

I turned and took in a breath as I met his shining blue eyes and boyish grin.

For a moment I was unable to speak. "Jens. What are you doing here?"

"My band has break. I fill in with Mr. Dorsey's band."

"That's quite an opportunity for you," was all I could manage.

He shrugged. "It is way to make money."

I stood, staring at him, barely able to form a thought. Stella finally nudged me and dabbed at her eyes with a handkerchief. "Well, I should leave. Stella's not feeling well."

He took my hand. "Please stay. I play now, but I would like to talk to you."

His hand was soft and fit mine perfectly. Goose bumps spread up my arm and I pulled my shawl tight around my shoulders.

"Do you mind, Stella?" She shook her head but gave me a disapproving look. "I'll call you tomorrow," I assured her.

"Yes. We still have so much to discuss for your *wedding*."

I squeezed her arm and whispered, "I'll be fine." She shrugged and left.

There was so much I wanted to say. But my only clear thought was of how I'd longed for his touch, the feel of his lips on mine; of how, when I was near him, it was like sinking into quicksand. The more I fought these feelings, the quicker I sank.

"I didn't think I'd be seeing you again, Jens."

"It is fate."

"Perhaps," I acknowledged, although fate had a twisted sense of humor to bring us together less than two months before my wedding. I knew I should leave before things became more complicated, but I couldn't. I followed him to a booth and sat through the first set.

The dance floor was overflowing, so that couples were dancing inches away from my booth. Jimmy Dorsey's band was as great as expected. The vocalist was an attractive man with wavy brown hair named Bob Carroll, but I couldn't keep my eyes off Jens. I hadn't expected to see him again, and now here he was, right onstage. Despite the time apart, it seemed that each time I saw Jens I was drawn to him even more. He was the forbidden fruit of my youth, and the taste had grown sweeter over time.

I ducked my head when I saw Lance walk by. Stella was right about his date. She had a white fur stole around her shoulders and a long dress that trailed behind her. She looked out of place among the more modestly dressed women from town.

During the break Jens came to my booth and sat opposite me, a cigarette in hand. "I have confession to make. I called your dorm. Your roommate say you come home for weekend."

"You did?" I tried not to smile, not wanting to betray my pleasure that he'd checked up on me.

"You still like school?"

I nodded. "Very much. Especially the choir. I have my first solo next month."

"That must be exciting for you."

"Yes, but it's not the same as singing on the stage of the Surf." I cringed at the memory of the last time I'd tried.

Jens flashed a mysterious smile. "Then it *is* fate that you come tonight. The stars are shining on you."

"What do you mean?"

He took my hand. "Come," he said, and pulled me toward the stage.

Jimmy Dorsey stood in the wings, wiping his forehead with a towel. "This the girl?" he asked.

Jens nodded. "May I introduce Lorraine Kindred."

Jimmy Dorsey was a bit younger than Daddy and had a loose, easygoing manner about him. He shook my hand and said, "We're happy to give the local kid a chance. You can sing a number at the start of the next set."

"What? I can't," I protested, a squeeze of panic taking hold.

"You must," Jens told me. "This is way to rid yourself of the regret of last time. You told me it was your dream."

I put a hand on my chest, steadying myself. "It was. It is. I mean, okay," I finally agreed, feeling shivery and excited.

I went to the restroom beforehand to freshen up, my hands in a nervous twitter as I tried to calm my wild red hair. At least I'd worn a nice dress. I was queasy and took a long drink of water. This *was* my dream. I realized that this would be the only time I'd ever have the opportunity to sing with Jimmy Dorsey; that it was probably my last chance to sing at the Surf Ballroom, too.

I decided to sing "It's Been a Long, Long Time." As I approached the stage, I had second thoughts. What if I froze again? Jimmy Dorsey stood in the wings, waiting. He smiled at me, a slight twinkle in his eyes.

"Ready for your debut?" he asked. "Are your parents in the audience?"

I shook my head. "My mother would never allow it."

"What Mama don't know won't hurt her," he said, winking at me. "You just concentrate on giving a good show up there. I'm going to introduce you."

Girls flanked the stage, enamored by his charisma. He looked like a movie star.

"Let's give this local beauty a chance to show off her voice, and from what I've heard, it's something your town should be proud of," Jimmy said into the microphone, and I had to concentrate to keep my knees from wobbling together as the crowd clapped and Jens whistled.

I took a deep breath and approached the microphone. "Thank you, Mr. Dorsey." He kissed me on the cheek and I got a strong whiff of cigarette smoke and hair tonic.

The music began, and I opened my mouth, not sure of the sound that would come out. My voice faltered at the first few notes. But then I heard the saxophone sound rise above the other instruments. I made eye contact with Jens to the side of me, and his encouraging nod quelled the nervousness in the pit of my stomach. I had trained with the choir. I was ready for this.

My voice became loud and clear and I let the song take me away. As my nerves settled, I relaxed, feeling as though I belonged on this stage. I looked at Jens as I sang and imagined I was serenading him under the apple tree near our barn.

Jens let loose with a brassy vibrato sound that made me weak in the knees. It was as though we were making love to one another right there on the stage. When I was finished, the entire audience rose to their feet and applauded. I covered my mouth with my hand, and tears welled up in my eyes.

"You were grand," Jimmy said. "You can sing with me any day."

I exited the stage and mouthed a "thank you" to Jens. The excitement had drained me.

I found my way back to the booth. I couldn't stop smiling.

Just then I heard Jimmy Dorsey say my name.

"I'm dedicating this next song to Lorraine Kindred. It's called 'Tangerine.' It goes out to a wisp of a girl with long red hair and a flawless voice. This song is for you." He winked at me.

I smiled again, my cheeks heating up at the attention now that I was out of the limelight. But Lance was swaggering toward my table, a smug grin on his face. Had he seen the way I looked at Jens?

If only I could escape to the restroom. I scooted to the edge of the booth, but Lance was faster than me and blocked my exit.

"I was just leaving," I said, hoping he'd move.

"So, the farmer's daughter is famous now. What does Scotty think of you singing?"

"He's at school," I said.

I chanced a glance at Jens. Lance must have followed my gaze because when I turned he was looking at Jens, too. He clucked his tongue and shook his head. "Scotty used to say you were the classiest girl in town. Turns out he was a sap. But I'm not. Tell that to your boyfriend up there."

"Where's your date, Lance?"

"I took her home."

"You should leave, too."

"Don't worry. I'm leaving this town for good. As soon as I take care of some business." Then he winked at me and sauntered off toward the bar, his drink sloshing over the side of his glass.

I stayed until the last set ended and the ballroom was nearly empty. I had to thank Jens and warn him about Lance. At least, that's what I told myself.

Forty-three

✦

1947

J ens held his instrument case in one hand, his other clasping mine. He led me to the side door and we snuck up the stairs. He held a finger to his lips until we reached the rooftop. I hadn't been up here since my double date with Scotty, Stella, and Lance years ago.

From the roof, we could see the lights of the boardwalk, and beyond that the open water. A cool breeze ruffled my skirt, but it felt good to be out of the smoky ballroom.

There was a single bench on the rooftop and he guided me to it. A full moon reflected shadows on the calm water. In the distance, dark clouds cut a line across the sky, promising rain.

I sat next to Jens, stiff and awkward, our arms touching. I nervously twisted Scotty's ring around my finger.

"Thank you for introducing me to Jimmy Dorsey," I finally said. "For the song. It meant the world to me."

"Maybe one day you be famous like Helen O'Connell."

"Really? Do you think it's possible?" For a second I forgot about the ring on my finger.

"Yes, very much. If it is your dream."

"I like school, but I'd quit in a heartbeat if I could perform with a band."

"Every band will want you, now that you sing with Jimmy Dorsey."

I wondered at how Jens could always make me feel special on my own terms, not in how it related to him. Around Scotty, I often felt like a cheerleader.

"What is your dream, Jens?"

He blinked at me for a second, as though it was painfully obvious.

"You," he said softly. "That is real reason I come here. I know what your letter said, but I hope to see you, to ask you face-to-face. To know the truth. If you are still *mein Schatz*."

What could I say? I couldn't deny the truth. I did love him. I feared my eyes betrayed me, that he could see how every bone in my body tingled at his nearness. But to say it out loud? What good would it do? I had already made a choice, one that came with a homemade dress and veil, and ninety invited guests, and a fiancé who had stood by me. I couldn't throw that away now.

"We shouldn't talk about this," I said, looking away. "It can't end well."

"It will never end well if you marry another. You are here now, with me. You must tell me."

I shook my head. "The war kept us apart, Jens."

"This *verdammt* war! The war is over now. But we are here, you and me, and this is all I care for."

The war wasn't over for everyone. "I'm getting married in two months, Jens."

"Do you deny you love me?"

"I made a promise . . ."

Jens jumped up and paced in front of me. "Was it a promise you could make?"

"Jens, when I didn't hear from you . . ."

Jens stopped pacing, his face reddening. "But I did write. I write and write and I never hear one word from you, and yet I still came to find you."

I felt tears swell in my eyes. "You told me not to wait. Those were *your* words."

He knelt in front of me and took my hands. "And now I regret that I say that. How can you marry him? You should be with me."

I closed my eyes. "Don't do this."

"Lorraine, listen to me. I love you more than anything. Does that mean nothing to you?"

"Of course it does." He was still on his knees, his face leaning in toward me. I felt myself moving toward him, closing the distance. At the last second, I pulled back. If I kissed him, who knew where it would lead? It was like playing with dynamite.

His shoulders sagged. "Then tell me you don't love me."

I gulped back a sob. "I can't!"

Jens tried to take me in his arms, but I pushed him away. "Jens," I pleaded.

He sat down again, lit a cigarette, and exhaled a long whisper of smoke that looked like a sigh. "I know you think you are doing an honorable thing, but is it honorable to marry a man when you love another?"

I looked down, trying not to cry, grinding a cigarette stub with my heel. I did love Scotty, just in a different way. And I couldn't change my mind now. Not after all that had happened.

I stood up. "I have to be up early . . ."

"No! Don't leave," he said, a note of panic in his voice.

"I have to."

"One last dance."

"What?" I shivered as a sudden wind whipped across the rooftop.

"Just one," he said. "Inside, where it is warm."

We walked downstairs. Everyone had left, and the lights were off.

"Mr. Fox did not know we were up there," Jens said, taking a long drag of his cigarette.

We walked through the darkened ballroom, where only the moonlight filtering through the lakeside windows lit the way. The chairs were piled on top of the tables. Polished glasses were stacked behind the wooden bar, which had been wiped clean. Beneath the bar an overflowing bucket of rags carried a stench of alcohol and cigarettes.

Jens's took my hand. His eyes locked with mine. "One last dance together." His voice sounded desperate.

I gulped. "There's no music."

"You can sing to me."

I dropped the shawl from my shoulders. Jens laid his instrument case on the floor and balanced his cigarette on the end of the bar. We danced across the empty floor, our heels on the hardwood the only noise to be heard. I put my head on his shoulder and hummed the tune I'd sung earlier. My voice started off smoothly, but a sadness crept in as we moved across the shadowy floor.

Our last dance. I would have to make this memory last for the rest of my life. The thought made me choke up; my voice cracked and I buried my face in Jens's shirt.

"Oh, *mein Schatz,*" Jens said softly. He lifted my head and his mouth moved toward mine. If he kissed me, I'd be lost completely. But he suddenly drew back at the sound of clapping.

A figure was standing near the bar.

"Who's there?" Jens asked.

The figure was silent. I could see the tip of Jens's cigarette glowing on the bar, but the rest of the room was dark. It wasn't until he was almost in front of us that I recognized him. Lance was carrying a long wooden club the manager kept behind the bar in case there were unruly patrons.

"If it isn't the farmer's daughter and the Nazi."

Jens picked up his instrument case and held it at his side. "I'm not a Nazi."

Lance laughed. "You think you got away with something last time.

But the residents of this town don't care much for your kind, especially when their sons were killed by scum like you."

"Don't listen to him, Jens," I said. "Not everyone is that way."

"What does Scotty think of a POW making time with his girl?" Lance asked.

The look on my face gave him the answer. He snorted. "Poor slob doesn't know you're two-timing him." Lance flashed that bullying smile he'd so often used in high school, when he had a younger student trapped against the lockers.

He took a menacing step toward Jens. "If Scotty had any balls, he'd have done this a long time ago. But since he's not going to fight for his own honor, I'll do it for him. I owe you one, anyway."

Lance was bigger than Jens and outweighed him, but he'd been drinking some. Not enough, though. The hate in his eyes appeared stronger than the drink had been.

The club came down unexpectedly. Jens blocked it with his instrument case, which cracked with the force. I screamed.

Jens scrambled to regain his footing. "Run, Lorraine!"

I couldn't move.

Lance struck again and Jens fell back against the stage, hitting his head on the hard floor. The club came down another time, narrowly missing his head as he jerked to the side. Jens managed to get back on his feet. He pushed himself into Lance's middle. They both went sprawling.

I grabbed a bottle of whiskey from the bar as the fight lurched in my direction. I threw the bottle at Lance's back, but I missed. It struck the bar and shattered, sending glass and whiskey the length of the bar.

Seeing this inspired Lance to grab a liquor bottle and break it against the edge of the bar. He thrust the ragged edges of the bottle at Jens, who jumped back. Lance ran at him and Jens grabbed his arm. The bottle went flying as they fell to the floor once more, a tangle of legs and arms.

The air had become thick and hazy, making it difficult to see what was happening on the floor. Then a rush of heat hit my back. I turned. The bar was ablaze! I took a step toward the kitchen to get water when I was forced back by a wall of hot air.

"Fire!"

The heat and my screams were enough to end the fight. The fire was spreading along the fronds of the palm trees, igniting the rattan furniture, and racing up the walls and ceiling. We watched in horror as the ballroom became engulfed in flames in less than a minute.

Lance ran toward the front door.

"It is locked!" Jens yelled at him. I tried to block Lance, but he pushed me out of the way and disappeared into a wall of smoke.

Jens quickly ran over and helped me up. The smoke burned my lungs. I coughed, barely able to breathe, and held my hand over my mouth.

"How are we going to get out? Should we try the roof?" I knew all the other exits were blocked.

"No." Jens grabbed his instrument case and pointed toward the lakeside windows. "Break glass." He threw his case at the window, but nothing happened. He picked up a chair and threw that at the window, but it only made a small chip.

"Table," he choked out, and I helped him drag a wooden table across the room. I could barely lift my side of it. I struggled under the weight, holding it by the legs as we lifted it to the height of the window. We battered it against the window, two, three times. Finally, a crack appeared.

One more thrust and the window shattered. Instantly, cool air rushed in. I gasped, pulling fresh night air into my lungs, coughing out the smoke. Jens lifted me up. My dress caught on the ragged glass and he tore at it, ripping it enough to push me out. I yelped as my arms brushed against the sharp edges.

As I glanced back inside, the wind was fueling the fire. The ballroom looked like a giant bonfire.

"Jens!" I grabbed his arm to pull him through the window.

"You call fire department. I get Lance out."

"No. It's too dangerous."

"I must try."

"No, Jens!" But he disappeared back into the thick smoke. I had to get help. Thunder boomed above me as I ran down the boardwalk toward Curly's Café. It was then that I remembered Carl Fox and his family, who lived in the apartment above the Surf.

I hurried to the front of the turret, sobbing and shaking, praying that Jens was still alive. I pounded on their door for several minutes before Carl Fox finally got up and came down.

"The building's on fire!" I yelled.

His face registered panic and he ran upstairs to get his wife and family. Mr. Knocke, who owned Curly's Café next door, hurried toward me.

"I called the fire department," he said, pointing to the smoke streaming out the rooftop. Mr. Fox was already coming down with his family. Neighbors were gathering outside, some of them carrying their belongings in case the fire spread.

All I could think of was Jens. Was he still inside? I ran back to the lakeside. It started to drizzle, but it was too late to contain the surging flames, which shot out the windows. I scanned the boardwalk and dock for Jens. There was no sign of anyone.

Then came an explosion, one that rocked the ground beneath my feet and nearly knocked me over.

"Jens!" I couldn't lose him! I shook with fear. "Jens!" I screamed again.

"Lorraine." His voice came from the direction of the lake.

I ran to Jens and nearly knocked him over, hugging him tight. "Thank God you're alive!"

He was kneeling over Lance, near the dock, pouring cold water onto Lance's face and arms. Lance was screaming. Jens had blood dripping from his hand and his face was cut. Fire trucks were approaching, their clanging sound waking the neighborhood.

"God was watching over us." Jens hugged me as he looked at the engulfed building. "But Lance has burns. He needs hospital."

He propped Lance up. "Can you walk?"

Lance didn't answer. His eyes were half closed. He staggered and Jens put an arm around his side. I held up his other side. We helped Lance to the front of the building, where emergency vehicles were parked. A crowd had formed. Lance's face had a bluish tint and was blistering on one side.

"He was drunk and stood too close to the building," I told them. Lance was in a stupor, unable to talk, reeling from the pain of his burns. He was coughing up black smoke. I wondered what he'd say later when he was more alert.

Lance was placed on a stretcher, and we were pushed back as they administered first aid.

Jens led me away from the vehicles. He held his cracked instrument case in his hand. "Why didn't you tell them the truth? That we were inside?"

"Jens, we must have caused that fire. Your cigarette was on the bar. What if it ignited the liquor when I threw that bottle?"

He put a hand on his mouth. "My cigarette! I . . . it was an accident. We will tell them."

Even if it was an accident, what would happen to him? A former POW? "Jens, listen to me. Lance was right. To them you're still the enemy."

He flinched at the word *enemy*.

"People won't understand. It's best we don't say anything, don't mention that we were inside." We watched the flames spewing from the building, neighbors carrying furniture out onto the road. "It was an accident," I repeated. "Or maybe it wasn't even your cigarette. It could have been something else."

I reached over and hugged him reassuringly. "You were so brave. You saved our lives."

A few people had wandered over to where we were standing with other spectators. Was that Mrs. Murphy, Stella's mother? The flames held their rapt attention, but I pulled Jens into the darkness of a neighboring willow tree, hoping she hadn't seen us.

We watched the fire burn, its flames licking the air as a light mist of rain fell around us.

"I sincerely hope it wasn't my cigarette," Jens said, shaking his head.

"It wasn't your fault. I threw the bottle. The whiskey probably caught on fire and we didn't catch it before it spread."

But even if it was an accident, if Jens was involved, wouldn't he be blamed? He was a recent German immigrant, a former POW, and that alone aroused suspicion. He could get deported. Or worse, he could go to prison.

I knew it wasn't rational, but it seemed as though the universe was conspiring to keep us apart. Or was this retribution for my betrayal of Scotty?

"We seem to be like oil and water, Jens."

Jens blinked at me. "I do not understand."

"Don't you feel as though the universe is working against us? That something is always keeping us apart?"

"No. I feel opposite."

"You said our meeting again tonight was fate. But I almost lost you. We both could have died in that fire."

"But we survived. We are here together."

I took a breath. The air was rank with smoke and ash. My eyes teared up, but it wasn't from the smoke. How could I tell him that Stella's warnings had come true? That this passion between us was dangerous?

"I love you, Jens. I nearly died when I thought I'd lost you. But I think you should leave."

He looked at me oddly. "No. Why?"

I started to say that it was for his own protection, but that wasn't the real reason. "It's for the best. I can't . . . I'm going to marry Scotty."

"How can you? After all we have been through?"

"Maybe it's *because* of what we've been through. I don't know, Jens. My first time singing at the Surf, and it burns down? When I'm with you, nothing else matters. I feel free to dream, to be who I really am. But I'm caught in a river made up of duty and lies. I've let it go too long now, and the current is too strong. There is so much that's expected of me, things I can't change. I can't turn back and I can't reach shore. You should understand about sacrifice, Jens. You lost so much in the war."

He put his bloody hands on my shoulders. "But not you."

Tears trailed down my face. "We were just another casualty. Like Pete and your brothers."

He opened his mouth, but nothing came out. It was as though my words had knocked out any remaining resolve. The willow tree above us caught the raindrops and the leaves trembled as they soaked in the moisture.

"It's too late for us, Jens." I touched a red scrape on his chin. "You should get those cuts looked at."

"I'm fine." He squinted at me as though he was in pain, but not from his cuts. "Are you certain this is what you want, Lorraine?"

I wasn't sure of anything right then. Perhaps I was still in shock, but I nodded, letting the tears flow. "I'm sorry, Jens."

I hugged him tightly, feeling his thin ribs, the concave stomach that still hadn't recovered from years of deprivation. We held on to each other for a long time.

"Goodbye, then, *mein Schatz,*" Jens said, finally pulling back and caressing my cheek, wiping away a bit of ash from my face with his fingers. Then he and his saxophone disappeared into the smoky night.

Forty-four

✦

2007

I grip my purse so tightly on my lap that my knuckles turn white. I'd expected that Daisy would be crabby because I forced her to drive here. But she's actually enjoying herself, sipping coffee and looking more relaxed than usual. She has the radio tuned to the Lifestyle station, meaning songs from her youth. Elton John is singing "Blue Eyes."

I'm the one who's nervous. I know it's just a museum. The POW camp was torn down years ago. A few pictures of a forgotten place shouldn't cause so much anxiety. But it was *his* POW camp. There's so much I don't know about the camp.

I've had second thoughts about going, ever since getting up this morning. I tossed and turned half the night, finally giving up on the idea of sleep at six, and tried to keep myself busy until Daisy arrived at nine. Now I try to make small talk about the weather and the upcoming harvest festival, but my heart isn't in it. I'm retreating back in time for every mile we drive. I'm remembering that year when everything in my life changed.

Daisy talks, though, noting the color of the leaves and the early chill in the air that we hope won't signal an early winter. I barely pay attention, but the sound of her voice is comforting, like a warm blanket on a cold day. Finally the Algona signpost comes into view. I tense, feeling anxious once again. Only my death grip on my purse keeps me from suggesting a retreat.

We drive downtown and follow a small sign to the museum, located in a former furniture building.

Daisy parks the car next to the curb out front. "We might be the only ones here."

I hope so.

She looks at me, at my grim expression.

"Mother, are you okay?"

I don't answer her. I take a deep breath and open the car door.

A man meets us inside the door, and we pay the small admission fee.

"Would you like a guided tour?" the docent asks.

"I'd prefer to start by just wandering around, if that's okay," I say.

"That's fine. If you have any questions or want a tour, I'll be here."

"Thank you."

Daisy looks confused, as though she can't understand why I would pass up a guided tour.

The exhibit is divided into three sections. One side holds camp-related information, including maps, pictures, and memorabilia. The middle contains cultural exhibits, such as art produced by the prisoners. The last exhibit is a tribute to area residents who took part in the war effort.

I start with a map that shows Camp Algona and its branch camps in Iowa, Minnesota, and North and South Dakota, and then move on to a picture of a truck similar to the one that brought the men to Daddy's farm, the familiar seven-sided white star on the door identifying it as belonging to the camp. I stop at a display behind glass that shows uniforms worn by the prisoners, luggage, and a guitar. There's even a replica of the barracks at Camp Algona. I never really witnessed how the thin, hard mattresses and old wood stoves of the small rooms could be so depressing. No wonder they didn't mind working on Daddy's farm.

Daisy is a few steps behind me. Neither of us speaks as we read and wander among the displays. There are oil paintings and sketches of farms much like the one I grew up on. Pictures of the camp soccer teams, clippings from the camp newspaper. Even the chess champion, Jakob. I let out a short breath when I see his smiling face staring back at me.

I come to a glass case that houses an instrument. A saxophone. Above it are pictures of the camp band. I catch my breath. There he is, proudly standing with his saxophone next to the other band members. I reach up and put my finger on the picture near his face.

It was such a long time ago. And it feels like yesterday.

Forty-five

✦

1947

The light rain didn't last long enough to help. News of the fire spread quickly, and the crowd grew as spectators kept watch through the night. Flames spewed so high into the sky that a fireman barely got off the roof before it collapsed. I cried, drenched and shivering underneath a worn blanket that someone had given to me, as the roof fell down.

When it was over, only three charred walls remained standing. At the same time, our town was spared tragedy because no one had been seriously hurt. Just a few months earlier, a fire at the Winecoff Hotel in Atlanta had killed over one hundred people. As quickly as the Surf had burned down, the newspaper said it was fortunate that Carl Fox and his family had escaped, and that no one else had been in the building at the time.

The hoopla surrounding the fire engulfed our small town. Stella was the first to call.

"Lorraine, I was scared to death. I shouldn't have left you there alone. I had nightmares about it."

"I was fine," I lied. "No one was inside except Mr. Fox and his family, and they all got out. But it was awful." My voice hitched as I remembered my panic as smoke filled my lungs, when I thought we wouldn't get out. Would I ever forget the anguish I'd felt when I thought Jens was dead?

"What happened with your musician?"

"Nothing. He . . . left."

"Thank God. The way you were looking at each other, well, I'm just glad Scotty wasn't there to see it."

So was I. I'd been careless, and in a small town where bad news traveled faster than good. No one knew that we'd snuck up to the roof except Lance, who must have seen us and hidden, then waited for us to come down. If Jens hadn't saved us, we'd all have perished in that fire. Would Lance say anything to the authorities?

"Everyone in town is just sick about this," Stella said. "Where are we going to dance now?"

"I don't know," I confessed, feeling the sting of guilt.

"Bad timing," Daddy had said that morning.

And he was right. Our town was still recovering from the war, and it needed the business the Surf brought. The loss was going to cost jobs.

"Do you think they'll rebuild?" I'd asked him, nervously twisting my engagement ring around my finger.

"Don't know that something like that can be replaced." He shook his head. "You'd think it was another Governor's Days with all the traffic coming through town to see the burnt remains," he said, and let out a scoffing laugh. "That place was a landmark for this community."

Even though I suspected that we'd caused the fire, people in town speculated that the building had bad wiring.

The papers reported that no one was injured in the blaze, and that small explosions were heard by spectators, supposedly caused by beer bottles.

There was no mention of Lance, or whether officials suspected he'd been inside at the time of the fire. I heard he'd been taken to Mercy Hospital in Mason City. This was one time I was glad Lance's family was above the law. No one would go poking around.

Scotty called a short while after I'd spoken with Stella. He'd heard that I had been a spectator at the fire and wanted to know all the details. Luckily, that's all he'd heard. My performance had been quickly forgotten in light of the devastating fire. I answered a few questions before complaining of a headache.

I was relieved that no one came to question me about the fire or about Lance. And even more relieved when I heard of plans to rebuild an even bigger and better Surf Ballroom, in a different location across the street.

But I still felt guilty. I should have told the authorities what happened. I should have admitted that we were inside. Even though I convinced myself that I was protecting Jens, I knew I was also protecting myself. I'd be kicked out of school if I was implicated in the fire. And what would Scotty think? He would never have done something like this. I knew I would never be able to look Mr. Fox in the eye again.

I returned to school just in time to study for finals and to perform in our spring concert. Daddy was too busy with planting to take time off to attend. Mom had no interest in coming.

The lilacs had bloomed the day before our concert, which Mr. Christiansen said was a good sign. The auditorium was full, and we walked in formation onto the stage in our long, flowing robes. When it was time for my solo, I stepped forward, careful not to trip. I stared up into the audience, not expecting any familiar faces. I was surprised to see Miss Berkland sitting in the second row. I folded my hands in front of me and opened my mouth wide, projecting my voice confidently.

> *Fair are the meadows*
> *Fair are the woodlands,*
> *Robed in flowers of blooming spring;*
> *Jesus is fairer,*
> *Jesus is purer;*
> *He makes our sorrowing spirit sing.*

I sang every stanza except the last one, in which I rejoined the choir, but not before I saw Miss Berkland wipe her eyes with a handkerchief. Afterward, she took me to lunch at the Bittersweet Café. We ordered egg salad sandwiches and lemonade.

"Your vocal notes were absolutely perfect, Lorraine. But you also have a sensitive soul. That comes through in your voice every time you sing."

"Thank you."

"I heard this wasn't your only recent venue," she said, raising her eyebrows.

I sucked in a breath, wondering what she'd heard. "It wasn't planned, I assure you."

"Don't apologize. I'm happy you had the opportunity." She leaned forward. "And I heard you were fantastic."

"I guess I won't be singing any solos from now on, since I'm not continuing with school, but perhaps when Scotty graduates next year I can help with the children's choir again."

"Nonsense. I've been trying to start a city choir for some time now. You'll be our star member."

I sighed and looked down at the napkin on my lap.

Miss Berkland reached across the table and patted my hand. "And who knows? When they build the new Surf, perhaps you'll be singing there, too."

I nodded, even as I knew that it would never come to pass, just as I knew I wouldn't finish college. Soon I would be Mrs. Scotty Bishop with a bouquet of red roses in my hands. This was the way it was supposed to be. This was what I'd chosen.

✦

When the school year ended I hugged Bernice and we promised to write, then I boarded the bus to Mason City. There was still much to be done before the wedding. I had invitations to send out, and had promised to help Mom make batches of dainty pink and green mints that we would store in the freezer until the big day arrived. I welcomed the busyness. It helped to keep the doubts at bay.

But coming home opened a floodgate of memories. I started to have nightmares where I was surrounded by fire, and would wake up thrashing in my bed. A few days after I came home I had a particularly bad dream. I stood at the kitchen sink the next morning, taking deep breaths, fighting panic and an urge to run as I remembered the engulfing flames and how Jens had almost died in that fire. The fact that I'd lost him forever since then.

I started shaking and crying, my tears dripping down into the cast-iron sink.

"Lorraine, what's the matter?"

I startled at Daddy's voice behind me and wiped my face before I turned around.

"It's nothing, Daddy."

"Nothing? This is supposed to be the best time of your life. Those don't look like happy tears."

"Just nerves, I guess."

"Nerves, huh? You sure about this marriage?"

"Of course. I know Scotty will make me happy."

Daddy patted a chair at the table. "Sit down, Lorraine."

I sat across from him, feeling like a little girl about to be disciplined.

Daddy leaned forward and spoke in a low voice. "I don't want your mother to hear this, and if you ever repeat it to her, I'll deny having said it. It would just break her heart. That being the case, there's something you should know."

He stopped and I thought perhaps he'd changed his mind. He sniffed and wiped a hand across his nose. He always had dirt under his finger-nails, as though this land had become an extension of him, a natural part of his body. "Pete told me he was going to enlist. He asked me for per-mission, and I gave it to him."

"Why would you do that?" I whispered. A gush of anguish swept through me. Why had he let Pete go?

"I know," Daddy said, reading my expression. "You think I ought to have made him stay. I think about it all the time, wishing I had that moment back. Wishing I had my son back." Daddy choked on that last line and coughed. "But he was of age, and I had the sense that he would have left regardless. I didn't want him going off and thinking that he'd abandoned us. And if I'd made him stay, he would have had to live with seeing his friends go off to fight for our country. Think about Norman, the shame he faced every day because he was 4F. The boy walked around with his deferment papers in his pocket, for crying out loud. Pete would have resented me forever."

I knew Mom would have preferred a little resentment rather than losing her son. "Why are you telling me this now?"

"Because forever is a hell of a long time. Pete made up his mind and did what he had to do, despite the consequences."

"I'm not Pete, Daddy."

"I know you're not. Just make sure you're getting married for the right reasons," he said softly. "You deserve happiness."

I reached over and hugged him. "Thanks, Daddy," I said, although he still had his head in the sand. Didn't he realize that Mom would never forgive me if I left Scotty at the altar, and neither would anyone else in town? That it might kill Mom? I thought of her weak, overworked heart, of how she could barely make it up the stairs, and these days often slept on the sofa. I thought of Scotty, of his earnest devotion. I thought of how much Daddy and Mom had suffered with Pete's death, how this would make up for some of the sadness. My marriage was no longer a matter of choice.

And now I wondered: had it ever been?

Forty-six

✦

1947

As scheduled, Scotty came home from school the next day. He'd gotten a summer job at the bank and we celebrated with dinner at the Northwestern Steak House in Mason City.

We gorged ourselves on steak, baked potatoes, and warm rolls, then split a piece of banana cream pie. The restaurant was crowded and the tables practically touched each other. A few people stopped to shake Scotty's hand, but he wasn't as well known in Mason City, so we didn't have many interruptions during our meal.

Scotty had gotten a fresh haircut and wore a new gray suit that he'd bought for his job. The white cuffs of his shirt rode up his arms and he kept tugging on them.

"I guess I need longer sleeves," he said. "Or I need to shrink a few inches."

"I heard there's a new store opening up for big and tall men in Mason City. Once you've made some money you can buy a shirt from there."

He nodded. "I don't want you to think I'm an old penny pincher, but we probably won't be able to go out much after we're married," he said. "Not for the first year, anyway."

"I'm not marrying you for your money," I said, squeezing his hand. It felt good to touch him again, to feel the way his large hands covered mine.

"That's good," he laughed, "because I don't have a lot of money." Then his voice turned serious. "But it will come, I'm sure of that. I promise I'll always be able to put food on the table, and God willing, we'll have a nice house someday for our family."

"I know we will. A girl can't ask for more than that."

Scotty cleared his throat. "You remember a kid from school, Zeke Woods? I ran into him the other day. He's working with Henkel Construction. He said something about seeing you sing at the Surf last month."

My hand became stiff. "I met Stella there. I told you I was there the night it burned down, remember? We talked about it on the phone."

"Oh, yeah." He casually brushed a pie crumb off the tablecloth onto the floor. "But how'd you end up singing with the Jimmy Dorsey band?"

I felt his eyes on me, and the light cashmere sweater I'd worn over my dress suddenly felt too hot. I gave a casual shrug. "I was in the audience. He asked me. Believe me, it was a complete surprise."

"It's not that there's anything wrong with that," Scotty said, his brows furrowing.

I sipped my water, my eyes focused on my glass, hoping he hadn't heard anything about Jens. "It was a one-time deal," I said. "It will never happen again. Besides, there won't be any dances at the Surf now."

"That's not the point. I mean, I know you sang a solo for your choir at school, but that's different than a ballroom. And I sort of thought you were done with all that singing stuff."

I put the glass down. "Singing stuff?" My voice took on a brittle tone.

"Don't get me wrong. It's not that I want you to sit around the house all day. I mean, I want you to have interests, Lorraine, and I'm all for you singing in church now and then. I just thought, well, with us getting married, that it would be enough for you."

He sounded an awful lot like Bernice—or worse, my mom. I ran my finger along the rim of the glass. Normally I'd have rushed to reassure him, but after spending a year away at college and having a solo part in choir, after singing with Jimmy Dorsey's band on stage at the Surf Ballroom, after surviving the terrifying ordeal of the fire, I couldn't just let singing go.

But Scotty wanted me to. I could hear it in his voice, a desperate quality that needed reassurance from me that life at his side would be enough.

I tried to smile. "Of course it's enough."

He let out a breath and squeezed my hand. "Good. I'm glad. I mean, I only want you to be happy, Lorraine."

+

A few days later, as I pulled the sheets through the wringer of the washer, I stared at the concrete floor and was reminded of the burnt brick walls of the Surf, the empty shell the building had been reduced to. It had been seven weeks since the fire. Would I ever be rid of that awful image, the fallen roof and charred remains? The dress I'd worn that night still smelled of smoke, despite the fact that I'd washed it several times since.

A knock on the kitchen door startled me. I wiped my hands on my apron, which was stained with egg and mayonnaise, and pulled at my tangled hair, remembering that Scotty would be over soon after work. I checked my watch. Scotty wasn't due for another half hour. It was probably Mr. Murphy from next door, coming to tell us the cows had broken through the fence again and were on his property.

I trudged up the basement stairs. I still had to change my outfit and finish the laundry before Scotty arrived.

As I reached the landing I saw a man standing at the screen door, his hand reaching out to knock again. My eyes followed the thin, long, musician fingers up the arm of the man dressed in slacks and a brown vest, to his face and soft, earnest eyes. It wasn't Mr. Murphy, and it wasn't Scotty.

I stopped, unsure if my legs would hold me up. "Jens?"

He spoke through the screen door. "Lorraine. May I speak with you?"

His voice was cautious, as though he expected me to slam the door in his face. I looked toward the sunroom. Was Mom asleep? Could she hear us?

I opened the door and stepped outside. "My mom is resting on the porch," I said in a low voice.

The sight of him was too much. His blue eyes searched mine with an unspoken question. I leaned against the door for support. I wanted to reach out and touch him, make sure he wasn't a mirage.

"How are you, Jens?"

"My name is Sid," he said.

"What?"

"I had it legally changed. I am becoming an American citizen."

"You don't have to change your name to become an American citizen."

"Yes, I do. Jens was poor German soldier, a man with little hope. But Sid, he is someone with a future."

He took my hand in his, sending a jolt up my arm, as if his touch had resuscitated me.

"I have thought every day of the fire," he said.

"So have I. I can't believe you risked your life to go back and get Lance. I'm not sure anyone else would have done that. And when you didn't come out, I thought that you . . ." The memory still made me tremble.

"I was scared, too," Jens said. "But not to go back for Lance. I was scared I would lose you. To do so was unthinkable."

I nodded, my throat tight at the thought of what I'd valued most in that critical moment, of what Jens had valued most. "I shouldn't have sent you away."

"We are in agreement on that," he said.

"Yes," I said, my mouth tugging into a small smile.

"I come to tell you. We have need of a singer soon," Jens said.

"You want me to sing with your band?" I said, shocked.

He took a deep breath. "More than that. I ask you to come as my wife. It is not an easy life on the road, but perhaps if we are together . . ."

It was then that I remembered Scotty. He would be here any minute.

"Jens, I'm getting married next week."

"Then there is still time."

"Time? No . . ."

"You're not welcome here!" I jumped as Mom's cold voice rang out behind me. "Leave our property."

Mom was still in her blue robe, tied at the waist with a double knot. She stood behind the screen door, one hand holding the neckline of her robe closed. Her hair was wound in bobby pins; little black edges stuck out the sides of her head. Her eyes were big and her mouth was tight, as though the pins were pulling her face back.

"Mom. Give us a moment."

Mom tightened her grip on the bathrobe and opened the door. "I most definitely will not. Lorraine, get in here this instant."

"I'm not a child. . . ."

"Then stop behaving like one. You're an engaged woman, for God's sake."

I turned at the sound of wheels on gravel. Scotty's black Ford was speeding up the driveway, kicking up a white cloud behind it.

Scotty parked next to the barn and bounded out of the car, reaching back at the last second for a bouquet of daisies. His hair was flattened down and he had a spring in his step that disappeared the moment he saw Jens.

"I'm so sorry, Jens," I croaked. "You have to go."

He took my hand again. "I cannot leave without you."

"Don't touch her," Mom said through clenched teeth. "You are the enemy!"

I didn't expect Mom to be courteous, but her downright malice made me cringe.

"Mom, go back inside," I pleaded.

"I was never enemy," Jens spoke in a determined voice. "I was forced to fight in a war I didn't want to be in. Then I was a prisoner of war. And now I will be American citizen."

"You aren't fit to be part of this country!" Mom said, and I looked down, blocking out her words until they became gibberish. I focused on the yellow smear on my apron, the metallic smell of egg that still lingered there. The stain resembled an empty nest, as if a bird had been frightened off by Mom's screaming. I wondered if Mom's voice would carry out to the east field where Daddy was planting.

I looked up to see Scotty smack his oversized hand on Jens's shoulder. "Take a hike. She told you to leave."

Jens broke away from Scotty's grasp, but not before Scotty pushed him down. Jens sprawled out in the dirt, then stood, putting his fists up. Scotty towered over him.

I quickly moved between them. "No! No fighting!"

"Tell him, Lorraine," Scotty demanded. "Tell him who you're marrying."

I wanted to shrink away and disappear into the tall clover that grew along the edges of the road. I turned toward Jens, who had put down his fists. "You have to go."

"I will leave if you tell me one thing," he said, brushing dirt off his shirt. "If you tell me you do not love me in front of everyone."

"Tell him, Lorraine," Scotty said, his voice wavering.

I met Jens's eyes and opened my mouth, but I was speechless.

"Tell him!" Mom's shrill voice commanded from behind.

I stood there, my mouth wide as a barn door. No sound came out.

In the distance the apple tree had burst forth in clusters of pink flowers, a promise of bountiful fruit. Jens and I had made our own promise beneath that tree.

I looked to Mom, and tried not to cry, but the words came out in a sob. "Jens is a good man, Mom. Why can't you see that?"

Mom's eyes were black slits, her mouth a straight line. "All I see is my daughter making a fool of herself," she spat out. "Your behavior is disgraceful!"

Hot tears ran down my face. Why did she have to be this way? "If I'm making a fool of myself, it's because I love him!" I shouted before I could stop myself.

"What?" Scotty looked as though I'd punched him in the gut.

Mom rushed to his side and put her hand on his shoulder. The bottom of her robe swirled in the breeze. "Scotty, she doesn't mean it."

Scotty shook his head. "Wait. What about us, the wedding plans? You know my cousins are coming from South Dakota. Is this because of what I said at the restaurant, about you not singing? Because we can work this out . . . we love each other, sweetheart."

"I do care for you, Scotty. . . ." I stopped and wiped my face, realizing how inadequate that sounded.

Scotty put his hand over his eyes and took a ragged breath. "This can't be happening."

I glanced down at the ring on my finger instead of at his wounded face. I couldn't look at him straight on. It was too painful. "I tried to forget him, Scotty. I couldn't."

Scotty's chin quivered. "Damn it, Lorraine. You took my ring."

The small diamond glistened in the sunlight. What could I possibly say?

"I love you, Lorraine. But I'm not going to beg." There was a strain in his voice that said otherwise.

"I wouldn't want you to," I said softly.

Mom put a hand to her pale forehead. "All that time I spent on your dress and veil. Are you just going to throw that away, too?"

Her voice had softened and her eyes had filled. I faltered and stepped back. She seemed so vulnerable in that moment. I felt the guilt press down on my shoulders at the thought of my wedding gown still hanging on my door, the intricate embroidery of my veil, of all that it represented. Fresh tears slipped down my face. "Mom, I love you. I didn't mean for this to happen. But I have to do what's right for me, just like Pete had to do what was right for him."

She stuck her hands in the pockets of her robe. "Right? You think because your brother got some posthumous award it made things right?" She scoffed, her tone changing quickly. "You're only eighteen. You can't make a decision like this; you're too young. Why don't you listen to me for a change?"

I shook my head. "I'm as old as Pete was. I've tried to make you happy, to make up for losing him. It's never enough."

In the distance a meadowlark whistled a carefree tune, and I thought of the day Pete left. I remembered his words when I'd asked him why he had to leave us. "I just gotta go. You'll understand when you're older."

It was no use trying to fight it any longer. My connection to Jens was unbreakable and undeniable. I took off the ring and walked over to Scotty. "I'm so sorry," I said as I held it out to him. He reluctantly took the ring and shoved it into his pocket.

"Why?" He sniffed, looking me in the eye.

I could only offer him the truth. "I can't live a lie."

"You should never have taken my ring." His words stung, but not as much as the accusing look he gave me.

"Lorraine." Mom put her hands on my shoulders as though she was going to force some sense into me. "Don't do this! You can still come inside and do right by your family and your fiancé. If you leave with that man, I'll never forgive you. Are you prepared to give up your family and home and everything for him? If you do, I guarantee you'll regret it forever!"

Forever. The word hung in the air. I loved Mom, but was my obedience ever going to be enough to keep her alive? What about *my* happiness? Daddy had told me I deserved to be happy. He'd let Pete go, and I knew he would let me go, too.

I took a last look at the house, and the barn, and the winding creek where Pete and I had caught crawdads, trying to etch them in my soul the same way my brother was. Then I looked at Mom, whose wild eyes demanded so much of me. Would she really turn her back on her only living child?

I finally glanced at Jens, who appeared to be holding his breath. My hands shook as I took off my apron, my fingers fumbling with the knot in the back. I gathered all my courage and handed the apron to Mom, then took Jens's hand in mine, a perfect fit.

"I know how much you've suffered, Mom. We all have. But forever is a hell of a long time."

Forty-seven

✦

2007

The boy in the picture stares back at me, a smile on his handsome face. My eyes are tear-filled. I'm shivering, overcome with the sight of him and the proof that the boy from my father's farm really lived here. There's so much I didn't know about the camp.

"Mother. Are you all right?" Daisy asks. Then she peers closely at the picture. "That's odd. It looks like Dad."

I open my purse and take a worn black-and-white photo from my billfold. It shows a young man in a white T-shirt and gray pants bent over a mound of hay. You can't see his face, but you can see his strong, tanned arms and his muscled physique. I show the tattered photo to my daughter and hesitate to say more. Sid had kept so much of this life private, and now it feels like snooping.

Finally I muster the courage to explain. "His name was Jens back then. He was a prisoner of war, and he worked on your grandfather's farm."

Her forehead creases. "But who is this?"

"It's your father."

"Dad came over from Germany after the war was over."

"Yes, he did, but he was here during the war, too. Your father was a

German soldier who was captured in Italy and brought to Iowa to the POW camp here. When Pete went off to war Daddy hired the POWs to work on our farm. Jens was one of those prisoners. That's how I met him."

She shakes her head. "Why would he change his name?"

"He wanted to leave his past behind. He chose Sid because when he was a young boy he heard the great jazz musician Sidney Bechet play in Germany and he was inspired by him. That's why he learned to play the saxophone."

"He was a prisoner of war?" Daisy puts her face up to the picture so that her nose is almost touching it. "Oh my God! How is it I'm just hearing about this now?"

"Your father never talked about his life before we married, except to say that we met at the Surf. We did meet there when he came back after the war. He was playing in the band, and I was engaged to another man. But when I saw him again, I knew that he was the one."

"Why would you both keep something like that a secret?"

"He was ashamed. He didn't think people would accept him if they knew. He shouldn't have felt that way, but it was a different time back then. There was a lot of fear and loathing of Germans during the war."

"But you lived in a small town. People must have known."

"Some did. I sang with your father's band and we traveled for several years before settling back on the farm. By that time people had forgotten, or at least didn't talk about it anymore."

"So he was ashamed. Why didn't you tell me?"

"I made a promise. But now that he's gone, well . . ."

Daisy shakes her head, her voice agitated. "I can't believe you kept this from me all these years! How could you?"

The docent peeks around the display.

"Look," I say, lowering my voice, "things were different back then. Your father wanted to be an American more than anything, and I respected his wishes. If that meant leaving out things you didn't need to know, that was a small price to pay."

"But, Mother . . ."

"You've always taken everything for granted, Daisy. You should be glad you're here, that your father cared about you enough to safeguard his own American identity. He didn't have it easy, you know."

Daisy's lips are tight. She isn't used to having me stand up to her. She looks down at the faded photograph. "He's so young. What did your parents think of you falling in love with a POW? Your mother, especially? She lost her only son in the war."

I hear a bitterness in my own voice. "My mother never forgave me." I still feel the ache of her final rejection in the hospital, when she barely acknowledged my presence at her deathbed. Daddy wanted me there, but Mom's grudge had outlasted all her pain. "We didn't move back to Iowa until after she died. By then I was ready to live on the farm again."

Daisy puts her hand over her middle. She looks at me as though it never dawned on her that her own mother had made such choices in her youth. "I wish I'd known this before."

"I wish I could have told you before."

She raises her eyebrows. "Why are you telling me this now? Is it because of your upcoming surgery?"

"No. Yes. I suppose that's part of it. I've been meaning to tell you since your father died. I just couldn't find the words. That was, until I went to the Surf again. It sparked the memories, and so much more." More than I can ever tell her.

She furrows her brow. "Now that I think about it, when I asked Dad about the war, he always clammed up. And when he was sick toward the end, he did talk about a watchtower and barbed wire. I thought he was hallucinating due to the meds, or living through some movie he'd watched."

"I think for many of the World War Two survivors it is like a movie," I say. "A way to keep it more distant and less real."

Daisy holds the picture out to me.

"No," I say, "You keep it now."

She puts it in her purse. Her eyes are wet and she wipes them with the corner of her hand. "Thank you."

"Look at this story." I point at a framed picture of two men and the words beneath. "One brother had immigrated to the U.S. before the war and settled in North Iowa, and the other was a POW at Camp Algona. The two men were reunited at the camp and they visited every week during the incarceration. What are the odds of such a thing happening? Your father wasn't sent here by pure coincidence, even if it appears that way to most people. There were too many strands of fate at work. We were brought together. I believe that with all my heart."

"That's a lovely sentiment, Mother," Daisy says. "But learning that my father was a prisoner of war isn't quite so lovely."

"Your father's heritage is nothing to be ashamed of. He was conscripted into the war like so many others. He didn't have a choice. And if he hadn't been captured, we never would have met, and you wouldn't be here."

"Like you said, it was fate. But it's sad that Dad couldn't share that with me. I feel as though I've been cheated somehow."

"Yes. I understand. That's why I had to tell you."

Daisy looks disappointed, though. She's quiet on the way home. I've changed her heritage, her view of her own identity. I know she resents that I didn't tell her the truth before. And I know it will take time to trust me again.

I think of my upcoming procedure, of my mother's fragile heart, which gave out on her at a young age. I hope we have that time.

It's not until Daisy has pulled up to the curb of my condominium that she speaks. "Whatever happened to the man you were engaged to?"

"Scotty Bishop? He married a girl who was crowned Miss Mason City, and they moved to Des Moines. I heard they retired to Florida some years back. Why do you ask?"

"I was just thinking of how hard it must have been for you to marry Dad, who was a German, especially after your brother was killed in the war. Did you ever have any regrets?"

I reach over and pat her hand. "Not a single one," I say.

Forty-eight

✦

2007

The warm air holds a crisp scent that means the Indian summer will be short-lived this year. I missed the harvest festival last year because of Sid. Now I walk through the park, where homemade jams, handcrafted jewelry, and tables of baked goods line the streets. The sound of polka music drifts from the bandshell. Wine and beer-tasting tents dot the sides of the park. It fills my heart to see my hometown overflowing with crowds shopping in the local boutiques, watching the pumpkin relay roll, and taking rides on the trolley. Babies in strollers, dogs on leashes, and young adults on bicycles are in abundance.

I make my way to the Arts Center, where visitors are admiring the hanging art and tables crowded with paintings and sculptures. I find the long table where the memory tiles are on display next to the written memories. The instructors are there, along with Jane from our condominium, all of them beaming with pride for their students.

"We have wonderful news," Jane says. "These tiles are going to be part of a memorial wall in the entrance of the Arts Center, along with the written pages. What a lasting tribute they'll make!"

"I don't know what to say. I'm speechless." I feel a certain pride in the tile I made, in the fact that I've created a visual memory, if only for myself. I look down at the image of the ballroom, the majestic turrets, the red-tiled roof, the fencing around the rooftop patio, and the lake in the background. And of course, the flames surging out from the top of the ballroom. Now everyone will see it and learn about the original Surf. I wish Sid could be here with me.

Other artists arrive. Many have families in tow, and I feel strangely alone. I'd mentioned it to Daisy, but she didn't seem interested. Group pictures are taken, as well as individual pictures that will be mounted next to the tiles on the wall display.

I'm admiring some of the other artwork when I look up to see Harry and Daisy studying my tile and sketch.

"We thought we'd see what you were up to," Harry says.

"This is really good," Daisy says, with a bit of surprise in her voice.

"Thank you. It turned out better than I thought it would."

"Well, I've always been very artistic. Maybe I got that from you."

Daisy has become so agreeable over the last two weeks that I'm not sure she's my daughter. We've never gone this long without fighting. I'm not sure if it's my recent confession or the fact that my surgery is scheduled for Thursday.

I lean across the table and whisper to her. "Did you tell Harry?"

"Yes. He's thrilled about our tarnished past. He thinks it's the best thing that's ever happened."

"At least it isn't dull."

"I prefer dull. But it's a side of Dad that I never saw before. I'm glad you told me." She gives my hand a squeeze, and I know that I did the right thing in telling her.

"I'm going to wander," she tells Harry, and moves on to the next table.

Harry is bent over, reading my written memory of the fire. His brows go down in a way that I know means he's struggling with something. He finally looks up. "You wrote that you were outside and saw the fire. But then you wrote that you helped the Fox family evacuate. That would be before the flames were visible outside. I don't buy it, Lorraine."

"Oh, maybe I didn't remember that correctly." Harry has always been too smart for his own good. But I've been carrying secrets around for an awfully long time.

Harry folds his arms. "I have a feeling you know more than you've been telling me, don't you?"

I let out a long sigh. "Okay, Harry. I have a confession. I was inside the Surf when the fire broke out. I was lucky to get out alive." It feels good to speak the truth after all these years.

Harry draws back as though I've gut-punched him.

"I should have told you from the start," I say. "I've never been good at disclosure. It's taken me my entire life to live up to that flaw, as you know from recent events." I motion toward Daisy, who's speaking with another artist.

He stares at me for a long moment. "You know what started that fire, don't you?"

"I think so."

His eyebrows go up.

"It was an accident," I assure him. "A neglected cigarette and spilled liquor on top of the bar. It spread so quickly that we barely got out alive."

"We," he says, "You weren't alone."

"No."

"Who else was there?"

"Does it matter?"

He lets out a forced laugh. "Yes. I feel as though I've been led on some wild goose chase this whole time. Are you protecting someone?"

"More than one person, actually. No one knew we were inside at the time."

He leans forward. "If it was an accident, then it's not as though we're going to bring charges sixty years later."

"This is a small community, Harry. You'd be surprised how it still might affect people today."

"If it was a cigarette like you say, how does that account for the explosion Mr. Fox heard?"

"The deep fat fryer was just on the other side of the wall behind the bar. There was an oil drum connected to it. I've always wondered if that caused the explosion."

Harry nods. "A deep fat fryer holds different levels of moisture. The old models were known to explode on occasion. But whose cigarette . . ."

He steps aside as a wheelchair is pushed past. Lance Dugan. He's hooked up to an oxygen tank, which is fastened to the side of his chair. He shows little reaction to the exhibits as a young woman pushes him through the center of the room. But when they pass my tile, the old man motions to stop.

"Maybe we can talk later, Harry," I say, excusing myself.

Harry moves to the side, but he's watching Lance. Lance's eyes flare with recognition as he stares at my tile.

"Hello, Lance," I say. "It's good to see you out."

He touches the faded scar. "Did you make this?" he asks, pointing to the tile.

"Yes," I admit.

"It's good," he says. "A nice likeness."

"Thank you," I say, feeling relieved.

"I used to go there all the time, you know."

"I remember."

He leans forward to read the written memory. His shaking hands pat it afterward.

"I was there the night of the fire," he says. "I was inside."

"I know." I glance back at Harry, who hasn't moved.

Lance peers at me closely and furrows his brows. "You didn't go with Scotty. You went with . . . someone else."

I can see the confusion in his eyes as he struggles to remember. "Jens," I say quietly.

"Yes. That was his name." He looks deep in thought when he suddenly bursts out, "War's a bitch, isn't it?"

"Mr. Dugan!" The woman pushing his wheelchair covers her mouth.

"Well, it is! But it's all water under the bridge. Right, Lorraine?"

"Right," I say, surprised he remembers my name.

"I never thanked you," he says, touching his scar again. "Or Jens."

I can see the fear in his eyes, perhaps from remembering how close he came to dying. My own heart still pounds at the thought of how I'd almost lost Jens. Even old age and illness can't erase the memories of that night.

"It's not necessary," I tell him. "It was a long time ago."

"Everything was a long time ago, wasn't it?"

I nod.

"You take care," he says, then motions for the woman to continue on.

Harry's eyes follow Lance and I can see him making the connection. It's the wrong connection, but my instinct is to let him draw it. If Lance hadn't started the fight, I wouldn't have broken the whiskey bottle on the bar, and it wouldn't have caught fire. And if Sid hadn't put his cigarette on the bar, or if we'd noticed the fire earlier, maybe we'd have had enough time to put it out. So many twists of fate, ones I've mulled over for the past sixty years.

I take a deep breath to calm myself.

"Are you going to tell me why you were inside the Surf with Lance that night?" Harry asks.

"Let's just say it was one of those childhood transgressions. The kind you'd just as soon forget about."

He sighs. "You're right, Lorraine. Water under the bridge. I guess that's a good conclusion for this investigation."

I nod. "Thank you, Harry." I feel lighter; the weight of the secrets I've been carrying all these years has faded away. Finally. Except for this last one. I still feel a compulsion to protect Sid, even after his death.

As Jimmy Dorsey once told me, some secrets are better left unspoken. This one I'll take to my grave.

Epilogue

✦

I wear a dress that hits my knees and has a short matching jacket. I dug it out of the closet, it's fifty years old, but it was a favorite of my husband's and it still fits, more or less. I spray a little vinegar-water solution on it to get rid of the musty smell, and dab Chanel No. 5 behind my ears. This is a special occasion. I'm not afraid of seeing ghosts at the Surf tonight. In fact, I'm counting on it. The cool night air carries the scent of the lake, and seagulls call out from across the road.

The Surf's parking lot is empty of cars. I recheck the invitation I received in the mail, wondering if I got the date wrong, or the time. I look at the fancy scrawl inviting me to a big-band performance with Ray Pearl and His Orchestra. I know it must be a tribute-style band in his memory, but I long to hear those old tunes, especially tonight. Is everyone else just fashionably late?

I walk up to the box office. A woman stands inside. Violet, with her dark bobbed hair and cherry lipstick, her jaw working its way around the glob of gum in her mouth.

"Violet?" I feel my pulse quicken.

"Hi, Lorraine," she says, as though she saw me just last week, as though years and death haven't separated us. "Would you like a ticket?"

I regain my composure. This is indeed going to be a special night. "Yes, please."

"One dollar," Violet says.

I fumble in my clutch and hand her a dollar bill. "Why isn't the marquee lit up?"

"This is a special dance. Only for invited guests. I love your outfit," Violet says. "You must be meeting someone special."

"I hope so." Seeing Violet makes it seem even more possible on this special day. "And in case I forgot to mention it, I appreciate all your hard work."

"You're so sweet," Violet says, and hands me a ticket. "I don't want to keep you, though. The place is already packed."

Packed? "But there aren't any other cars in the . . ." I stop, wondering who could be inside.

"Go in and see for yourself," Violet says, and blows a huge pink bubble, then inhales, causing a popping sound inside her mouth.

I open the door, not knowing what to expect. From the lobby I can see the dance floor is already crowded, just like the old days. But as I step down onto the shiny floor and look more closely, I realize the guest list for this dance *is* most unusual. Some of the people on the dance floor are old musicians, long-departed ones. Everyone is dressed in clothing from another era. I look up on the stage and draw in a sharp breath. The past flickers before me like an old-time movie and I feel the years roll back. Ray Pearl and His Orchestra are playing a ballad while Darlene Benson sings. Just like the opening night back in 1948. It isn't a tribute band. It's the *real* one.

I stand near the wall, taking it all in: the music, the smiling faces, the atmosphere. Whatever rabbit hole I've fallen into, I have no desire to climb out.

A man with dark hair and a twinkle in his eye approaches. Jimmy Dorsey. "Can I have this dance?"

I flush at the sight of the charismatic man standing in front of me, but shake my head. "I'm afraid not, Jimmy. I'm meeting someone special tonight."

"Lucky man."

He pulls a cigarette from his pocket.

"No smoking allowed here," I say. "It's bad for your health."

He waves the cigarette in the air. "Who'da guessed? I'll be outside if you need me."

The band is playing an old song called "Meet Me Tonight in Dreamland." I sing along with the tune.

> *Meet me tonight in dreamland*
> *where love's sweet roses bloom.*
> *Come with the love light gleaming*
> *in your dear eyes of blue.*

Odd how these words still speak to me, and how the lyrics of long-ago songs seem to have stayed in my head for so many years.

I look at my ticket. Booth 110 has been reserved for me. I sit down and wait, my hands tight in my lap, feeling more nervous than I have in years. The floor seems especially smooth and sparkly tonight, as though it's been buffed and waxed for the occasion.

Why had Sid and I stayed away from this place? We should have been dancing here every week! There was so much we should have done, so much we never had time to do. Time moved too quickly. We always thought we'd have more of it.

We'd both been surprised when he became ill. After all he'd been through, after surviving the war and the POW camps. Cancer seemed too ordinary a disease for someone who'd been through all that.

"Lorraine!" Miss Berkland stops at my booth. She's younger and thinner than I remember her ever being while she was alive, and she has her hand on the arm of a young man with an irresistible grin. "Will you be singing tonight?"

"Singing? I don't know. Is that possible?"

"Of course! Sly and I are doing a duet," she says, motioning to the man next to her, whose dark eyes shine with a certain kindness.

"You simply must sing for us, too. See you later, dear," she says, and smiles at me.

It has been so many years since I sang a solo. Sid and I had spent three years touring with the band, until I'd finally been offered a recording contract. I remember looking at my husband, asking if I should sign it.

"It's your dream, Lorraine," he'd told me. "I'm just along for the ride."

But then I'd gotten news that Mom was dying, and suddenly I'd ached for the farm and the life I'd left behind. I knew Sid wanted to settle down, too. We made it back shortly before her death, and Daddy welcomed us with open arms. I never looked back and never regretted it. My life has been a happy one.

I know that aging has caused my voice to lose its clarity, tone, and range. Of course, in this magical place, perhaps it is possible to sing again. But there's something else I'm dreaming of tonight. A special someone.

My thoughts are interrupted by the sight of a familiar young man in uniform. Pete! He's standing by the wall next to his buddies Mike Schmitt and Jerry Ashland. He eyes a pretty girl walking by and raises his glass of beer in a toast to me from across the room.

I start to get up. But before I can stand, a hand gently presses down on mine. I gasp and cover my mouth with my other hand.

I've imagined this moment so many times, but now I don't quite believe my eyes. His blond hair is neatly combed and his dimple more pronounced. He's dashing in his white suit and black bow tie. He looks like the boy I knew so many years ago.

He takes my hand and I stand. "Happy anniversary," he says, drawing me close to him.

"I wasn't sure you'd show up," I say in a quivering whisper. My eyes brim with tears. "I thought you'd be mad at me because I told your secret."

He shakes his head. "How could I be mad at you? It was the thought of you that kept me going during the years at the prison camp. I wouldn't have survived if you hadn't kissed me that day in the barn. If you hadn't told me you loved me. You made my life worth living. You know I love you no matter what, Lorraine."

He kisses me and I forget everything. I'm a young girl again. I'm no longer in Iowa. I'm in a tropical paradise under a dark sky, watching a band play next to the flickering lights of the palm trees, while clouds float across the ceiling. I smell a whiff of salt air and see the waves washing against the shore on the far wall.

"This can't be real," I say.

"Don't I feel real to you?" he asks, and his accent is thicker, like it was when he was young. He squeezes my hand and brings me closer.

"Yes. But this is impossible."

"Wasn't our love impossible?"

"If this isn't a hallucination, then what is it? A dream? Am I dead?"

"It's magic, *mein Schatz.*"

Magic. Is it a twisted magic caused by a failing heart? But everything feels so grounded. I drove here in my car, walked across the hard pavement, put my keys and ticket stub in my clutch, which is sitting on top of the booth.

And the love of my life is holding me, ready to waltz across the crowded dance floor. We're among the spirits of this place who fell in love here, whose essence is part of the clouds floating above our heads and the floor beneath our feet. It's like coming home again.

"I don't care what it is, Jens," I whisper into his ear, and it feels good to use his real name again. "As long as you're here with me."

The band is playing the song, "I'll Be Seeing You," and despite the crowd, it feels as though it's just the two of us on that floor.

And then we danced.

Author's Note

✦

Not many people are aware that approximately seven hundred POW camps were scattered across the U.S. during World War II, housing more than four hundred thousand German soldiers by the end of the war. Every state (with the exceptions of Nevada and Vermont) had POW camps that were demolished shortly after the war ended. The POW camp in Algona, Iowa, housed ten thousand Germans over the course of the war, with an average of 3,261 from April 1944 to February 1946. The POWs worked on neighboring farms in the community as well as at local factories. The Camp Algona POW Museum in Algona, Iowa, has done a good job of collecting artifacts pertaining to the camp.

There is no record of how many POWs migrated to the U.S. after the war. Those who did were often sponsored by the employers they'd worked for as POWs. I spoke with descendants of former POWs who had migrated to Iowa after the war, and they maintained that the POWs had been treated well in Iowa, that there was nothing for them back in Germany but devastation and ruin.

More than 2,600 ballrooms once dotted the landscape of the United States. That number has dwindled to one hundred. The Surf Ballroom is listed on the National Register of Historic Places. The original ballroom burned down in 1947 from unknown causes, and I took creative license in imagining the fire and its cause. The new Surf was rebuilt the following year across the street. Virtually every musical legend has played there. Although many big bands performed throughout the years, the Surf is better known as the place where Buddy Holly, Ritchie Valens, and J. P. "The Big Bopper" Richardson gave their last performances before their plane crashed in a field north of Clear Lake, Iowa. Every year a "Winter Dance Party" is held on the weekend closest to February 2, the anniversary of their final performance.

My own parents met at the Surf, as have thousands of couples over the years. If there are ghosts haunting it, they must be the ghosts of people who found it a magical place.

Acknowledgments

✦

I've been fortunate to have my writing hand held by editors, encouraging friends, and relatives. Mary Logue read an early version of this story and convinced me it was worth pursuing. Alexandra Shelley knew how to ask the right questions, and turned a scattered mess of a story into a publishable draft with her professional guidance and detailed critique. My agent Irene Goodman unfailingly encouraged me while pushing me to higher standards. This story would never have seen the light of day without her.

Thank you to everyone at Thomas Dunne and Macmillan, especially my editors Melanie Fried and Anne Brewer who championed this book, assistant editor Jennifer Letwack, copy editor Anna Leuchtenberger, and all who worked on bringing this story to light.

This book owes its creation and fulfillment to many oral historians, some I've known my whole life, and others I met while researching this book. My aunts Dixie Mennen and Betty Smith were both generous in sharing their memories of the Surf Ballroom and the big bands that played there, as well as the effects of World War II on their hometown and their own personal lives. Jean Casey, former director of the Clear Lake Library, referred me to H. Duesenburg, who volunteers in the history center and knows almost everything about Clear Lake. He helped me find pictures, posters, and old newspaper articles about the Surf Ballroom. Laurie Lietz, executive director of the Surf Ballroom and Museum, provided me with additional support and materials. Andrew Thoreson answered my fire-related investigation questions. Ralph Beha helped with the German translation. Dr. Richard Rattay shared his father's story as a former POW who later resettled in Iowa.

My critique groups The Intrepids and Whole Novel Group have kept me on a writing schedule for years. They offer wholehearted support while challenging me to do better, and my life has been enriched by their friendship. I owe Janet Graber a special thank-you for reading many versions of this story over the years, each time with fresh insight and helpful suggestions.

I wouldn't have written this story if my parents hadn't met at the Surf Ballroom, if they hadn't fallen in love and provided nurturing lives for their seven children in North Iowa. I hope they're enjoying a special dance in celebration of this book.